The Winter Baby

Sheila Newberry was born in Suffolk and spent a lot of time there both before and during the war. She wrote her first 'book' before she was ten – all sixty pages of it – in purple ink. Her family has certainly been her inspiration and she has been published most of her adult life. She spent forty years living in Kent with her husband John on a smallholding, and has nine children, twenty-two grandchildren and five great-grandchildren. They retired back to Suffolk where Sheila still lives today.

Also by Sheila Newberry

Angel's Secret
Bicycles and Blackberries
The Canal Girl
The Daughter's Choice
The Family at Number Five
Far From Home
The Gingerbread Girl
The Girl With No Home
Hay Bales and Hollyhocks
A Home For Tilly
Hot Pies on the Tram Car
Molly's Journey
The Poplar Penny Whistlers
The Punch and Judy Girl
The Watercress Girls

Sheila Newberry

The Winter Baby

ZAFFRE

First published in Great Britain in 2017 by

ZAFFRE PUBLISHING
80–81 Wimpole St, London W1G 9RE
www.zaffrebooks.co.uk

A CIP catalogue record for this book is available from the British Library.

ISBN: 978–1–78576–307–6

also available as an ebook

1 3 5 7 9 10 8 6 4 2

Typeset by IDSUK (Data Connection) Ltd
Printed and bound by Clays Ltd, St Ives Plc

Zaffre Publishing is an imprint of Bonnier Zaffre,
a Bonnier Publishing company
www.bonnierzaffre.co.uk
www.bonnierpublishing.co.uk

To John, my late husband, who took our large family on many adventures while I, more of a dreamer, just closed my eyes at the cry of 'Jump, Mum! Dad will catch you!' And of course he always did.

For my father, John Langley, who served with The Buffs in the Middle East, including Egypt.

Also remembering my wonderful Irish grandfather, Ernest Meehan, larger than life, who played his banjo at family gatherings and always included 'I'll Take You Home Again, Kathleen' and 'Danny Boy'.

Preface

One afternoon around fifty years ago, my husband John and I visited an old brickworks near Westerham, in Kent. We were house-hunting and the deserted property was reached through a little wood with a stream running by. We came across a large sunken area surrounded by brick walls, a well with a rusting bucket and a pile of bricks in the corner. Beyond was a big barn, with windows almost obscured by cobwebs. On a rise to the right, in the middle of a grassy plot, was the house we had come to view. Its bricks were patterned in soft shades from yellow to blue. Whoever had owned the property at the turn of the twentieth century had built an imposing residence. Inside, however, was a shambles, and although there were stairs leading up to where the bedrooms would have been, they ended in space for there was no upper floor. Yet someone *had* lived there, for there were broken chairs, a dusty, sturdy table and a fireplace, albeit not connected to a chimney.

We looked at one another – we had small children; this was not the place for us. They would no doubt love the wood that went with the property, but I knew I would be nervous there on my own with the little ones while John was at work in London all week. So we walked away, and before long we had found a new home – a smallholding in the Weald of Kent – and our *Knee Deep in Plums* days began . . . Yet that abandoned house and the forlorn pile of bricks in the yard has been with me ever since. It deserves a story, I feel.

Prologue

1903

The girl had been wandering for some days on the North Downs, stumbling along what she believed to be the old Pilgrims' Way. She'd lost track of time in her confused state, but she knew it was coming up to Christmas. Snow was falling thick and fast and she had no feeling in her feet, which were encased in boots with worn soles and cracked leather uppers. The dark, threatening sky above contrasted with the thick layers of snow-on-snow on which she staggered step by step; the cruel wind whacked her back and she cried out in agony. She clutched her shawl around her shoulders, dislodging the bundle fastened with odd pieces of string. She groaned as she bent slowly to retrieve it.

'I must carry it; I can't leave it behind, it's all I have . . .' she muttered. These lucid moments were fleeting.

She'd kept to the track, seeking shelter the first night after she fled in an abandoned shepherd's hut. The door hung off its hinges and the bitter wind invaded the cracks in the wooden wall slats. Others had been there before her; she'd sorted among the debris they had left behind and found an empty brown beer bottle with the stopper lying nearby. Water, she thought, suddenly aware of how thirsty she was. I might be able to fill the bottle from a well on a small farm on the way – but where am I going? Home, she told herself. She sank down on a heap of old straw against a wall, closing her eyes, but she couldn't escape the awful smell that assailed her nostrils. She could guess what the rusty bucket in the corner contained.

She endured another sleepless night in a crude shelter in a field. There was a red-streaked sky in the morning: shepherd's warning – she must keep moving. Now, at dusk, alone in a white world of snow, she was retching, although her stomach was empty. She became aware of the muffled sound of bells. Am I dreaming? she wondered. Where am I? What am I doing here? Is it Christmas? Am I nearly home? The pain washed over her again, and near to collapse, she groaned, 'If I lie down in the snow, I won't be here tomorrow.' In her distress, she thought she heard a voice urging her to carry on. Who is it? she wondered, and who am I?

In a brief respite from the flurries of snow, she noticed that there was a hamlet below the ridge. She had previously avoided descending to these small villages along the way, but now she plucked up the courage to follow the lights beaming from a row of cottages. The bells had become clearer, though they were not as sonorous as church bells, and through a window she glimpsed a circle of people around a table, each with a handbell, ringing in turn.

A woman came into the room with a tray full of glasses, steam rising from a bowl of punch. The bells were put down as she placed the tray on the table and began to ladle the punch into the glasses. A man went to add a fresh log to the fire that already roared up the chimney, then crossed to the window to close the curtains, but a small gap remained so that a chink of light was visible from outside. The girl moved away from the window. She leaned against the rough stone wall next to the front door and glimpsed a lovely wreath of holly fastened there. She pricked her finger as she touched it hesitantly, but her hands were so cold she didn't feel anything. There was singing coming from the house now.

'It came upon the midnight clear, That glorious song of old . . .' They must be practising the bell-ringing and carols for Christmas, she thought.

Suddenly she heard organ music and felt drawn to find out where it was emanating from. Whoever was playing stopped abruptly. She saw a chapel further along the cobbled street; finding the oak door unlocked, she ventured inside, but no further than the porch, where she found a settle. This would be her bed for the night. She would be safe here, she was sure. There were notices on the walls but the light was too dim to discern them.

She rested her head on her bundle and shivered. *Charity is cold* – the words were jumbled in her head. She had no coat, just the shawl, and she tucked her numbed hands underneath it. She was too weary to attempt to remove her boots from her sore, blistered feet. They were smeared with clay after her slithering descent from the rough grass on the edge of the snow to the terrain below.

The inner door opened and a figure emerged from the chapel: a tall, well-built woman carrying a lantern. She looked down at the girl huddling on the settle, taking in the pale face and the shabby clothes, recognising fear in the blue eyes looking up at her.

'There is nothing to be afraid of,' she said gently. 'You are welcome to rest here. I would offer you a bed for the night, but we have six sons still at home. I'll come back soon with food for you. I am the minister's wife.' The girl's eyes flickered and she nodded.

Later, the minister's wife supported her with an arm around her narrow shoulders while the girl sipped hot soup from a tin mug. She broke pieces of soft new bread into a dish and added a chunk of cheese. 'Eat what you can, it will give you strength,' she said.

The empty crockery was packed into a bag, and from a reticule the woman produced a warm red and green plaid cape. 'Let me help you put this on, my dear. It will be too large, no doubt, but wrap it around you and it will be as good as a blanket. I haven't worn it in ages but I brought it here from Scotland when I married – I am glad for you to have it. In the pocket you'll find a lucky piece of white heather; I put it there twenty years ago.'

When the minister's wife returned the next morning with porridge and a bottle of tea, she found that the girl had gone. Her footprints had already been obliterated by a fresh fall of snow. She didn't even tell me her name or where she was going, the woman recalled. In fact, she didn't speak at all; she appeared to be suffering from shock. I can only pray she reaches her journey's end safely . . .

PART ONE

1903–1907

Oh! I will take you back, Kathleen,
To where your heart will feel no pain,
And when the fields are fresh and green
I'll take you to your home again, Kathleen.

'I'll Take You Home Again, Kathleen,'
Thomas P. Westendorf, 1875

ONE

Soon after dawn, the girl left the Pilgrims' Way and the Downs, but she lost her bearings again and it was late afternoon before she emerged at a junction of five roads. She rubbed ice from a sign that told her she was at Hawley's Corner. She'd heard that name but she couldn't quite remember why or when. There was a hill ahead. She hesitated, too exhausted for a climb and suffering from hunger pangs, as she had not eaten anything since last night. Earlier, she had dipped her bottle in a trough after she saw an old shepherd deliver water to his small flock of sheep, but the bottle still smelled strongly of beer and she only managed a mouthful before she spat it out.

She followed one of a warren of unmade roads where she could just make out through the swirling snow a lone farmhouse and outbuildings surrounded by fields cloaked in dazzling white. Home, she thought, she was almost home . . .

She was unaware that someone was following her along the lane until she turned her head after discerning muffled footsteps. Coming towards her was a big fellow with a cap pulled down over his ears and a muffler round his neck. He carried a large spade, which made her panic. She tried to run towards the house but her legs gave way and she collapsed in a heap on the snow. She hadn't quite made it, despite all her efforts, and she was so weary that she didn't struggle to get up or even cry out. She had reached her journey's end.

Through a mist of pain and fear she looked up at the man bending over her. He pulled his cap off and stuffed it in his pocket, thinking it might alarm her. His curly hair was ruffled and his smiling face made her wonder: am I in heaven? Is this an angel?

He put down the spade and asked gently, 'Will you allow me to help you?' When she didn't answer, he lifted her up into his arms, and with long strides reached the farmhouse gate, calling out, 'Mother, can you come? We have a visitor . . .'

The door opened and light spilled out across the drive. It illuminated the name over the lintel: Home Farm.

The man lowered his burden gently, supporting the girl until her feet reached the ground, where his mother was ready to guide her into the warm house. He went back to retrieve the spade, which his mother had asked him to bring in from the barn in case the snow built up round the house during the night. There were already icicle spears hanging from the gables and window frames.

The girl was supported by the woman into a large room just off the hall. There was a low black-beamed ceiling, whitewashed walls patterned by shadows from flickering candles in polished brass candlesticks, and bare floor-boards with colourful rag rugs. In the centre of the room was a long table with benches on either side, and at both ends an oak carving chair with a cushioned seat. On the table was an embroidered cloth runner, with a yellow bowl in the centre brimming with rosy-cheeked apples. She had an overwhelming feeling that she had been in this room before – was it a long time ago?

A Border collie had made himself comfortable on the long black horsehair sofa drawn up to the cheerful log fire, but was told firmly, 'Down, Bob!' His mistress helped the girl to swing her legs up and to stretch out on the sofa with a couple of plump cushions behind her back. 'Let me help you out of your cape. I'll shake off the snow and hang it up to dry. You were fortunate to be wearing it in this weather, eh? I am Jessie Mason – Danny, who carried you here, is my younger son.'

As she said this, another large man appeared in the doorway. He had a mop of thick dark hair and a shaggy beard. The girl on the sofa gave a strangled cry at the sight of him. She covered her eyes with her hand, an involuntary gesture, as if expecting a blow.

'Can I help, Mother?' he asked. He had a deep voice and a slow way of speaking.

'You can, Sam. Fill my small washing tub with water, make sure it's not too hot, and find a flannel piece and a bar of soap. The young lady will need to soak her feet, I think, and I will help her wash herself. Could you bring me the nightgown I've been airing by the kitchen range, please? Also, a big towel from the cupboard,' she instructed him. 'Danny will be back in a minute – you should both stay in the kitchen while I attend to our unexpected visitor, and give the stew on the hob a good stir. We'll need a cup of strong tea before supper, I think.'

'Here's Danny now,' Sam said. He closed the door, but the girl could still hear muted conversation in the hall as Danny divested himself of his outer garments and boots, then the young men went to fetch the tub and the other things their mother had asked for.

'Don't worry about my boys; they are gentle giants, I always say, and will do anything for anyone,' Jessie said proudly. She sat down on the end of the sofa and began to gently ease off the girl's boots. 'You can't hurt this old piece of furniture; it's easy enough to wipe down. Now, my dear, will you tell me your name? That's all I need to know; you needn't tell me the story behind your distress till you feel ready.'

'Kit . . . Kathleen,' the girl said faintly. Her eyes closed.

Now that the girl's head was uncovered, Jessie saw long, tangled black hair in need of a wash, like the rest of her, and she put two and two together – black hair and blue eyes, a soft lilting accent. 'You are from Ireland, I believe?' she asked. 'A long way from home.'

'Home . . .' the girl murmured. She gave a deep sigh.

'I believe you are,' Jessie said softly. 'Your poor feet – I need to put salve on them, then bind them up. Oh, here comes the tub. I hope they remembered newspaper to stand it on. Sam, look in my box on the dresser and bring the ointment and a roll of bandage – oh, and scissors. Then take these boots to the kitchen. They need a good clean, as you can see.'

Danny, unlike his older brother, was clean-shaven, with copper-coloured hair, the same shade as his mother's neatly coiled bun. She appeared small beside her large sons, but was actually a few inches over five feet tall, with a face creased with laughter lines.

'I hope I didn't frighten you?' Danny asked the girl. She didn't respond. Her eyes were open now: they were blue, he saw, mirroring his own. He surprised himself with the thought that fate had brought her here.

'Kathleen,' his mother said.

'I was lost,' Kathleen whispered unexpectedly, turning her face away from his gaze. She sounded so desolate, he thought as he left the room.

Jessie turned away while Kathleen undressed, and rolled the soiled clothes into a sheet of newspaper. 'I will wash these for you tomorrow.' She hesitated. 'I have some garments that belonged to my daughter . . .' She swallowed hard, and then said, 'I lost my Mary four years ago, when she was only thirteen. I still miss her, but you have to carry on, don't you?'

She turned back to tuck the big towel round Kathleen and gave a gasp, quickly suppressed, when she saw what had been disguised by the girl's long full skirt. There were bruises on her arms too, as if someone had brutally restrained her, and raised red weals on her back. Jessie, shocked, dipped the flannel in the water and tenderly washed her visitor like she would a young child. After all, she thought, she's not much older, it seems.

After Kathleen had soaked her feet in the tub, Jessie bandaged them up, then Danny carried her in his strong arms into the kitchen, where his brother was laying the table for supper and pots bubbled on the range. Kathleen's face rested against his jersey. He saw her wrinkle her nose. 'You can smell the hosses, I reckon. I'd just bedded them down for the night when I came upon you struggling along in the snow.'

She found her voice: 'Horses.' She sounded reproving.

Danny caught his mother's warning glance, and interpreted it: don't ask questions.

'Here's the strong tea you ordered, Mother,' Sam put in. 'Drink up while I dish up the stew. I added the dumplings to the gravy, by the way.'

'You'll make someone a good husband one day, Sam.' She sipped her tea gratefully.

'Not till I've built my house first,' he replied enigmatically.

Kathleen gulped when a bowl was placed before her.

'Take it away, Sam, and add it to Danny's plate,' Jessie said. 'He's been working hard all day.'

'And I haven't, I suppose?'

'Well, you could hardly dig clay today or build walls, could you? You've been full of grand plans ever since your uncle left you the old brickworks. Danny put *his* half-share into livestock,' Jessie reminded him.

Danny interrupted. 'He has his dreams and I have mine, that's all I have to say. But Mother, we've frightened our visitor, she's weeping.' He pushed back his chair. 'I'll make her some bread and milk, shall I? She might manage that.'

Tears coursed down Kathleen's pale cheeks, but she didn't sob. Jessie went to reassure her. 'Put our plates in the warming oven, Sam,' she said. 'Danny, yes, bread and milk – now why didn't I think of that? And Sam, you help me get Kathleen upstairs. She can sleep in my room so I can keep an eye on her. The spare bed's made up. Danny, you can bring the bowl up when it's ready. And she'll need the stone hot-water bottle . . .'

'Hold tight as we go up the stairs,' Sam said gruffly to Kathleen.

She turned her face, avoiding contact with his beard.

'I'm sorry.' He smiled ruefully. 'A beard gives me some protection as I work outside in all weathers. Here we are. Mother, open the door. I'll put her on the bed, then you can see to things.'

Kathleen couldn't speak. Was she dreaming – would she wake up and find herself still struggling through the snow?

Jessie sat down next to her on the bed. 'I would like to give your hair a good brush if you can sit up. You'll need to anyway when your sop arrives . . .'

'Sop?' Kathleen asked, her voice just a whisper.

'Bread and milk, my dear. It was often the only thing I could eat when I was expecting my babies. You'll feel better once you get that down you.'

'You know?' the girl faltered, as Jessie gently dealt with the tangles in her hair.

'I do indeed, but I also saw that you had been beaten. Was it . . .' she paused, 'the man concerned?'

There was no response.

'Have you anyone to go to in times of trouble?'

The words spilled forth this time. 'No. I thought the Pilgrims' Way would absolve me.' She couldn't tell Jessie any more, it was all too painful and raw. She had managed to blot out the most recent and terrifying events, but she feared what might happen if they resurfaced.

'My dear, I'm sure you are absolved already.' Instinctively Jessie knew that was the right thing to say. She imagined the girl was a Catholic.

Danny delivered the bowl of bread and milk, and the hot-water bottle swathed in a small hand towel. 'I hope you will sleep well tonight,' he said, smiling encouragingly at Kathleen as Jessie propped her up in bed with a pillow.

He turned to his mother at the bedroom door and said quietly, 'Doc Wiseman is coming to check the foal over tomorrow morning – would you like him to see her?'

'Danny, he's a *horse* doctor!'

'Maybe now, but he was once a doctor in a hospital, in the country where he was born, before he came here as a refugee. He won't charge you for advice.'

'I don't know how long she will be with us. Perhaps, though, this is her journey's end. Only she can decide that. It would be good to have another woman in the house.'

When Jessie turned back to the bed, she saw that the bowl was empty and the girl was asleep, the spoon still in her hand. She tucked the bedclothes round her and sighed. Her daughter had slept in that bed during her final illness, and now she had another young girl to look after.

Downstairs, Danny told Sam, 'I'll take the dog out as usual.'

'It's still snowing, don't go too far,' Sam said. He grinned at his brother. 'Though I don't suppose the weather will cool your ardour. Marion, no doubt, is waiting for you to knock on her door, eh?'

'Don't marry me off just yet,' Danny retorted. 'But at least I'm not in love with bricks, like you!' He dodged the cushion Sam aimed at him.

After Danny had gone out of the front door with the collie following to heel, spade in hand in case he stumbled into a snowdrift, Sam stoked the fire and gathered up the newspaper that had been under the tub. An item on the inside pages caught his attention:

MISSING GIRL

Police were called to an altercation at a large house in Croydon. Neighbours reported seeing a young woman they knew as Kitty, a servant in the house, running off down the street, with a man in pursuit. The man, who was rumoured to be her employer's long-time companion, returned alone more than an hour later. He told police he was only trying to help her, but she had eluded him. Later, a woman's body was removed from the house. Her identity and cause of death have not yet been established.

The date on the newspaper was five days ago. The newsagent kindly supplied them with unsold papers, which were useful for many purposes.

Sam would never know why he acted then as he did, tearing out the damp page, screwing it up and putting it on the fire. He watched as it blazed up, then dwindled into ash.

TWO

Doc Wiseman straightened up, rubbing the small of his back. Jessie pulled the covers over Kathleen's exposed body. Doc asked why she'd wanted him to call, rather than the village doctor. 'I only prescribe medicine for animals,' he said.

'It seemed a good idea,' she told him. 'Danny told me you were once a people's doctor before you took to the horses.'

'Ah . . . it is true, I qualified in medicine many years ago. This was in eastern Europe in the 1870s when many like me were persecuted – I am a Jew, as you may know. I took the first job I was offered when I came to England.'

Kathleen closed her eyes and turned her head away from their gaze. She hadn't answered any of Doc's queries. He was a short, stocky man of indeterminate age and he had a swarthy complexion and dark brown eyes. His hair, neat beard and bushy eyebrows were iron grey.

Doc cleared his throat and motioned Jessie to follow him out on to the landing and to close the bedroom door behind them.

'Well, Doc?' she prompted him.

'What do you know?' he asked her.

'Not much – only that she came here by the Pilgrims' Way. I saw the injuries when I bathed her last night, and her . . . delicate condition, of course. I think she comes from Ireland.'

'It is possible,' Doc said slowly. 'She also suffered blows to the head, which seem to have affected her memory. The body heals more quickly than the mind. As for her pregnancy, I estimate that she has about a month to go. Whether the stress of recent events will result in a premature birth, I cannot say. She needs complete rest, good nourishment and care. Are you prepared to do this for a stranger?'

Jessie didn't hesitate. 'Of course, Doc. Do you have any idea how old she is?'

'It's hard to say – maybe seventeen or eighteen years old. Her youthfulness will aid her recovery.' Mary would have been the same age, Jessie thought.

Doc began to descend the stairs and Jessie followed. 'I'll see you out,' she said.

'I am returning to the stables; Danny said I should come here first.'

'Tell me what I owe you, Doc.'

'I too can do a kindness, Jessie, remembering what others did for me. Let me know if your visitor has any further problems and I will come.' He donned his hat and overcoat and ventured out to his conveyance.

'If you don't need me, Mother,' Sam said, emerging from the living room, 'I'll go down to the brickworks. Things to do.'

'Not outside, I hope? It's going to snow again, I think.'

'Well, I need to bring you back some of the wood I sawed up. I want to start tidying the big barn where Uncle lived while he was building his house. He got as far as digging the foundations and I owe it to him to finish it. I will work here as usual, I promise, and I'll go there when we are not so busy.'

'I am glad of that, Sam, but you'll also need to get the brickworks going again,' Jessie reminded him. 'You'll need a great many bricks to build your house.'

After several days in bed, Kathleen felt strong enough to come downstairs. She washed herself in the bowl on the washstand and then determined to dress without Jessie's help. Earlier, Jessie had put a pile of clothes on a chair without comment. The garments had obviously been kept in a chest with camphor.

Jessie had also brought a large parcel containing baby clothes, which had been stowed away after she suffered a late miscarriage when her daughter was six years old. They had hoped for a sister for Mary. There were three little nightgowns in soft cream flannel, which she had hand-sewn herself; a crocheted woollen shawl used by both boys as well as Mary; and other useful items, including a dozen new terry-towel napkins, neatly hemmed. She put this parcel in the top drawer of the bedroom chest. Better to be prepared, she thought. Doc's predicted two weeks after Christmas, but I'm not so sure . . .

Kathleen took her time dressing. Mary must have been sturdily built, as the clothes were roomy. Like the cape the minister's wife had given her, which covered a multitude of sins . . .

She had a short rest after donning drawers, chemise and warm woollen stockings. Then she pulled over her head a flannel petticoat, followed by a thick serge skirt and a hand-knitted jumper in white wool with a cable pattern. She felt under the bed and found the carpet slippers Jessie had placed there. It helped that the slippers were large, because of her bandaged feet.

Now for her hair. Her bundle was in the washstand cupboard. Jessie had not presumed to look within it, any more than Kathleen would pry into the chest of drawers. She untied the string and uncovered the treasures inside. Fragments of memory were stirred by a framed picture of her parents, a prayer book, a rosary, and her birth and her parents' marriage certificates in a brown envelope, though she merely glanced at these, finding it difficult to take it all in. She kept looking and found her mother's wedding ring from her first marriage on a silver chain, a small packet of love letters with a red silk rose written by her father to her mother in their courting days, and a rag doll that Kathleen had taken everywhere with her when she was young. She wrapped most of these things up securely again, except for the doll, whose name she couldn't recall, which she placed on her pillow, and the silver chain with the ring, which she fastened around her neck. Finally she pulled out a leather pouch containing her mother's silver and blue enamel-backed brush and comb.

She was sitting brushing out her long hair, wondering how she would manage to descend the stairs, when Jessie came to see how she was getting on.

'Shall I braid your hair for you?' she asked, and then ventured, 'Could you get in touch with your mother?'

Kathleen shook her head.

'Or your father?'

Again Kathleen said nothing, but there were tears in her eyes.

Jessie bit her lip to stop herself crying too. She realised that Kathleen couldn't bring herself to talk about the trauma she had obviously endured; what this young girl needed now was care and reassurance. Jessie, being warm and maternal, instantly decided she would provide that. 'Time to make lunch. Danny will be hungry as usual! I'll take you downstairs.'

'Sam?' the girl asked unexpectedly. 'They argue . . .'

'Oh, they are great pals really! Sam's at the brickyard. He'll be back soon, I hope, with more kindling. He owns a small wood. *Not* a place I'd like to live on my own!' Jessie chatted on as they went slowly downstairs and into the living room.

'It's a day for stoking the fire and existing on what we have harvested and stored especially for weather like this.'

'What kind of farm is this? Is it arable or a dairy farm?' Kathleen asked.

Jessie replied instantly, pleased by her interest and wondering whether Kathleen herself came from a farming background. 'Well, there's the apple orchard, where we have Cox's Orange Pippin, Charles Ross, which you can eat as well as cook, and Blenheim Orange. We also grow strawberries, and vegetables such as peas, beans and potatoes. The fruit all goes to Covent Garden, but we sell vegetables locally and use a lot ourselves, of course. As for animals, we buy young lambs to fatten up, and our milk comes from a couple of goats – did you notice that it tastes different from cow's milk? I make butter and cheese from it too. Then there are the hens; of course they're not laying in this cold weather, but I have eggs in isinglass in the pantry.' She paused for breath, hoping she was not talking too much, but Kathleen was obviously listening.

'Am I a burden?' Kathleen asked, her lips quivering.

'My dear, of course not, I'm happy to see you recovering.' Kathleen smiled, so Jessie continued, 'Do you recall anything more about why you wanted to, as you said, absolve yourself? Or about where you came from?'

Kathleen's smile vanished; she frowned and shook her head.

'I'm sorry. I thought you might be ready to confide in me.' Jessie bit her lip. 'Join old Bob on the sofa, he's taken a fancy to you; he growls if he doesn't like someone. I'll heat the soup and lay the table, eh?'

After Jessie had gone to the kitchen, Danny appeared. He removed his boots before coming into the living room to check the fire was going well. Kathleen lay asleep on the sofa, the dog curled up at her feet. She didn't stir as, on a sudden impulse, Danny leaned over her and kissed the top of her head.

As he straightened up, her eyes opened and she demanded, 'Why did you do that?'

'I couldn't resist it,' he smiled. 'I thought of Sleeping Beauty and how *she* was woken by a kiss. I didn't mean to frighten you.'

She sat up and said, 'Don't do it again.'

Rebuffed, he went out of the room without another word. Upstairs, he sat on his bed, head in his hands. Whatever was I thinking of? he asked himself. What would Marion say if she knew I was attracted to another girl – one I know nothing about? Sam was right when he said I might be full of desire for Marion but I shouldn't contemplate marriage at my age. I shouldn't have got angry with him and told him to mind his own business . . .

Downstairs, Kathleen was trembling. The dog licked her hand, sensing her distress. She sighed. 'I do like him, I do . . .'

Jessie escorted Kathleen upstairs after supper that evening and helped her into bed.

'I was born here, you might like to know,' she said impulsively. 'You have only seen this side of our home. As our family grew larger, so did the house – you can even see the join on the roof! The kitchen has been enlarged too. The parlour is over the way, but it isn't used except on special occasions, and upstairs are five bedrooms, including one in the attic. It's not possible to heat them all, but they'll be in use again in the spring.

'My father and uncle built this place – we were a houseful then: my parents, my uncle, my two sisters and two brothers. I was the youngest; the others married and moved away. When I wed Wilf, he joined the workforce as well as the family. The farm was left to us because we built up the business, but the others shared the money, so we had to work even harder. Sadly Wilf passed away not long before Mary, but I was thankful he didn't know she would be following him. I still have the boys, of course, and Danny has promised that when he marries he will bring his bride here. Sam . . . well, he is a difficult one to fathom. I suppose what I'm trying to say is that you are welcome to stay here until the baby comes, and after, if you wish . . .'

'Tell Danny,' Kathleen said suddenly, 'that I can help with the horses.'

Jessie smiled at her acceptance. 'You should do so yourself, Kathleen, and perhaps you might say sorry for hurting his feelings earlier?'

Kathleen looked down, thinking to herself, does he tell his mother everything?

Christmas was almost upon them before they knew it, and they were busy with the preparations. Kathleen wasn't able to help much for it was obvious that the baby would soon put in an appearance. She managed to assist Jessie with the baking, sitting at the kitchen table, which Jessie had scrubbed clean for pastry rolling.

'You know how to cook, I see,' Jessie said as Kathleen mixed the dough. She passed her the jar of mincemeat. 'Made with windfall apples, of course. Nothing is wasted here.'

'Could I bake some soda bread?' Kathleen said unexpectedly.

'Of course you can! Oh dear, I really must ice the Christmas cake soon . . .'

Sam came in through the front door, stamping his snow-clogged boots on the mat. 'Mother,' he called, 'come and see what I've brought – had to drag it here on the old sled on top of the logs.'

Jessie went to see. The door was still wide open, letting in blasts of cold air; outside was a Christmas tree blocking the path.

'I saw Danny on my way up and he said he'll be back in ten minutes to help me carry it into the hall. I'll fetch the big pot from the outhouse. How about a cup of something – I wouldn't mind a dash of whisky in it!'

'I'll ask Kathleen to make a pot of tea. Are you finished for the day?'

'At the brickworks, yes. Plenty to do here, though; tomorrow is Christmas Eve, after all.'

As Sam went out to join Danny, Jessie said to Kathleen, 'I made another two cakes besides the Christmas cake, because both the boys have birthdays in January: Sam will be twenty-three on the third, and Danny nineteen on the fifth – how time flies, eh?'

'My birthday is on the fifth too,' Kathleen said suddenly.

'Ah . . . how old will you be then, my dear?' Jessie mentally crossed her fingers, worried that she was stepping over the boundary.

'Eighteen,' Kathleen revealed. She looked sad. Turning seventeen had been a nightmare that still haunted her; had she really lost her memory, or was she deceiving herself? she wondered.

Jessie put her arms round her and hugged her close. 'You will be a young mother by then, Kathleen. I will help you all I can, I promise.'

THREE

Christmas Eve was on a Thursday. It remained very cold, and although snowfall was intermittent, there were treacherous icy patches along the lane and the strawberry fields were hidden under a frosty coat. The only splash of colour came from the scarlet berries on the holly tree near the back door, and there were birds continually quarrelling over this bounty.

It was traditional to decorate the tree the day before Christmas, and Kathleen was given an old box of decorations to sort through.

'I did this on the farm,' she mentioned.

So that's why she thinks of this as her home, Jessie thought. 'You have an artistic bent,' she said. 'Mary was the same . . .' Jessie bustled about making cocoa, calling out to Sam and Danny, who were outside bringing in more logs for the fire. 'Nice hot drink in here for you, boys!' Then, to Kathleen, 'Why not take your cup up to bed with you? You look very weary.'

Kathleen climbed the stairs slowly, pausing now and then, aware of a dragging pain in her lower back. Should I mention it to Jessie? she wondered. She heard the boys in the kitchen and decided to wait until Jessie joined her upstairs. Though this might not be for some time, she realised, because there were still things to prepare for Christmas Day.

She undressed slowly: a big effort tonight. It wasn't late, probably not much past nine o'clock. As she folded her petticoat, she noticed a damp patch on the back, but more ominous was a spreading scarlet stain on her underwear. She felt clammy and afraid. She needed to go out onto the landing and call down to Jessie, but she wasn't sure she could make it; her legs were so wobbly. She heard with relief the sound of someone coming up the stairs.

She called out weakly, 'Jessie – hurry! I need you.'

The door burst open and there stood Sam. Kathleen was past caring now. 'Sam, the baby – get Jessie.'

'Hold tight!' He didn't know what else to say. 'Mother!' he yelled. 'Kathleen needs you – quick!'

Jessie had followed him up. 'I'm here, my dear. Sam, will you go for the midwife? Take the buggy, and make sure there's oil in the lamp. Mrs Buss is aware that she might be needed.' Sam turned to leave. 'Oh, and tell Danny I could do with his help – he's not squeamish, having been with the mare when her foal was born.'

'I'm not a horse!' a weak voice reminded them from the bed.

Danny pounded up the stairs two at a time as Sam closed the front door behind him. He knocked lightly on the door but opened it at the same time. 'What can I do?'

'Open the press by my bed and find two big towels for a start – I thought ahead and filled it with the necessary linen. Then we must wrap her lower half in one towel, and cover my bed with the other, as we must move her there before stripping her bed and protecting the mattress . . .'

With Kathleen swathed in the towel, Danny lifted her up and carried her across the room to the big bed, where he deposited her gently. She freed her hands and reached up to hold his. Her grip was surprisingly strong.

Danny turned to his mother. 'She won't let me go,' he mouthed. Sweat glistened on Kathleen's forehead and she groaned as the pains increased.

'Stay with her,' Jessie advised. 'I'll tackle her bed.' She covered the mattress with layers of brown paper, then an old sheet. 'Bring her back and I'll make her as comfortable as I can. She'll need the other towel to lie on again.'

As Danny obeyed his mother's instructions, the groaning became louder.

'Fetch up a canister of hot water, Danny, then fill the kettle and set it to boil again,' Jessie said. She poured cold water into a small basin on the washstand, in which she soaked a flannel, wringing it out and placing it on

Kathleen's forehead. She had something to say before Danny returned.

'Kathleen, dear, may I take your ring off the chain and put it on your finger? Nurse Buss is likely thinking you are a young married lady, you see. For tonight you will be Mrs . . . what is your surname?'

'Clancy,' the girl murmured. She didn't demur when Jessie slid the ring onto her finger.

'I assume this is your mother's wedding ring? You will be reminded of her, I'm sure. She must have had small hands like yours, Kathleen.'

Kathleen was quiet now, her breathing coming in short gasps.

As Danny came back into the room with the hot water, he said, 'I can hear voices outside. I'll tell Nurse Buss to come straight up, shall I? Then Sam and I will keep out of the way.'

'The cocoa is cold.' Kathleen tried to struggle up.

Jessie nodded to Danny. 'Take the cup away, Danny.'

As he did so, he whispered to Kathleen, 'Good luck.'

'Stay – hold my hand,' she pleaded.

'I'm sorry, they won't allow me to,' he said. 'I really would if I could.'

Nurse Buss was a large lady and she too was rather out of breath. 'Didn't get time to even put my corsets on,' she said. 'Now, Mrs . . .?' She looked at Kathleen's hand, noting the ring.

'Clancy, but she is called Kathleen,' Jessie supplied.

'That's nice – do they shorten it to Kitty, I wonder?' Nurse was talking to put her patient at ease as she prepared to make her examination.

'No!' Kathleen yelled, becoming agitated.

'Don't fret, Kathleen . . . Easy now, try and relax. Good gracious, things are happening fast!' said Nurse Buss. 'The pain will soon be over. Are you ready to help me, Jessie?'

It was midnight; as the clock began to chime, the winter baby was born, at this very special time . . .

Danny hadn't gone downstairs; he was standing outside the door, alarmed at the shrieks coming from the bedroom. Abruptly the cries ceased, then he heard agitated voices.

'The cord's round the baby's neck!' Jessie exclaimed.

'Stand back, I'll deal with it,' Nurse Buss replied. 'Oh my word, it's a wonder the baby wasn't throttled as it came out.'

'Why isn't the baby crying?' Jessie asked, sounding panicked.

'I'm doing everything I can . . .'

Danny couldn't stand it. He dropped the cup, which broke and spilled cocoa onto the landing, and opened the bedroom door to see the nurse swinging the baby by its heels from side to side. At that moment the little bundle gave an indignant cry. Nurse Buss turned it right way up and belatedly announced, 'It's a girl! About five pounds – early, but all there!'

Danny rushed over to the bedside, where Kathleen stretched out her hand to him once more for comfort.

'It's a girl,' Kathleen murmured.

'I know, I heard,' he said.

'I must be dreaming,' she said, sounding far away.

'Is he the father?' Nurse Buss asked bluntly.

Before Jessie could answer, Danny heard himself saying, 'Yes.'

'She's not *Mrs* Clancy then,' Nurse Buss said, 'but I won't give my opinion. I won't spread the news; I don't approve of that. She's been through a lot, poor lass, and there's more to do here, so go downstairs, Danny, and tell Sam to make a big pot of tea.' She turned to Kathleen and gave her the baby to hold. 'She's not cleaned up yet, but nor are you. Is that basket ready to put the baby in, Jessie? Does she have a name?'

'Heather,' Kathleen said. Her lips trembled as she looked down at the baby's little wrinkled red face. 'A lucky sprig of heather.'

Jessie asked tentatively, 'Could her second name be Mary?'

'Mary was my mother's name . . .' Kathleen drew a deep breath. 'Oh, what's happening now?' she cried.

'Take your granddaughter, Jessie, while I deal with the afterbirth. And keep the boys at bay until we've seen to it,'

Nurse Buss said in her forthright way. 'Have you a nightgown and a shawl for this little one?'

'Yes, they're in the chest of drawers.' Granddaughter, Jessie thought. Goodness knows what my Danny has committed himself to, but whatever transpires, I'll love this little girl like one of my own, like the baby I hoped to have . . .

'You shouldn't have said that,' Sam said bluntly to Danny. 'How could you have been responsible? Kathleen only turned up here a few days ago. You may have let yourself in for a packet of trouble. She's a victim of bad treatment, that's obvious, but we know very little about her.'

'Except she was desperate for someone to help her, Sam. She trusts us, I can tell, and Mother already treats her like a lost daughter.'

'That's what I'm afraid of. Suppose Kathleen has done something terrible and that's why she got beaten up?' Sam couldn't help recalling the paper he had burned the night she arrived at their house.

'Don't be silly, she's too young for that.'

'And you, Danny, are not quite nineteen. Neither of you is grown up yet, but someone got her with child, didn't they? Besides, you've got a sweetheart. Marion is probably dreaming right now of her future with you. Don't tell me you think you're in love with Kathleen!'

'I feel I want to look after her – she seems innocent, despite having a baby. You'd better not say any more, Sam!'

Tempers were flaring now, just as Jessie came in to tell Sam that the midwife was ready to leave, adding to Danny, 'Kathleen wants to thank you for what you said, though she knows you spoke on impulse so you are not to worry about it.'

Danny felt embarrassed when he ventured near the bed, for the baby, wrapped in a blanket, downy dark head still damp from her first bath in a basin, was cuddled in Kathleen's arms. Seeing his flushed face, she twitched the sheet to conceal her bare breast where the baby was attempting to suckle.

'Don't worry,' he said awkwardly. 'You wanted to say something to me?'

'Yes. Thank you for trying to cover up for me not being married, but people will soon guess the truth. Anyway, Jessie says a baby is always a blessing, in or out of wedlock.'

It was the most she had said since she had arrived at Home Farm; the shock of giving birth before her time appeared to have changed things.

'She has your dark hair,' he observed. 'Sleep well tonight, Kathleen.'

'I hope I haven't upset all the Christmas plans,' she said, sounding sad.

Jessie, coming into the room at that moment, put in, 'Of course you haven't. You'll have to stay up here to rest, Kathleen. Nurse Buss will be calling daily for a week, and those are her orders. You'll be up and about again to see the new year in, I'm sure! Our friend Mrs Amos and her daughter Marion are coming to share Christmas Day with us as they always do, so I will have plenty of help in the kitchen, and we'll make sure you don't miss out on your Christmas dinner!' Jessie smothered a yawn. She had instructed Sam to put the gifts round the tree, but she couldn't come to bed yet herself.

'How kind you all are,' Kathleen said to them. She closed her eyes; she needed to say a little silent prayer of relief for her baby's safe arrival and to confess that she was still more confused than joyful. She ended with *Please let me stay here forever; I am safe here.*

Jessie leaned over the bed. 'The baby's asleep. Your milk won't come in for a day or two, but both of you are getting used to the idea, eh? Pass her to me and I'll settle her in the basket. You should have a nap too. I'll be up later to see to you both. Goodnight, Kathleen.'

Kathleen awoke in the night, shaking and dripping with perspiration. She called out to Jessie, who had not long been in bed herself, and Jessie padded on her bare feet over to the other bed. 'Hush, Kathleen – don't wake the baby. What's wrong?'

'I had a bad dream . . .'

'What about?'

'There was a man chasing after me; I thought he would catch me, take me back.'

'Back where? To where you came from, before you found the Pilgrims' Way?'

'I don't know . . . He had a black beard.' Kathleen shuddered.

'Oh that's why you were alarmed when you first met my Sam – it wasn't *him*, Kathleen, you know that! Your memory is coming back, perhaps.'

'I don't want to remember! Except . . . it was something to do with the baby. He said I had to be punished.'

'Did he . . . was he the one?'

'He was accusing me, but I got away!'

'It was only a bad dream,' Jessie said, trying to sound convincing. 'Go back to sleep and forget it; that's the best thing to do. You are with friends here; we'll protect you, I promise.'

At her own bed, she turned and reminded Kathleen, 'It's Christmas Day. How wonderful for your baby to be born on such a blessed day.'

FOUR

Danny collected Marion and her mother at mid-morning on Christmas Day, after he'd fed and watered the horses and chickens, and milked the goats. Meanwhile Sam saw to the fires and the stove. They wouldn't exchange their modest presents until the afternoon; the parcels were still round the tree. The guests also had gifts to distribute at the farm.

Marion and Danny had been friends since childhood; she was already nineteen, a few months older than him. This past year had seen a change in their relationship. Marion had grown into an attractive young woman with a curvaceous figure and blonde hair piled on top of her head. She no longer had any plaits to pull, which Danny had once been prone to do. Danny had changed too; he was no longer a skinny youth. He'd shot up in height and Marion had realised with surprise that he was disturbingly attractive, something she had not been aware of before. Their days of rough-and-tumble together, scrambling up haystacks and playing ball games in the field, had passed. Sam would say that they mooned at each other nowadays, but Marion had been well counselled by her mother and allowed Danny to go so far but no further when the two were entwined – as Sam also put it – under the porch when reluctantly parting at night.

Mrs Amos was a widow like Jessie, and Marion was her only child. Together they worked their smallholding further along the lane. They had a fine flock of Rhode Island Red chickens, and like Danny and Sam, they had chores to do before taking the rest of the day off.

'The capons smell good, Mrs Mason,' Mrs Amos observed, sniffing the aroma in the kitchen. The chickens, ready for the oven, had been her contribution to the dinner. Despite knowing each other for years, the two women still addressed one another formally.

Jessie indicated the piles of vegetables awaiting attention on the table. She was glad she had sliced and salted down the runner beans early in the autumn, as they could be tipped straight into a saucepan after rinsing. The Christmas pudding rocked merrily on the stove. There would be custard to make later, and Jessie had already whipped up the cream and put the jug on the marble slab in the pantry to keep cool.

'Marion and I will see to the table in the living room,' Danny offered. 'She'll make sure everything is in the right place.'

'The best silver, mind,' his mother told him. 'Remember forks and dessert spoons for the pudding today.'

'I suppose that leaves me to do the potatoes,' Sam said with a wry grin.

'Cut the ones for roasting into quarters,' Jessie reminded him. 'Mrs Amos and I will tackle the sprouts – Danny picked them with the frost on them first thing.'

'I nearly got frostbite in the process,' Danny said ruefully.

'You've given almost all the carrots to your horses; it's lucky I've got the big swede, plus parsnips, onions and red cabbage,' Jessie told him. 'Go and help Marion, then.'

Marion was polishing the wine glasses with a clean cloth. 'Mother's brought you six bottles of her elderberry – how many sitting at the table?'

'Five, though maybe Doc Wiseman'll turn up. Mother said he was welcome to join us. She knows what he likes, and though he says he isn't kosher, whatever that is, he mainly eats vegetables. But that isn't a problem here.'

'What about your visitor – I hear she's just had a baby? You didn't tell me about her! I think Mother knew but she didn't say anything. I expect she thought it was none of our business.' Marion sounded rather cross.

Danny encircled her waist with his arms as she bent to position the final glass to her satisfaction. 'How about a kiss for Christmas?' he asked boldly.

'Answer my question first – why didn't you tell me? We shouldn't keep secrets from each other.' His hands moved to cup her breasts. 'Danny! Someone's bound to come in here any minute – keep your hands to yourself!' she said, disengaging herself.

'Kathleen – that's her name – only had the baby last night, just after midnight, so it's a Christmas baby. I'll take you upstairs later to meet her, eh? Then you'll see she's just a girl.'

'She's old enough to have a baby. And why should I want to meet her?' she pointed out, before he kissed her to prevent any more questions. Then her arms went firmly round his neck. 'Are we going to tell the family today about our plans to get engaged?' she asked him. 'Mother's already expecting an announcement.'

Sam coughed to let them know he was about to come into the room. Had he overheard their conversation? Danny wondered. They sprang apart and Marion busied herself with the cutlery. Danny winked at his brother. 'Mother said use the best rush mats; they're in the end drawer. I suppose you've come to help.'

Sam batted him lightly on the head with one of the mats. 'Watch your step!' he advised him.

Christmas dinner was a long-drawn-out affair. The capons and ham, which had been cooked with a couple of bay leaves, were carved by Sam, and the vegetables were served: the red cabbage finely shredded, the swede mashed into a golden mound, the parsnips roasted with the potatoes, the carrots glistening with butter, the bright colour of the sprouts rivalling the green of the finely sliced runner beans. There were sausages rolled in streaky bacon, bread sauce and stuffing, delicious redcurrant sauce, and the little silver dishes lined with blue glass were filled with salt, pepper and mustard. The elderflower wine loosened tongues; there was much laughter and joking.

Between courses, Danny reached for Marion's hand under cover of the red-and-white-checked tablecloth, but she snatched it away. When Jessie served Kathleen's modest portion into a bowl, it was Danny she asked to take the food upstairs. Sam had said he would shave his beard off, but he hadn't done so yet, and she didn't want Kathleen getting upset today.

Kathleen was dozing when Danny tapped politely on the door and came in with the tray, which he placed on the bedside table. 'Merry Christmas, Kathleen.' He touched her shoulder gently.

She opened her eyes then and sat up, hair tumbling round her shoulders, and he plumped up the pillows behind her. As he leaned over, on an impulse he gave her a brief kiss on her cheek, which was damp with tears. Before he realised what she was about to do, she turned her face and kissed him full on the mouth. He could taste the salt on her lips.

'Why did you do that?' he asked, straightening up before putting the tray on her lap.

'Because I wanted to,' she replied honestly.

'I thought you didn't like me taking liberties.' He sounded bemused.

'I don't – but I suppose you have been kissing your girlfriend under the mistletoe.'

'Oh, we don't need mistletoe for that!' Danny said.

'Thank Jessie for the delicious food,' she said. 'It's lonely up here – will you come up again later, please, Danny?'

He didn't answer, because at that moment there was a knock on the front door.

'That must be Doc Wiseman; I'd better let him in. Enjoy your dinner, Kathleen.'

'You're very quiet, Danny – everything all right upstairs?' Jessie asked later.

He nodded. 'Shall I bring in the pudding?' he asked.

'No hurry, Doc's not finished his dinner yet.'

There was no pudding for Kathleen because it was considered too rich for a nursing mother. 'It could upset the baby's tummy,' Jessie had said. She left the washing-up to whoever was willing to do it and went upstairs to see to Kathleen and the baby.

Kathleen had only eaten a small amount, so Jessie removed the tray. 'I expect you miss your family today, Kathleen?'

Tears spilled from the girl's eyes. 'I've just realised that now I'm a mother, I have to grow up and behave like one. I don't think I'm ready for that. I'll never have a sweetheart now, will I? I won't get married in church in a lovely white dress. I know I must learn to love my baby, and I'm so fortunate to be here, but . . .'

'I know, my dear, I know,' Jessie told her, and just at that moment the baby woke, gave a little hiccup and began to cry.

'I don't want to feed her,' Kathleen wept. 'Is it wicked to say that?'

'Of course not, but my dear, please try.'

In the parlour downstairs, Sam wasn't joining in the jolly banter. He was perplexed about his feelings after Danny had taken Kathleen her Christmas dinner. Why hadn't Danny realised it was bound to make Marion suspicious? he wondered

There was no announcement either, no toast to celebrate good news as Marion had hoped. She didn't look at Danny and she moved away to sit beside her mother. Mrs Amos whispered something to her and Marion shook her head. 'He thinks perhaps we're too young. I think he's changed his mind . . .'

'He can't do that,' Mrs Amos said firmly. Marrying her daughter off to someone like Danny who had prospects was the first step in her plans for her own future.

Doc Wiseman was the only one who offered to visit the new mother and her baby and to congratulate Kathleen. He felt in his waistcoat pocket and produced a silver florin, which he pressed into her hand. 'A little gift for the baby,' he said, and then added, 'Our good Nurse Buss might not approve, but I think you might be brought downstairs for the ceremony round the tree, and the others can admire your bonny baby!'

'Danny . . .' she said.

'I'll take you myself,' Doc replied. 'Jessie will bring the baby, I'm sure.'

Marion didn't look at Kathleen or the baby. She was aware that her mother was watching her. She knows how I feel, she thought. Danny overstepping the mark like that, touching me – I could read his thoughts all right!

'Hold him off,' her mother had advised, only last night. 'He thinks you're a ripe apple ready to be picked.' I am, Marion privately agreed, but she wasn't sure she was ready for all that yet.

Kathleen sat next to the tree and Jessie cuddled the baby, while Sam called out names and handed over parcels. Kathleen received a pair of sheepskin mittens, so warm and cosy that she put them on immediately. 'Hand-made,' Danny told her proudly. 'I stitched them myself. They are from all of us; Mother made a pattern and cut them out.'

Mrs Amos nudged her daughter. 'There's your present from Danny, open it,' she demanded.

Marion unwrapped a fine cobweb-patterned woollen shawl. 'You didn't make *this*, Danny,' she said flatly.

He grinned. 'Of course not! But I chose the best in the shop.'

The lamps were turned low and they sang carols round the tree by candlelight, beginning with 'Away in a Manger', with a howling accompaniment from the dog, and later there were hot mince pies and Christmas cake, and the wine was drained to the last drop.

When the baby became restless and it was her feeding time, Danny offered to take Kathleen and Heather upstairs. Marion said in his ear, 'Can't Sam do it?'

Danny whispered back: 'She's afraid of his beard.'

'You're making a fool of yourself,' she hissed.

Doc Wiseman had good hearing. 'I brought her down and I must see her settled for the night. Are you ready, Kathleen?'

'Thank you all,' she said tremulously. 'Happy Christmas.'

The party broke up at midnight and Danny took Mrs Amos and Marion home. Marion clutched her present and wondered if he really loved her as he insisted he did. Their parting kiss was brief and all he said was 'See you tomorrow.' She didn't answer.

Doc Wiseman sat in his study and by candlelight opened the diary he had kept all year. He was nearing the final entry, to be made on New Year's Eve. He wrote: *My friends made me very welcome today, but it was not the same as last year. There will be, I think, big changes ahead for the Mason family.*

FIVE

'I hear you have been a naughty young mummy,' Nurse Buss told Kathleen. 'Jessie says you refused to nurse the baby, despite the fact that your milk is now established. If you carry on like this, your breasts will become very painful. Are you willing to try again?'

'I can't, I *can't*!' Kathleen cried. 'I haven't enough up top.' She stared at Nurse Buss's impressive bosom. She regretted saying to Jessie before Nurse arrived, 'She had no trouble feeding *her* children, I'm sure!'

Jessie had rebuked her. 'Nurse Buss was never able to have children of her own, Kathleen. She's a very kind person, and *she* didn't judge *you*.'

'I'm sorry, I shouldn't have said that. But you all expect me to be a good mother when I never wanted to be a mother at all – well, not until I was in my twenties. I haven't, you know, got over what happened.'

'How can we help you if we don't know what did happen?' Jessie asked, but Kathleen didn't answer. She didn't know herself, she thought; her mind was too muddled.

Now, realising that different tactics were needed, Nurse Buss said soothingly, 'All right, my dear. It won't hurt little Heather to have goat's milk; Jessie knows how to boil up feeding bottles and prepare the milk, after all. But you mustn't blame us if you suffer as a result of not relieving yourself.'

'Jessie said I would have to bind my chest, and it would take a few days to stop the milk, that's all.'

'I want you to promise me you will cuddle the baby as before while you give her the bottle,' Nurse Buss said. 'Are you seeing to the napkins? You mustn't expect so much of dear Jessie; she is a busy person, you know.'

'I bathed Heather myself today.'

'That's encouraging. You will be able to go downstairs in a couple of days, something to look forward to, and I've told Jessie I think I know where she can get a second-hand perambulator for you. I must get on – I'll see you tomorrow morning, eh?'

Marion made up her mind. She would tell Danny that if there was no engagement announced on his birthday, she would consider their romance at an end. I nearly gave myself to him, she thought. I might have ended up like that girl they've taken on even though they don't know anything about her.

First, there was New Year's Eve, followed by the first day of 1904. Kathleen and her baby joined the family downstairs and Heather slept most of the time in her Moses basket, which Jessie had made comfortable with flannel sheets and a soft blanket. Jessie had been sewing again late at night, taking in the seams of a red velvet dress with a white lace collar that had been worn by her daughter during her last Christmas. She made the alterations when she was alone because she couldn't help shedding tears as the memories came thick and fast. She said to herself firmly, 'Mary would approve, I know. She loved that dress.'

Kathleen glowed in the red dress, and with her long black hair loose, apart from a matching headband, she looked very different to the girl they had taken to their hearts the day she'd arrived in a snowstorm.

Jessie, of course, was aware of the attention paid to Kathleen by her sons. She sighed and decided that she must have a word with young Danny. Surely he doesn't intend to break Marion's heart? They seemed so in love, she thought.

Sam's feelings were harder to fathom. Jessie's opinion was that he took after his father; he was not impulsive like Danny, but if he committed himself to someone it would be for ever.

Sam planned to celebrate his birthday evening with his brother and their friends at the local inn, the Old Ship, in Tatsfield. His present from Jessie was a smart waistcoat with a guinea in the pocket. He confided to his mother it would also be a chance to talk to Danny about recent events. Mrs Amos had told Jessie that Marion was heartbroken by his rejection.

'I saw the sign to Tatsfield when I reached Hawley's Corner,' Kathleen mentioned.

'It's a friendly village,' Sam said. 'Many of the original houses were built on the escarpment of the Downs. There's a nice village green, and a pond too. We are on the outskirts here, so we like to meet up with our old school friends when we get a chance.'

'I wish I could go with you,' she sighed.

Jessie, shocked, actually reproved her. 'Women are not allowed in the saloon, Kathleen. Anyway, you are not well enough to go out yet.'

Kathleen bit back a retort; she knew that Jessie was right. Not only was she still recovering from the trauma that had forced her to run away, but Nurse Buss had told her it would take at least six weeks before she got her strength back after childbirth.

Jessie regretted snapping at Kathleen, but she was genuinely glad she had been able to help her by taking her in. She would need to economise for a while, she thought, after paying the midwife's fee, but it's only money, she told herself, and Kathleen had repeated her intention to work and earn her keep when she was able. They'd just have to wait and see.

At midnight, Kathleen awoke to hear muffled laughter on the stairs. It sounded as if one of the brothers was staggering, and the other was hanging on to him with one hand and the banister with the other. Danny! she thought. He's drunk – and Sam's likely the same.

She pulled the covers over her head. The baby gave a wail and Jessie roused herself and went over to the basket. Kathleen pretended to be asleep.

'There, there, my darling, Grandma's here: I'll warm up your bottle for you when those boys are safely in bed.'

The birthdays on the 5th were more sober affairs. Danny wondered if Marion would turn up as originally planned, but he hadn't changed his mind about the engagement.

In the kitchen after breakfast, Jessie gave him a pocket watch, which had belonged to his grandfather, and a new pair of rubber wellington boots. Sam presented him with a tweed cap to wear when riding his mare.

'I'm sorry,' Kathleen faltered. 'I haven't a present for you, Danny, and you've all been so generous to me – I've got boots too.'

'You can give Sam and me a birthday kiss,' Danny said with a grin.

'They're pulling your leg,' Jessie told her, but Kathleen, blushing, went first to Sam and then to Danny. Neither of them bent down, so she had to stand on tiptoe and grasp their shoulders before she could bestow a peck on their cheeks.

There was a burst of laughter from both of them. 'I didn't mean it, you know,' Danny admitted. 'But we enjoyed it,' he added.

Kathleen flounced over to the Moses basket, turning her back on them, feeling humiliated. She lifted Heather up and went into the living room to tell old Bob all about it.

SIX

January had been plagued by squally weather, but February 1904 would prove to be the wettest month on record; it certainly lived up to folklore, where it was known as 'February fill-dyke'.

Doc Wiseman declared Kathleen fit to begin work at the end of the month. His opinion had been sought because Kathleen believed Nurse Buss would advise her to stay at home with the baby. Jessie agreed with Doc. 'Best time for you to do it, before she's crawling into everything.'

Kathleen was aware that Jessie took everything in her stride, and that little Heather was well looked after. She's just like a grandma to my baby, she thought.

Now Kathleen squelched in her new boots along the muddy lane beside Danny. They had eaten breakfast before six o'clock and it was still dark out; they needed the lamp to light their way so they could avoid the puddles. Danny also carried a large container of water, which he had pumped up earlier. He glanced down at Kathleen; she was wearing the voluminous plaid cape for the first time since she'd arrived at the farm, and an old cloth cap she'd found on the hallstand. She'd bundled her hair under it and turned her collar up.

It was warmer in the stables. Besides the mare and foal, there was a young gelding still to be broken in, a huge plough horse, a grey pony, which pulled the buggy, and an aged donkey that the boys had ridden when they were young. These all needed their breakfast rations of hay while the straw and muck were shovelled up and deposited on the growing heap of manure a few yards away outside. Although Kathleen didn't enjoy this task, she was determined to show she could do it. She looked forward to helping with the grooming, especially the beautiful chestnut mare, Red Ruby; the gelding, Jack Spratt, had a glint in his eye.

Danny had other jobs to do, too. He let the chickens out into their run, filled their water container and scattered corn for them. He called Kathleen to feel in the nests to see if there were any eggs. 'There's a basket on a nail in the barn.'

She found six big brown eggs, still warm, which she took while the hens were busy pecking up the grain in the pen.

Danny went on to check the goats and to show Kathleen how to milk them. She wasn't too sure about their horns and their dancing hooves, which could easily become a kick if they objected to her presence, she thought.

'You've milked a cow, surely, on your farm?' he asked her.

She shook her head. 'We only kept horses, racing ones, like Red Ruby.'

Another revelation, he thought. Following advice from his mother, he did not comment.

She managed to get a few squirts of milk in the bucket, and then became aware that a fierce-looking billy goat was eyeing her over the half-door that kept him in his pen. She panicked and almost knocked the bucket over as she fled outside, where Danny was tying up a loose panel in the fencing. 'Danny, the billy goat will get me!' she panted.

'Don't be so silly,' he told her. 'But I'd better take over before you, well, kick the bucket, eh?'

Kathleen watched from the doorway as he sat on the stool and began to hum a tune. The goats seemed to calm down and listen. He had names for them: Dotty and Spotty.

When he didn't speak to her, she sneaked back to the horses and located the grooming tools. Surely he would appreciate that, she thought.

'Why did you go off like that?' he demanded later. 'You can help me take the milk back to the farm, and I expect Mother will brew some tea and give us a biscuit or two.' He looked at her thoughtfully. 'You're good with horses; I might teach you to ride, eh?'

Kathleen snapped back, 'I expect I could teach you a few things, like not using a whip!' She had spotted the crop among the saddlery.

'I have a light riding crop, true, but I just flick it now and again to urge a horse on,' he said crossly. Then he remembered belatedly what Jessie had told him about the raw red weals on Kathleen's back when she first arrived. 'I'm sorry,' he said.

'What for?' she flared. 'No one is going to beat me ever again!' She pressed her face against the mare's flank, trying to hide the fact that she was crying.

'Oh Kathleen,' sighed Danny, turning her gently to face him. This time she buried her face against the harsh wool of his jersey. His arms tightened around her.

'You smell of farms,' she said in a muffled voice.

He shook with laughter. 'What d'you expect? You'll smell like that at the end of today, I reckon. Fortunately you took off your smart coat. Hey, isn't that one of my old jerseys?' He lifted her off her feet so that they were face to face. She clung to him and closed her eyes. It was a moment when anything could have happened, and they were so close she was aware that his heart was beating fast, like her own.

She wriggled free from his grasp. 'Well it's my working jersey now. Jessie said you wouldn't mind.'

'I don't, but it swamps you, like your cape; there's hardly anything of you since you've had the baby.' His face showed his concern. He couldn't help comparing her slight figure with Marion's delectable curves.

'You've been ignoring me since my . . . our birthday, you *and* Sam,' she reproached him.

'Why do you think that is?' he said softly. 'I let Marion down because she was jealous that I was paying you attention. It'll take time for her and me to get back on the old footing.'

'Is that what you want?' she challenged him.

He handed her the cape. 'Why should I tell *you*? Come on, Mother will be waiting for the milk.'

'But what about Sam? I thought he liked me too.'

He handed her the lighter bucket. 'Well, you and I have something in common –horses – but Sam is only interested in building his house and making bricks.'

'Oh good, here you are at last. Heather needs her bottle,' Jessie said, as she took the milk into the pantry. 'Have you finished your chores in the barn, Kathleen? When you're cleaned up, will you bath and dress the baby? I would like to go up to the village later and I thought you could come too with the pram and we might meet some of my friends. At least the rain's let up for a bit.' She looked at Danny. 'Did she do well, Danny?'

'Yes, she did,' he replied. 'Tea up, Mother?'

'Wash your hands in the scullery first; I don't want you poking in my biscuit tin till you have,' Jessie warned him. 'Fill Kathleen's big jug from the copper water too, before I put the clothes to boil.'

'Yes, I'll wash up upstairs and get changed, then see to Heather,' Kathleen said. She'd already taken her boots off; they would need to be cleaned of mud and straw, she thought, before she walked into the village.

Danny kept his boots on as he sipped his hot tea. His mother washed the flagged kitchen floor several times a day, but that was expected of the women of the house.

'She'll need some breeches if she's going to ride,' he told her.

'I know what you're thinking, Danny, but I put Mary's old breeks in the ragbag – I'll have a look for them later. Mary was only twelve when she wore them, but I reckon they'll fit our Skinny Lizzie.'

'Sam gone down the brickworks?' Danny enquired, changing the subject. He wouldn't admit to himself how aroused he'd felt when he'd held Kathleen in his arms at the stable. She thinks of me as the one who saved her that day, he thought, and I suppose I am, but I should have told her gently that I am spoken for. The trouble is, I can't stop feeling the way I do, and Marion is aware of that . . .

'Not yet,' Jessie said. 'He went upstairs for something. He's tidied up the yard and filled the water buckets. He'll be down for his tea shortly.'

'If you see Mrs Amos . . .' Danny began diffidently.

'I'll tell her, shall I, that you want to make up with Marion?'

'How do you always know what I intend to do, Mother?'

'You're my son, aren't you? I know you from A to Z!' Jessie replied. 'Well, I suppose I had better take Heather upstairs for her bath.'

As Jessie was about to climb the stairs, baby in arms, she met Sam coming down. 'Turn around. You can deliver Heather to her mother and save my legs,' she told him. He hoisted the baby to rest comfortably against his shoulder. Heather wasn't afraid of his beard, he thought ruefully.

He knocked on the bedroom door before he ventured in.

Kathleen was standing at the washstand, clad only in her chemise. 'Thank you, Sam. Put Heather in her basket on the stand, will you?'

He did so, and then backed out of the door without a word. He'd glimpsed the scars on her back before she had turned round, and the sight had shocked him.

Jessie pushed the pram up the hill while Kathleen held one side of the handle, finding it to be hard work. 'The wheels need a spot of oil,' Jessie observed. The sun briefly shone before it disappeared between two ominous black clouds. A few spots of rain was all that fell, though, for the moment.

There was plenty of hustle and bustle in the heart of the village, round the green.

'What a wonderful pond!' Kathleen exclaimed. 'And the cottages – the bricks are such a lovely colour! It's like a picture book. Is that the school?'

Jessie nodded. 'The boys did well there,' she said proudly. 'Sam's still a keen reader. He has all the latest novels; he's ordered *Nostromo*, though I'm not sure what it's about. It's written by Joseph Conrad – have you heard of him?'

'No – I haven't had time to read lately. I loved *Black Beauty*; it was a birthday present when I was ten, but that was left behind.'

'Remind me to buy that new *Daily Mirror* newspaper for Sam. He says there's much more news in it than the local paper; he likes to know what's going on in the world,' Jessie said, adding. 'He asked me to buy you a bar of chocolate, too.'

'Trying to fatten me up,' Kathleen said ruefully. 'Look, someone's waving at you.'

'That's Mrs Amos – you didn't chat to her on Christmas Day, did you? She's Marion's mother.'

'I didn't speak to Marion either; she's Danny's girlfriend, isn't she?'

'Well she is and she isn't. They had a bit of a falling-out, but I'm going to offer the olive branch.' Jessie waved vigorously in return.

'Not the day for a walk,' Mrs Amos said, looking under the hood of the pram at the baby. 'Don't keep her out too long in this miserable weather. When you've done your shopping, call in at my place on the way home and we'll have a nice hot cup of tea.' She rustled a paper bag in her basket.

'I couldn't resist these Kentish apple cakes in the baker's, even though I've got some scones in the tin at home!'

'I'm just going to the newsagent's for a newspaper for Sam and ten cigarettes for Danny, and then we can walk back together. I thought of taking Kathleen round to look at the church, but I reckon the skies are about to open, don't you?'

'You shouldn't encourage Danny to smoke; Marion disapproves of the habit,' Mrs Amos said, looking at Kathleen, who remained silent.

'Will Marion be at home?' Jessie asked, tucking her purchases under the pram cover.

'She will. She's busy with her sewing – she's thinking of going to the Big House, as they've asked her if she'd like to work part-time there. They need someone in charge of the linen, and she's very neat with her darning.'

'Oh, is there not much profit in the poultry nowadays? We're getting very few eggs ourselves at the moment, but when it's your living . . .'

'She thinks she might as well earn some extra money, enjoy herself, if there's no wedding on the horizon.' Again Mrs Amos looked long and hard at Kathleen.

Jessie was indignant. 'Danny hasn't been unfaithful to her, if that's what you're getting at. You can keep your cakes! Kathleen and I will go straight home from the shop!'

Kathleen didn't speak until they were back indoors. She'd changed the baby and settled down on the sofa to give her the bottle of milk that Jessie had warmed up. Jessie took off her boots and sat beside them. 'I'm sorry Mrs Amos snubbed you like that, Kathleen. I suppose Marion is hoping to make Danny come to heel. They can think what they like, but I brought my lads up to respect women, not . . . I'm sorry; perhaps I shouldn't have said that, my dear.'

'It's my entire fault,' Kathleen said, dampening the baby's dark hair with her tears. 'It always is.' She glanced down at her mother's wedding ring. I wish that what Danny told Nurse Buss was true, she thought. I wish he really was the father of my baby . . .

Jessie couldn't bring herself to tell Danny about the falling-out with Mrs Amos. When he said that evening that he was going out for a while, she just nodded. 'Don't clatter about when you come home; I feel like an early night.'

'What do you want?' Marion demanded when she opened the door that evening to find Danny and old Bob on the step.

'Aren't you going to invite me in?' he said. 'I've got something to ask you.'

'If you're about to say what I think you are, the answer is no, Danny Mason. You . . . you *jilted* me!'

'How can you say that? We weren't engaged, after all.'

'But we were about to be, until you set eyes on that little Irish girl – when she'd just had a baby, too! How could you!'

'I feel sorry for her, that's all,' he said in his defence. Then he turned, and Bob, who had been quivering on the cold step, rose to follow him. 'I'm sorry, but if you can't trust me, Marion, it's no good me trying to explain. I'm seeing another side of you, I'm afraid. I thought we were in love . . .'

'So did I, but I was wrong!' She slammed the door before he could say any more.

Jessie was weary and still upset about falling out with Mrs Amos, so she went off early to bed as she'd said she would. 'I'll take Heather up with me, shall I, since she's fallen asleep after her bottle. You enjoy the fire for a bit longer, Kathleen, and drink your cocoa, eh?'

Kathleen put another log on the fire. Sam arrived home; she supposed he had been to the pub. He looked in to say goodnight. 'Where's Mother?' he asked.

'She's gone up already. Goodnight, Sam,' she said.

'Danny not back yet?' he asked as he turned to go.

'Wasn't he in the pub with you?' Kathleen asked abruptly.

'I wasn't there, I was at Doc Wiseman's, and he invited me to have a game of chess. Satisfied?' He didn't wait for an answer.

Kathleen was anxious, not satisfied. She watched the fire die down as she waited for Danny to come home. Around midnight, she closed her eyes and sleep overtook her.

She woke suddenly and became aware that she was not alone. Danny was slumped with hunched shoulders next to her on the sofa, and Bob was stretched out on the rag rug, warming up. The room was dark, apart from the glow from the fire. He must have snuffed the candles out.

'Oh, you've woken up at last,' he said. 'You'd better get off to bed. I'm not sure I'm steady enough to go upstairs.'

'You smell of beer – and cigarettes,' she told him, shocked.

'It's none of your business,' he said, his voice slurred.

'I'll help you up to your room. Jessie won't be happy until she knows you're there.'

She tried to pull him up; he swayed and clung to her. 'Let's go, then.'

'We've got to go to work in the morning,' she reminded him.

Sam was standing at the top of the stairs in his night-shirt, looking down on them as they struggled up step by step. 'Leave him to me,' he said briefly. 'I'll put him to bed.' The door to their shared bedroom was open and he steered his brother inside. Kathleen made her way past the empty room that she knew had been Mary's, and crept as quietly as she could over to her own bed.

A voice came from the other bed. 'Thank you, Kathleen,' Jessie sighed.

Kathleen undressed quickly, left her clothes in a heap on the end of the bed and slid between the covers. Jessie had provided a hot-water bottle earlier, and she warmed her feet on it gratefully. She hoped Heather would not wake again for a few hours. She lay for a while feeling forlorn. They were a happy family till I came, she thought. Oh why do I always upset folk wherever I go?

SEVEN

Kathleen awoke with a start. It took her a few moments to realise that she had overslept; that Jessie's bed and Heather's Moses basket were empty. The little clock on the washstand was ticking away noisily as usual, and she checked the time: 7.30 a.m.! Someone had delivered her jug of hot water, which was still steaming, so whoever it was had seen her sleeping, she thought.

She washed and dressed hurriedly. On top of the now folded clothes she had discarded she saw a pair of corduroy knee breeches and some thick socks: oh, so I'm expected to go to the stables as soon as possible.

As she reached the stairs, she heard a rumbling noise. It must be Danny snoring, she thought indignantly; like a . . . pig!

She rapped on his door and said loudly, 'Wake up!' before going downstairs. She was greeted by Sam in the hall carrying the milk pails.

'Good morning,' he said, as if nothing was untoward. 'Have your breakfast and then we must get to the stables and see to the horses. Danny not stirred yet?'

She shook her head. 'I don't think so. Heather?'

'In the kitchen with her doting grandma.' Sam actually smiled. 'No one's cross with *you*, Kathleen; you were a great help last night. Lead the way, these buckets are heavy.' As he followed her, he added, 'Those breeks fit you like a glove.'

Kathleen couldn't think of anything to say to that, but she was blushing because of where his gaze was riveted.

'Your scrambled eggs will be all rubbery, I'm afraid; they don't like being warmed up,' Jessie said, and then, with a smile, 'Oh, I'm glad the breeches look good on you! Not that I usually like women in trousers – they are hardly a feminine garment, are they?'

As she ate her breakfast, Kathleen thought ruefully: I read more into Sam's opinion than I should have . . . How could I look attractive in well-worn breeches with a big patch on the bottom? She smiled at her own foolishness and glanced at Heather, kicking her legs up and down in the pram, gurgling. She's a very happy baby, she realised, thanks to dear Jessie. I wasn't sure I could love her, but now I know I do. It is a good feeling.

Jessie poured fresh cups of tea and then sat at the table for a short rest. 'Kathleen, Sam and I were talking earlier, and I think it's time you and Heather had a room of your own,' she said.

Sam put in, 'Mother needs a good night's sleep now that she looks after the baby most of the day while you are working.'

Jessie frowned at her elder son; it wasn't his place to reprove Kathleen, she thought. 'You can have the room next to mine, so I'll be nearby if you need me in the night,' she added.

'But . . . that's Mary's room, isn't it? Where you keep all her things,' Kathleen faltered.

'My dear, the trunk can remain in the corner, but Mary was a happy girl, always smiling, until she caught scarlet fever. So my memories are of her as she was before she was ill, and I know she wouldn't mind you being in that room.'

'Danny and I can move the furniture around as you would like it,' Sam offered. He saw the tears glistening in Kathleen's eyes and added, 'You are one of the family now, and the baby is too. We'll take care of you . . . Now, shall I wake my brother up nicely, or pour a jug of cold water over his head?'

'You'd better not,' Jessie warned him. 'The water would go all over the bedclothes!'

'Oh well, drink your tea, Kathleen, and we'll get on with our jobs at the stables. Then I'll take you to the brickworks and you can decide if you'd like to help me as well as Danny.'

'You could share me, you mean?' she asked naïvely.

Sam laughed out loud at her remark, and Kathleen caught a flash of his good white teeth, usually obscured by the beard and moustache. She suddenly realised that he was clean-shaven today. Jessie was smiling too, as she scooped the baby up from the pram and exclaimed, 'Damp pants again – time to change your napkin, young lady. Sam, off you both go, and be back for lunch at one.'

They did the usual chores. Kathleen scraped the stable floor clean and spread fresh straw. Then came the enjoyable part, she thought, with currycomb and brush, teasing out tangles in the horses' tails and manes.

'I could do with a stepladder,' she said as she stretched up to groom Big Ben, the shire horse. He was patient, not skittish like Red Ruby.

Sam was attending to the donkey's hooves. 'He doesn't get enough exercise, unlike the buggy pony, I'm afraid. Still, in a year or two, Heather will be able to sit on his back. I hope she has a feeling for horses like you; they like to nuzzle in your soft little hands. Maybe my big hands are too calloused because of the bricks.'

Kathleen felt a warm glow inside. They really do want me to stay, she thought. 'Has the foal a name?' she asked.

'Danny didn't say.' The foal was red like her mother, with a white flash on the forehead.

'Mother suggested Grasshopper, after the local legend. Did she tell you about that?'

She shook her head, so he went on, 'The Greshams from Holt in Norfolk acquired the manors of Titsey, Tatsfield, Westerham and Lingfield in the sixteenth century. They have a grasshopper on their coat of arms. The founder of the family was said to be Roger de Gresham, who was discovered as a newborn baby abandoned in a field; he was saved by a lad studying grasshoppers chirping in the long grass, where the baby was hidden. Later, Sir Thomas Gresham built the original Royal Exchange in London, which was destroyed in the Great Fire of London . . . Am I boring you, Kathleen? You look far away.'

'No, I think the story of the grasshopper is . . . entrancing!' she said. 'Carry on.'

'Well, Thomas Gresham was also involved in foiling the Gunpowder Plot, Guy Fawkes and all that, in 1605. The interesting connection with Tatsfield is that the felon who betrayed his fellow conspirators escaped and galloped on his horse past Church Corner in the village, or so they say . . . You're yawning, I see, so I'll stop the history lesson there.'

'Sorry, I was listening, honestly, but I was looking at the foal and thinking that Grasshopper is a good name. And

I was thinking about what Jessie said: that you were very clever when you were at school.'

'Oh, did she say that? I wanted to go on to university and study history, but my dad . . . Well, he said, "Learn to do a hard day's work first, boy!" When he died, I knew I'd have to help support my mother, especially when we lost my sister too. Danny, of course, is her favourite son, though she'd never admit it, so he gets away with a lot that she wouldn't tolerate from me.' He smiled at Kathleen, 'It doesn't worry me. He'll inherit the farm one day and I already have the brickworks! Let's go there now, eh?'

They went through a five-barred gate and along a wide path with woodland on either side. They came upon the brickworks suddenly, and after stepping down from the buggy, went down steps into a hollow. Kathleen surprised herself when she literally skipped round the circular courtyard where the bricks were originally dug and fired, which was now sealed off with many odd bricks in different shades of yellow, red and blue. There was a pump in one corner and a pile of bricks the other side. Beyond was a field, where Sam explained that a pit would be dug, since the old one was exhausted.

Kathleen saw on a rise to one side a range of black-tarred barns. 'That's where my uncle lived for years on and off,' Sam pointed out. 'I used to come here with him sometimes and learn all about brick making. I'll build my own house alongside the big barn when the clay pit is ready.'

They pumped up some water for the pony, now cropping the grass. Then Sam took Kathleen into the big barn, where he boiled a kettle on a small stove. They sat together on a wooden settle, talking while they munched on the rather stale biscuits Sam produced from a tin and sipped hot tea. She wondered whether the biscuits dated back to his uncle's time there.

She felt relaxed in Sam's company. He doesn't affect me like Danny does, she thought. I suppose I was looking for love, but this is not the time or place. Sam treats me like a sister.

As if he was reading her thoughts, he said suddenly, 'Danny is hoping to mend the rift with Marion, you know, but she has a jealous nature.'

'Surely she isn't jealous of me? I'm not pretty like her, and my past life . . .' She paused.

'No,' he said quietly, 'you aren't pretty; you're beautiful, Kathleen. Your past is past, as far as I'm concerned. I don't want to know what you are unwilling to tell us.'

'Are you . . .?'

'Am I falling in love with you? Who knows – I certainly don't. But I enjoy your company. I'm five years older than you, but you have more experience of life; you are already a mother, though you obviously aren't grown up.' He gently tweaked her hair. 'You are very desirable, though,' he said pensively, thinking, why on earth did I tell her that?

'Why don't you kiss me?' she faltered.

'Because one kiss wouldn't be enough. Now let me tell you how we make bricks,' he said briskly.

She spotted a folded newspaper on the cluttered table. 'I'd like to read the paper while I drink my tea.'

'The news is a few days old, nothing interesting. I brought it along to light the fire.'

There was something he didn't want her to see, about the mystery in Croydon.

The coroner reached his verdict. The woman, now identified as Mrs Viola D'Estrange, aged around sixty, was said to have died from natural causes, although she had unexplained injuries. Her male companion, in his forties, unnamed, attempted suicide after questioning, and is now confined in a secure hospital. The girl in the case, believed to be the niece of Mrs D'Estrange, is still missing. There is concern for her welfare as she was heavily pregnant at the time she disappeared.

Sam crumpled the paper and tore a couple of sheets into shreds. He wouldn't forget the words, he thought. He put the paper in the rusty grate and lit a corner of it. It flared up instantly.

Kathleen watched, puzzled. Why hadn't he added some wood to the brief blaze?

'Shall I tell you how we make bricks?' Sam asked eagerly.

As he went on to explain the process, Kathleen snuggled up close to him, and he suddenly noticed that her eyelids were flickering. 'Have I sent you to sleep? I apologise if you were bored.'

'No,' she said dreamily. 'It's just that I was wishing you would kiss me – oh, not in a romantic way, but you see, when I was a little girl, my father used to pick me up and hug me and kiss me whenever I was crying or sad, and call me his princess.'

'Ah, so you need a fatherly kiss now and then?' He stroked her cheek with a finger. 'Well I don't mind that, so long as you're not thinking of marrying me – or Danny, who is far too immature.'

He hugged her and then kissed her, but it was not a fatherly kiss at all. It left them both breathless for a minute or two. Sam was worried he had taken advantage of her vulnerability, while Kathleen couldn't help thinking: if only it had been Danny . . .

'Time to go home,' Sam said unevenly. 'There might be a surprise for you, I hope, if Mother's managed to get Danny up and out of bed.'

Jessie looked keenly at Kathleen's flushed face when they walked into the kitchen as she was dishing up stew and dumplings on to the dinner plates. 'Your bedroom is ready for you,' she said proudly. 'Danny moved your bed and the baby's things in there earlier. Did you have a good day?'

Sam answered for them both. 'A surprisingly good day, Mother. Kathleen knows how to make bricks now.'

EIGHT

After a cruel winter, it was a record year for sunshine from spring to a glorious summer. Crops ripened early in June, including the strawberries in Kent. The local pickers arrived soon after dawn; fruit picked then would be taken to Covent Garden market by horse-drawn spring vans for sale the same day.

Young Heather was now sitting up, though not yet crawling, so Kathleen wheeled her pram along to the strawberry fields and parked it under the shade of a tree opposite her designated row. The lines of leafy green plants with their hidden bounty stretched as far as the eye could see.

Jessie would check on the baby from time to time; she didn't pick the fruit herself, but organised the army of pickers and the trays of strawberries awaiting collection. Danny and Sam carried these and loaded them when the big vans arrived. Jessie had a notebook and pencil in her pocket. The pickers' tally must agree with her diligent counting.

Heather wore a sunbonnet and a muslin dress to protect her from sunburn, but as an added precaution, Jessie advised Kathleen to smear cold cream on the baby's exposed limbs. Kathleen mused that her own fair complexion was more in need of protection, for Heather's plump, dimpled cheeks were a peachy shade. She also had beautiful brown eyes. Kathleen could not acknowledge to herself why this must be.

Heather played happily with her teething rattle and soft toys and watched proceedings. The youngsters who came along with their mothers liked rocking the pram and making the baby gurgle with laughter. Jessie noted the remains of a strawberry that one of the children had obviously given the baby. Heather had sucked the juice, which had dribbled down her front, then thrown it overboard, like her toys, which her small admirers retrieved constantly.

When a break was called, Kathleen returned to give Heather a drink of water and a hard-baked rusk, for her front teeth were about to erupt. Kathleen herself drank from a bottle of cold tea, made without milk and sugar. She enjoyed the fresh taste of the new Typhoo Tea that Jessie had decided to try.

The pickers lay about under the hedges that bordered the strawberry rows. Kathleen spotted a familiar face – Marion, her hair glinting gold in the sun. She'd shortened her skirt by pulling the excess material through and above her belt, and Kathleen could see her shapely legs and dimpled knees. And here I am in these grubby breeches, she thought with a pang, one of Danny's baggy old shirts with the sleeves rolled up, the ankle boots I wore when I came here, with my hair tied back like a horse's tail and this awful straw hat that Danny says he'll give to the donkey later . . .

Tucked under her arm was a cushion covered in sacking, on which she shuffled along what seemed an endless row of plants. She loved the sensation of parting the foliage and discovering the fruit clustering in the cool shade beneath. The redder the berry, the sweeter the taste, she'd discovered. She had eaten her share of them, hoping she was not observed. The experienced pickers were already halfway up their second row; they didn't crawl, but went swiftly between the plants, bending their backs to the task, picking the berries with a skilful twist of the stem. The little green cap must remain, or the strawberry was not acceptable. 'Hello, Kathleen, how are you?' Marion asked pleasantly. 'I didn't recognise you at first. Surprised to see me? Danny and I are together again, as you know. I am allowed home from my job to help with the picking, which I do every year.'

Kathleen had not been aware that Danny was reconciled with his first love, as he paid her scant attention nowadays. This saddened her, because she no longer felt close to him, or as though she could cling to him as she had when she first arrived. Sam was a different matter; he treated her as if she were a younger sister, but she couldn't forget that moment of unexpected passion the first time she had visited the brickworks. This had not been repeated. She suspected that Jessie had spoken to both her sons.

As Kathleen made her way back along her row with her basket, she glanced back and saw that Danny had arrived after attending to the early morning stable duties. He helped Marion to her feet and the pair embraced briefly before they returned to their respective tasks. He's ignoring me, she thought sadly. I was a fool to think he had feelings for me, but I miss him. He was my confidant; I can't tell things to Sam the way I could to Danny.

Danny shaded his eyes with a hand as he scanned the rows until he saw Kathleen moving slowly along on her knees, searching for the best berries. He sighed. She must think I was never attracted to her, he thought, but I must be aloof because I was forced to choose between her and Marion. The trouble is, I can't stop thinking about Kathleen and wondering what might have been, but I have to do the honourable thing by Marion. I hope Kathleen hasn't been hurt too much by all of this.

A newcomer arrived and stood looking at the pickers as they worked. It was Doc Wiseman, box camera in hand. The girl in the next row to Kathleen said, 'Turn your head and smile! He takes pictures of the strawberry pickers every summer for the local paper.'

'I don't know if I can stand up. My knees are really sore in spite of the cushion,' Kathleen said faintly.

'Oh go on – I see Danny's girl is posing for him already!'

'She's much better looking than me,' Kathleen said dolefully. 'I'm not sure I want folk to recognise me dressed like this.'

'They don't give our names,' the girl assured her.

Kathleen stretched her aching back and saw Doc coming along the row ready to take their picture. Maybe the newspaper readers will think I'm a boy, she thought hopefully.

Danny followed him up. He helped Kathleen to her feet and stood between the two girls. 'You tower over them, Danny; put a hand on each of their shoulders – young ladies, display your baskets of strawberries.' Doc encouraged.

Someone else was rustling along the row towards them. 'Wait for me, Doc!'

As Marion approached the group, Danny moved back so she could stand in front of him between the two other girls. His arms encircled her waist. It was an intimate gesture.

Kathleen heard him whisper to Marion, 'Let your skirts down or your mother will be shocked when she sees the photograph.' Marion likes to be the centre of attention, Kathleen thought ruefully

'I really came along to tell you all it's time to go home,' Danny said. 'We pack up at one o'clock, as any fruit picked once the vans have gone cannot be kept until tomorrow. Mother said feel free to take your final basket home to your family; we'll see you at five a.m. tomorrow,' he added to the other girl. 'I'm going to check on the horses now, Marion; they went into the paddock first thing. Would you like to come with me? Then I'll take you home.'

They went across the rows in a zigzag fashion towards the stables and the field beyond. Their laughter drifted back to the little group. Kathleen couldn't help thinking that as the horses were outside, the two of them would be able to have a roll in the hay. After all, when you were young and eager, and no one else was around . . . It was never like that for me, though, she thought. I was a prisoner in that place.

She walked alongside Doc Wiseman; they could see Jessie waiting for them with Heather. Kathleen pushed the pram while Jessie went ahead.

'You look a different girl; happy, Kathleen,' Doc told her.

She smiled. 'Due to hard work – I've got muscles now – and good food, Doc.'

'My dear, it is love that has made you bloom.'

Kathleen blushed and said impulsively, 'You're wrong if you think it is one of Jessie's boys – it seemed that way at first; however they treat me like a sister.'

'I was referring to the love you have been given by Jessie. She knew nothing about you, but she took you into her home and cared for you.'

'You took your time,' Jessie greeted them. 'Will you join us for dinner, Doc? It'll be salad and stuffed tomatoes; we have a glut of those now.'

'Thank you, the right fare for a hot day,' he said. 'I wonder, will Danny be back later? I wish to discuss something with him; you also, Jessie.'

Jessie sighed. 'Who knows? Time means nothing when you are, shall I say, smitten?'

Kathleen lifted the baby from the pram and went to her room to see to her, and to have a quick wash in cold water before she shed her working clothes and changed into a frock. All my clothes once belonged to Mary, she thought, and I'm grateful for them, but when I get my strawberry money, I'll buy a dress that fits me.

'Well, Heather, are you ready for your bottle?' She gave the baby a kiss. 'Jessie says you look more like me now you've grown some hair on your head, and I'm glad.'

'I'm sorry,' Danny murmured as he rolled away from Marion in the hayloft.

Marion reached out to him again – she was ecstatic, not upset. 'Now you'll *have* to marry me, Danny Mason!' She had unbuttoned her blouse herself, and for the first time he had been allowed to caress her bare flesh and they had thrown caution to the winds.

He didn't answer that; he detached himself once more, and helped her down the loft ladder. She encouraged me, he thought, but that's no excuse.

'I'll take you home,' he said. 'Your mother will be wondering where on earth we are.'

'She'll know,' Marion said. 'Mothers always do.'

Mrs Amos didn't ask why Marion looked dishevelled, saying merely, 'Come in, both of you. Better have a wash before you sit down to lunch. At least the food didn't spoil as it's a cold platter today, what with this heat.'

Danny said awkwardly, 'Mother will wonder where I am . . .'

'Nonsense. I'll be round to see her shortly, as I hope you've got some good news for me?' She exchanged a glance with Marion, and they both smiled.

At that moment, Danny realised that what had just happened between him and Marion must have been with Mrs Amos's encouragement. He was trapped. What could he do except say, 'Yes, Marion and I intend to be married.'

'As soon as possible, just in case,' Marion said, sounding triumphant. 'If Mother will give her consent, as I'm under twenty-one.'

'I shall be glad to do so. You will have to go back to your job when the strawberry season is over and work a week's notice. I will discuss a date with Mrs Mason – September sounds right, eh?'

Danny had to make something clear before it was too late. 'It's always been understood that when I got married, my wife and I would live on the farm – after all, Mother needs me, and I have the stables to consider.'

'I will miss Marion, but I've had help with the poultry while she has been away and I think I can manage, though I might need a contribution now and then to the bills.' Mrs Amos looked meaningfully at Danny. He was relieved. For a moment he'd thought she would announce her intention of moving to the farm with her daughter. He realised that he was trapped in any case.

'Oh, you're here at last,' Jessie greeted him. 'Doc Wiseman was here, but he had to leave for an appointment. He says can you call in on him one evening; he has something important to ask you.'

Danny sounded subdued. 'I'll see him soon, but not tonight, Mother. I have other things on my mind.' He looked over at Kathleen, with her baby in her arms. She had combed out her hair and wore a pretty summer dress. I'm a fool, I know that, he thought, but now it's too late. Suppose I've put Marion in the family way?

'Were the horses all right?' Kathleen asked. 'I missed them today.'

He nodded. 'Mother, I need to tell you something, but I'll get cleaned up first.'

'I think I can guess what it might be, Danny,' Jessie said quietly. 'I'll come up to your room in ten minutes.'

At the end of the first week, there was excitement when the strawberry pickers opened the local paper to see the photographs taken by Doc Wiseman.

Kathleen was relieved; her new friend Isobel was right. The caption simply read: A BUMPER CROP OF STRAWBERRIES! And below that: SOME HAPPY PICKERS! Her eyes were drawn to the couple in the middle: Danny and Marion.

She had shed a few tears that night, after hearing the news about the forthcoming marriage, and was glad she no longer shared Jessie's bedroom. She realised that the trauma she had been through had made her desperate to find someone to love and care for her. Now that her emotions had stabilised, she was aware that she was not ready for such a relationship yet. She was not even sure which brother she cared for the most. However, Danny was now out of bounds.

Danny had had his chat with Doc Wiseman and had come home very excited. 'Doc wants to join me in my venture at the stables. He's saved a lot of money over the years and wants to invest in a couple more good horses – he believes in me, Mother!' he said to Jessie.

'So do I, son,' she said quietly. 'Is Marion pleased?'

He bit his lip. 'I haven't told her yet, she's too busy with the wedding plans.'

The following week, Kathleen was at home with Heather after working hard all morning, and was resting on the couch when Jessie answered a knock on the door. She called out to Kathleen, 'A surprise visitor for you!'

Kathleen was trembling as she wondered who on earth it might be. She laid the sleeping baby down and wedged a cushion beside her, in case she rolled over and slipped off the couch. Bob twitched an ear, alert even when he appeared to be asleep nearby.

A tall woman clad in grey stood in the hallway. For a long moment she said nothing, then she held out her arms. 'Kathleen! I know your name now. I recognised your picture in the paper; my husband spotted that the photographer was an old friend of ours, Dr Abraham Wiseman, so he got in touch with him and discovered that you were here. I have worried about you ever since you went off in that awful weather – I thought I should have taken you home with me that night, even though we are a houseful – but here you are, safe and sound, with a beautiful baby, and I want to give you a big hug!'

'The minister's wife,' Kathleen said faintly, relieved that it was not another face from the past. Then her knees buckled and she fell to the ground.

When she came to, she was lying on the couch with Jessie bent over her, wafting a bottle of smelling salts under her nose. The minister's wife was jiggling Heather, now wide awake, on her hip. Kathleen spluttered and pushed the bottle away. She sat up. 'What happened?' she asked.

Jessie stroked her forehead with a damp cloth. 'You passed out – you panicked, Kathleen. Who did you think it might be?'

'I'm not sure,' she said slowly, 'but I'm sorry if I alarmed you.'

Sam, who had arrived home while Kathleen was lying in the hall, and had carried her into the living room, had been dispatched to make tea, the universal panacea. He came into the room now with a tray, which he placed on a low table.

'Let me help you sit up, Kathleen,' he said, sounding concerned. He moved her carefully and put a cushion behind her back. 'There. Now would you like me to hold the cup to your lips so you can sip the tea when you're ready?'

Still a bit disorientated, she said, 'Oh, I do like Typhoo . . .' He laughed and she told him, 'You have such good teeth.'

'All the better to smile at you with! But I hope I don't look like a big bad wolf.'

'Oh I do like you, Sam . . .'

Jessie and the minister's wife – who told them cheerfully to call her Min for short – sat down and sipped their tea, too. Heather lay on the rug and amused them with her gymnastics. Bob the dog watched her with his head on his front paws, for he had taken on the role of looking after her when he sensed it was necessary.

Sam held the cup steady as he said he would, and Kathleen drank her tea in little gulps. She was feeling stronger by the minute. 'You were out in the field in the blazing sun for eight hours, running backwards and forwards to see to Heather. It's no wonder you fainted,' Sam said. Turning to Jessie, he asked, 'Could she have the day off tomorrow? That would help.'

'Of course she can,' Jessie agreed.

Min said in her ear, 'What a thoughtful son you have, Jessie.'

'They are both good boys, and now it seems I have an adopted daughter and granddaughter, after losing a precious daughter four years ago.'

Danny came in accompanied by Doc Wiseman. 'What's wrong?' he asked anxiously when he saw Kathleen.

'Nothing at all,' Kathleen answered. 'But as Doc will have told you, I'm sure, I have had a great surprise – meeting the lady who helped me along the Pilgrims' Way.'

'Any chance of a cup of tea for Doc and me?' Danny asked. 'Marion was helping me get the horses into the stables, but we took her home before we came back here.'

'I'll make a fresh pot,' Sam said.

'There's a fruit cake in the tin,' Jessie called after him. 'Slice it up on a plate!'

'I must go,' Min said. 'My brood will be home and waiting for their supper.'

Kathleen said, 'You will come again, won't you? I wore your warm cape all winter, you know, and the sprig of lucky heather is still in the pocket. I am so grateful to you; I wouldn't have got here without your help.'

'It is always good to hear of a happy ending to troubles,' said Min, 'and here you have a new family and a new life.'

NINE

On a sunny day in September, Danny turned to watch the progress of his bride down the aisle. Sam, his best man, gave his arm a squeeze of encouragement. Danny felt uncomfortable wearing a starched white shirt and high stiff collar with a tie instead of his usual neckerchief. His suit wasn't new, but it had belonged to his late uncle and had not been much worn, due to it not being suitable wear for the brickyard. Jessie had altered it to fit him.

At Marion's insistence, there had been no intimate moments for the two of them since the occasion that had precipitated their marriage. There had been no mention either of any pregnancy. Seeing Marion in her simple ivory gown with a band of flowers holding her veil in place, it became obvious to him that she still had her curvaceous figure but was not carrying any extra weight. He glanced at Sam, and because he knew his brother so well, he could guess that Sam was thinking the same.

Doc Wiseman had been asked to give the bride away, as Marion was determined to charm him now that he was involved in the enterprise with Danny. It will be the three of us, she thought, and Jessie, of course, but she will continue with her work and not interfere with us, I hope . . . As Marion walked past the front pew, she saw Kathleen holding the baby up to show her what was happening. She gave the girl a triumphant little smile before taking her place beside Danny and passing her small bouquet of red roses and asparagus fern to her mother.

Jessie, sitting next to Kathleen, squeezed her hand. Poor girl, she thought compassionately. She believed Danny was her knight in shining armour, and perhaps she had hopes she would be the bride today. But Danny, I am sure, will keep the promises he makes to Marion. Love will grow from friendship; I know that.

It was a simple ceremony: vows were exchanged, the wedding ring slid onto Marion's finger. Danny already wore a signet ring, which had been his father's. The choir led the singing of 'Love Divine, All Loves Excelling' and the minister gave a little homily as expected. Then the small wedding party left the church to the pealing of wedding bells. Jessie held Sam's arm, and Kathleen, with Heather, followed them out into the bright sunshine.

The wedding breakfast was held at the farm; Jessie and Mrs Amos had worked hard to provide this, and Kathleen and Sam had promised to do all the washing-up later.

There was no honeymoon as such, for work was always a priority. Sam had decided to move out to the barn at the brickworks, though he was to help on the farm part-time as before, and Jessie insisted that until he had a stove to cook on, he should still have supper every day with the family. Marion, of course, would now assist Danny and Doc at the stables. What would Kathleen do?

Kathleen didn't say much as she dried the dishes after the celebration meal, but Sam whistled cheerfully as he washed up in hot water with plenty of soda in it. The wedding party had trooped into the parlour, which Kathleen had helped to clean and polish. She and Jessie had filled vases with flowers from the garden, and the lid was up on the piano, which Marion could play by ear; it was called vamping, with the left hand striking the chords while the right hand produced the tune. The lyrics were printed on song sheets: 'Nellie Dean', 'In the Shade of the Old Apple Tree' and 'Love's Old Sweet Song'. Heather was bouncing on Jessie's lap to the music. She was nine months old now, crawling and already pulling herself up by anything she could grab and hold on to in order to stand up. The furniture was pushed back, the carpet rolled up, leaving the floor clear for dancing.

Will anybody invite me to dance? Kathleen wondered wistfully. She wore the dress she had chosen from Jessie's catalogue, for which she was paying a shilling a week from her wages. Blue like her eyes, it was made of soft cotton, with puff sleeves and a full skirt; the latest fashion, just right for whirling round a room, but the washing-up must be done first, so she had donned an apron to protect it.

Sam said, 'I don't mind missing the dancing; I tried once, and my partner said my feet were too big!' He gave her a sideways glance; was she fighting back tears? Though Danny hadn't given her any encouragement since he and Marion had announced their wedding plans, and nor had Sam himself.

Upstairs, the newly whitewashed rooms – the spare bedroom and the one next to it – were ready for the bride and groom. The spare room was now Danny and Marion's bedroom, and the other room, which the brothers had shared all their lives until now, was to be a small private sitting room.

'Where are you sleeping tonight?' Kathleen asked Sam.

'On the sofa, I suppose, with old Bob!' he replied with a grin. 'I'll be officially leaving home tomorrow!'

'Will you be all right at the brickworks, Sam? Have you a bed?'

'Two beds actually. There are stacks of furniture upstairs,' he said cheerfully. 'It will be a bit strange not to share a room with my brother, but now Marion can put up with his snoring, eh? What about you?' He turned to face her, drying his hands on a tea towel. 'I know you were – well – drawn to Danny, if that's the right way to put it. But if it's any comfort, he might be thinking he has married the wrong girl right now.'

'Don't say that!' she exclaimed. 'It was far too soon after . . . I was too full of emotion after what I'd been through. I've got things straight in my mind now.'

'Good. So have I, I hope. I would like you to move in with me.'

For a moment she didn't know what to say, and then she blurted out, 'Are you asking me to marry you, Sam? You said you weren't ready for that yet, didn't you?'

'I'm not,' he said quietly. 'And it's the same for you, isn't it? Though I believe you would have changed your mind if Danny had asked you.'

'That's not so,' she cried. She wanted to tell Sam that she still thought of the day he had kissed her, the first time she went to the brickworks. He had shown restraint ever since. True love was slow-burning, she could see that now.

'I am asking you to work with me to make a home out of that barn, and to help me achieve my dream. I don't expect you to do the heavy manual labour, though. I intend to set up the business with the money my uncle left me. I'll employ a couple of chaps who have experience in the industry – we'd need to get in a stock of your favourite tea, because you'll have to keep the workers fed and watered! You'll be happy to hear that I'll have a cart to transport the bricks to customers and I'll let you choose the horse. It might not be a smart buggy, but you would be able to go out and about too.

'I know Mother will be glad to look after Heather, just as she does now, but the baby could be with us whenever you're not working. It isn't practical or safe for a toddler to be around when we are busy with the bricks, though, is it?

Also the smell is very pungent when they are being fired. I realise it would not be a comfortable place as it is here, yet . . .'

'I'm not worried about that, Sam. I'd be independent, more or less, wouldn't I? But people might talk.' And it will be difficult to leave Home Farm, she thought.

'You're wearing a wedding ring, aren't you? And I promise not to . . . take advantage of you, Kathleen.'

She experienced an unwelcome flash of memory about someone who had done just that, and the next thing she knew she was weeping in his arms and clinging to him. 'I'll work hard, Sam, I will.'

He disengaged himself gently, fetching a kitchen chair for her. 'Hush, Kathleen, or someone will come to see what's wrong. Sit down. I'm going to make us a cup of tea.'

'You do like me, Sam, don't you? I trust you!'

'I won't let you down, I promise.' If only he could bring himself to say how he really felt about her, but he was holding back because of the secret she would not tell, and also because he could not reveal what he had discovered. 'I'll talk to Mother tonight if I get a chance,' he said.

Marion had changed into her nightgown and was lying in the big double bed with the brass rails, which had been brought down from the attic. It had been up there since

Danny's grandparents had died. Danny waited for a while before he came into the room. He glanced at his new wife, who feigned sleep, and then proceeded to undress himself. The candle snuffed out, he climbed cautiously into bed. As he settled down, he suddenly became aware that she was shaking with laughter.

Her arms went round him and she whispered exultantly, 'Together again at last!'

Danny had to know, so he asked, 'Marion, you're not expecting, are you?'

'Silly boy, of course not. Mother gave me some advice before we . . . you know.'

'Are you following that advice tonight?'

'Of course I am. Mother said men can't be trusted in that respect.'

'Don't you want a family?' he demanded.

'Not yet – do you?'

'When you let me think you might be . . . well, I came round to the idea,' he said, hurt at the deception.

'Silly boy,' she said again. 'Stop talking, will you?'

He turned away from her. 'I think we should get a good night's sleep, Marion. It's been a very busy day after all.'

Now it was Marion whose pillow was damp with tears. She didn't fall asleep until the early hours, and then was woken at dawn by Danny with a kiss. 'I'm sorry, Marion, about last night. Will you forgive me?'

'I should be saying that, Danny. I shouldn't have listened to Mother, but it's difficult not to when you're an only child and you are all she has.'

'Let's make a fresh start today. Are you coming down to the stables with me this morning? We will be alone there except for the horses. Kathleen is going to work with Sam from now on, Mother told me that late last night. Please be nice to her; she wants to be your friend, I know it. Nothing happened between the two of us, I swear to you. Perhaps you and I have married too young, I don't know, but we both have to grow up quickly, eh?'

A discreet tap on their door made them start. Jessie called, 'Breakfast in half an hour! Did you have a good night – oh, sorry, not the thing to ask of newly-weds!'

Danny and Marion looked at each other and burst out laughing. 'Mother, as you say, don't ask!'

Jessie had enjoyed a good sort-out upstairs the past week. 'Haven't looked at any of the furniture for years, and guess what I found? A high chair and a cot for Heather! They need a good scrub and a coat of paint, of course.'

Kathleen, busy spooning bread and milk into Heather's mouth while she sat on her lap, said, 'Oh good. She only just fits into the basket now. Jessie, before the others come down, I want to say how kind it is of you to go along with our arrangements.'

'My dear, Sam's made a good choice.'

'There's nothing more to it,' Kathleen told her.

'Not at the moment, perhaps, but nothing would please me more. I really would be Heather's grandmother if you two—' She broke off as Sam came in for his breakfast.

'We two what?' he queried with a grin.

'You know,' Jessie said, passing over his plate of eggs and bacon.

'Do I?' he said too innocently.

This time she ignored him. 'Pass Heather to me, Kathleen, and I'll see to her upstairs. Your breakfast is in the warming oven along with Danny's and Marion's. They should be down shortly, I hope.' She paused. 'Are you moving out today?' she asked.

'No, probably in a day or two, Mother,' Sam replied.

'You see, I believe I'm about to have another lodger. Doc has to find new rooms. His landlady told him that her son and his family are coming to care for her now she's not so capable as she was. When I've cleared the attic room and the attic itself, Doc says that will be ideal for his needs. Only a few months ago, it was just you boys and me; now we will soon be bulging at the seams.'

'He will pay, I presume, for you to look after him?' Sam asked.

'Of course! I will employ someone to help me here too.' She looked at Kathleen. 'I want you to feel this is still your home, Kathleen. Your room will be ready for you at any time, but I will call it Heather's room now, eh? Oh, here they come at last.'

'My fault,' Marion said apologetically, sitting down at the kitchen table. 'I didn't know what to wear. I shall need some breeks like Kathleen. I'm looking forward to being with the horses; I rode a lot when I was a child.'

Danny tweaked her hair, piled on top of her head. 'Have you ever milked goats?'

'No, but I like a challenge,' she said, looking at Kathleen, who flushed, because this was something she had not taken to at all.

'We must go.' Sam pushed back his chair. 'I expect you want to give Heather a hug, so I'll fetch the buggy now while you do that.'

Upstairs, Jessie saw Kathleen's eyes well up as she kissed the gurgling baby. 'Don't worry about leaving her this morning, Kathleen – grandmothers all over the country look after the children while their mothers are at work . . . it's traditional.'

Marion soon got the hang of milking the goats. She showed Danny the two brimming pails. 'Haven't you got a yoke to carry them?'

'Not that I know of,' he said.

'We . . . Mother has one in her barn; we ought to go over later on to see if she's recovered from yesterday.'

'Sleeping off all those glasses of elderberry wine, I guess.'

'Oh dear.' Marion became agitated. 'Has she fed the poultry, do you think?'

'Don't worry. She told me her new assistant would see to everything this morning,' he assured her. 'Time to feed our hens and collect the eggs,' he reminded her.

Later, when they were about to take the milk back to the farm, they looked in on the horses in the stables. They would return later for the jobs to be done there. As Marion stroked the mare, Danny came up behind her and encircled her with his arms, his hands sliding up to clasp her full breasts. He whispered in her ear, 'Sorry again about last night. Can I make up for it as we did before?'

'Do you mean . . .?'

'Yes, and don't pretend you weren't thinking the same,' he said, as he helped her up the ladder into the hayloft.

Jessie cuddled Heather close before she put her in the pram for her morning nap. 'They're taking their time bringing home the milk, Heather; I wonder why?' She dabbed at the dribble on Heather's chin with her bib. 'But we can guess, can't we?'

I'm not too old to remember all this, she thought, although my Wilf was fifteen years older than me. I was nineteen too, when I married him. I was twenty when Sam was born, so I'm only just forty-four now, but no one seems aware of that. I've been Mother for so long, and now I think of myself as a grandmother . . . Wilf liked me to let down my hair; he said it was russet like the autumn leaves. But now I've reached a turning point in my life.

TEN

By October 1904, Kathleen mused that she seemed to have been in Kent forever. Here she was, settling into the Barn House with Sam, almost a year after her arrival and her adoption by the warm-hearted Mason family, and the birth of her daughter, Heather.

She had spent many hours scrubbing walls and floors, mixing whitewash in a bucket and applying it liberally to brighten the place, and looking after Sam and the workers. Sam had done his best to help her by providing a copper to boil the water, which he pumped up for her use every day, and installing a second-hand range for her to cook on. She made regular batches of soda bread, as her mother had done back in Ireland. In the larder, she kept a round of strong cheese, wrapped in muslin, slices of which, with chunks of the new-baked bread, she handed out to the workers outside. Butter and milk were provided by Jessie, and Sam insisted they pay for these, but they were glad of the vegetables and apples they were given.

'Next year,' Kathleen said, 'if Sam digs me a garden, I'll grow my own.'

The new clay pit was taking shape, but if the weather worsened, work on this would have to be abandoned until spring. At the moment, snow and blizzards seemed to be confined to Scotland and the northern counties.

Kathleen's pots and pans were cast-offs from Jessie's kitchen, but they gleamed on the shelves Sam had put up for her, and she spent her evenings making rag rugs, with Jessie's encouragement, to cover the wooden floors so they were warmer to tread on. Laundry was done in the scullery, where another wood-fired copper had been installed for boiling the linen. She strung the washing between the trees and imagined that it fluttered like flags in the wind. The sight of it made her feel less isolated.

Kathleen had a companion, a small Labrador pup who made extra work with his occasional puddles and muddy footprints. She named him Oliver, because she had been reading *Oliver Twist*, who'd asked for more, and her little Ollie was a great trencherman, as Sam said. Kathleen was working her way through the bookshelves, for Sam had brought piles of his books here. She peeped into *Nostromo*, by Joseph Conrad, but it was, in her opinion, a man's book, by a writer who had been at sea for most of his life. She sometimes recalled the journey by boat from Ireland, when she had been terribly seasick, then travelling to the place, where . . . She blanked out the rest in her mind. What does it matter now? I am safe here, she thought.

Every afternoon, Sam took Kathleen over to the farm to spend a few precious hours with Heather, and then returned at supper time, when his mother would cook for them. Kathleen appreciated this, but she hoped that soon *she* would make the evening meal for the two of them, in their new home. They stayed until Kathleen put Heather into her cot and kissed her goodnight, and then the two of them returned to the Barn House and sat together in the living room with a strong fire going.

On Friday nights, the hip bath was placed near the hearth, and Sam filled it with hot water. 'You first,' he insisted to Kathleen. 'The water will be black when I've finished with it.' He tactfully held up his newspaper and turned his head as she dropped her towel and stepped into the water. He took his turn when she swathed herself in the towel and tiptoed away into her bedroom.

One evening, when she reached for the towel, the pup, in playful mood, seized a corner of it and tugged so that the covering slipped. Kathleen cried out, 'Stop it!' Without thinking, Sam dropped his paper and rushed over to remove the dog. Kathleen had quickly turned away from him, and he saw close up the scars on her back, not as livid as they had been, but a permanent reminder of what had been inflicted on her merely a year ago. He shooed the pup away, retrieved the towel and draped it round her shoulders.

'Please don't cry, Kathleen,' he said softly. Then he guided her out and opened the door to the small room where she slept.

'You saw, didn't you?' she managed. 'I will bear those scars for life – who will love me once they see those?'

He picked up her nightgown and gave it to her. 'Here, put this on and get into bed. I'll make a hot drink, shall I?'

'After you've had your bath, Sam. Thank you for not saying what you really thought.'

'What I really thought was: why have I been so stubborn? Why can't I tell Kathleen how I feel about her? You must know I love you, but the last thing I want to do is compromise you.'

'If you . . . if you want me to be really happy, you will give me a fatherly kiss.'

'I certainly don't feel fatherly at this moment,' he said, 'Can you wait until I'm clean like you, and have emptied the bath, taken Ollie out and made the cocoa?'

She smiled and wiped away the tears. 'Don't be too long,' she said.

Sam took his time over the evening chores, and then accompanied the pup outside to ensure that there were no puddles in the night. It was about an hour later that he looked in on Kathleen and saw she was fast asleep. He sighed, snuffed out the candle and retreated to his own bedroom next door with both mugs of cocoa. Clean sheets, he thought gratefully. She always thinks to change the beds when we have a bath.

Around midnight, he woke suddenly to find Kathleen beside his bed.

'You didn't come back as you promised you would,' she cried accusingly, hurt in her voice.

He sat up. 'Kathleen, please go back to your bed. You'll catch cold . . .'

'You can't deny you care for me, Sam, and you must know I feel the same about you. I was ready to prove it tonight, but you changed your mind.'

'Kathleen, I was eighteen when my father died; he was strict, not easy-going like my mother, but he told me the facts of life when I was younger. He said I should always respect women because they are superior to men – that I must be honourable and decent towards them and follow his moral code. An impulsive act, he told me, could lead to an unhappy marriage. He was a good man and he made my mother happy, I know that. Now do you understand? I want to marry you Kathleen, when you feel ready for that. But before it can come about, I need to know what happened to you before you arrived at Home Farm in such distress.'

'You know I can't remember all of that,' she cried.

'I think you don't want to recall it; you've closed your mind to it. Let me help you deal with it, please.' I have a secret to reveal too, he thought, about what I discovered in the newspapers. I feel guilty about concealing that.

'I'm shivering . . .' was all she said. She stretched out her arms in an imploring gesture.

'Wait a minute and I'll take you back to your room and tuck you up,' he told her.

He picked her up, and a few moments later she was settled back in her own bed. He bent over and kissed her. 'Goodnight, Kathleen. We are learning to live together; getting to know each other better. I'm not impulsive like Danny. It may not be a conventional courtship, but that's how it is.'

Doc Wiseman was moving into his new quarters in the farm. Sam offered to convey his possessions in his cart. He and Danny carried these between them up to the attic rooms and set them in place.

'I don't have many worldly goods,' Doc commented. 'I learned to travel light to survive when I left the place where I was born. I have an affinity with Kathleen in that respect: neither of us likes to look back.'

In the bedroom there was a narrow single bed and a bedside cabinet fashioned from a stout apple box, which he'd upended and inserted two shelves into. On top of the cabinet was an oil lamp and a single photograph in a silver frame; the image on it was somewhat blurred, but it was of a young woman with a child in her arms. Jessie, without commenting on the picture, spread one of her patchwork quilts on the bed. 'Would you like an extra pillow?' she enquired. 'I have several spare.'

'Thank you, but no, I am used to one flat pillow.'

The grey-looking pillow was filled with flock, not feathers like Jessie's, but at least he hadn't rejected the old washstand by the window, she thought. He had hung a rather threadbare towel on the rail. Where will he put his clothes? she wondered. Coming to a decision herself, she shouted, 'Sam, there's a chest of drawers in the attic. Will you bring that in, please? Oh, and the spirit kettle, we don't need that now, and a big jug for water.'

The space adjoining the bedroom was the place Doc had chosen to have his desk, a table where he could play chess, and two odd chairs. There was a skylight above, making this a good room to work in. Doc was busy stacking boxes into a pyramid in a corner; they appeared to contain documents and other paper.

'Here's your ink stand,' Danny said, putting it on the desk.

'Thank you, you are all so kind. I shall be very comfortable up here.'

Jessie and her sons exchanged a worried glance. We could have done so much more if we had been allowed to, she thought, but we have to respect his wishes . . .

Marion, who was looking after Heather while Jessie was busy, came in with the little girl in her arms. 'Heather seems to be running a temperature – she refused her bottle and is grizzling most of the time. D'you think . . .' She held the baby out to Jessie.

'Allow me to take a look at her,' Doc said. 'It will be easier if we do that in her bedroom.' He picked up his black bag. Jessie knew he had a stethoscope and other medical aids. She supposed he had brought the rather battered bag with him when he came to England.

At Doc's request, she laid the baby down on what had been Kathleen's bed, and he began his gentle but thorough examination. He didn't speak until he had finished. Then he turned to Jessie, who was looking anxious.

'Her chest is rattling; she is very hot and seems unwell. Where is her mother?'

Sam answered. 'Kathleen thought she should stay out of the way this morning. I was going to bring her over here as usual this afternoon.'

'Well I think you should do that now. And tell her to pack her a bag – Jessie cannot be expected to care for a sick child on her own.'

When Sam arrived back at the Barn House, he found Kathleen just taking a batch of soda bread from the oven. She looked up. 'You're earlier than I expected. I haven't made lunch yet, Sam.' Her face was flushed from the heat of the stove.

'Kathleen,' he said quietly, 'Heather is unwell. Doc said for you to pack a bag, as she will need you to look after her until she recovers.'

She plucked at his arm. 'Sam, is it serious?'

'Doc didn't say,' he replied.

'Will you be all right on your own?'

He smiled wryly at that. 'As you have discovered, Kathleen, I am self-sufficient, but I admit that you have made a home out of a shack.'

'Is that all?' she said tremulously.

'You know it isn't, but please hurry,' he said.

Kathleen sat on her bed, sponging her little daughter's forehead with a flannel dipped in cool water. 'It is important not to wrap her in too many blankets,' Doc advised. 'You need light coverings while her temperature is high. Too many cuddles are not advised. Although you'll need the fire going night and day in the bedroom, and a kettle steaming on the hob.'

I am facing up to my responsibilities at last, Kathleen realised. Heather is so well looked after here, but she needs her mother now.

Just then, Heather looked up and murmured, 'Mumma.' She had only recently begun to talk.

'Oh Heather, I will be a better mother from now on – I promise!'

A knock on the door, then Danny came in with a tray. 'Nourishment – you must eat, Kathleen, you didn't have any supper. How is Heather? Marion has become attached to her, you know, and she is worried about her.'

'I hope you will have a baby of your own before too long,' Kathleen said, experiencing a twinge of jealousy. Marion had seen more of her daughter than *she* had since she'd moved to the Barn House with Sam, she thought. 'Doc says she is on the mend; he had feared she might develop bronchitis.'

Danny sat himself down on the chair by the bed and gently stroked Heather's soft dark hair. 'She looks more and more like you every day,' he said softly. 'Are you happy with Sam? Will you marry him eventually?'

'*Dada*,' the baby said clearly.

'I wish I was, you know . . .' Danny cleared his throat. 'Mother says those are the first sounds a baby makes, it doesn't mean—'

'I'd better put her in her cot, I think,' Kathleen said. She had mixed emotions about what he had said. 'You asked if I am happy with Sam; well I am. We're not married yet, nor are we behaving like a married couple, but that will come in time, I hope. Sam will be Heather's father then,' she added firmly.

'Marion and I have had no luck with conceiving so far, but Mother says it is early days. Well, goodnight, Kathleen – I can't help thinking what could have been if—'

'Don't! Please don't, Danny.'

Sam had been sawing logs all afternoon; there was plenty of dead wood to clear near the Barn House. This would be his occupation now: delivering logs to customers, stockpiling them for Christmas. It would be their only income until they could dig clay again and get on with brick making, what with the severe weather they were experiencing. Though he was still able to employ his workers to help with the wood, which was important for them and their families.

It was almost dark before he went indoors and made up the fire. The place looked empty without Kathleen; no welcoming cooking smells wafting from the range. He sat down heavily on the one armchair. I must get a lady's chair for Kathleen, he thought. She usually sat by his feet on a tapestry stool, with Ollie beside her. The dog missed her too.

Will she come back? he wondered. Although Heather was very attached to Jessie, he knew that she needed her mother. He decided to tell Kathleen that now the place was more comfortable, Heather should come and live with them.

Having come to one decision, he made another. It took him a good hour to achieve, but he moved Kathleen's bed from her room into his bedroom, and placed the two beds together. He would get a double bed when he could afford one, but for now they could share this arrangement. Heather's cot would be in the other bedroom, close by.

Ollie gave a reproachful whimper and pushed his food bowl across the floor.

'Sorry, old boy, I'll get your supper and then I must find something for me – there's all that soda bread and plenty of cheese, eh? I hope it isn't too late to make all these changes, and that Kathleen won't decide to stay back at the farm . . .'

A week later, Sam brought Kathleen and Heather home. He took Kathleen right away into what had been his bedroom. She looked at the big bed, the new coverlet, and then at Sam. 'I don't understand . . .' she faltered.

Sam was holding Heather, who was wriggling to be put down. She could walk now, although she still sat down unexpectedly sometimes with a grin on her face. 'Dada,' she said approvingly now. He took her hand.

'Come and look at your room next door, Heather, and see what is in there for you . . .'

Kathleen followed them. There was a cot ready made up. 'I bought it second-hand, but it was only used by one child before,' Sam said.

A soft toy sat on the pillow. 'It's a frog, Heather,' Kathleen said through her tears. 'Shall we call him Froggie?' She passed the green velvet frog in the red waistcoat to her daughter. 'Dada bought him for you.' She tried not to remember Jessie's face as they had waved goodbye this afternoon and driven away. 'Be happy!' Jessie had called. 'Love one another . . .'

'We'll see you tomorrow!' Sam had replied.

Heather was tucked up in her cot, and after she fell asleep during a lullaby, Kathleen went hesitantly along to her new room. Earlier she had unpacked her bag and put her treasured possessions in place. Sam was outside with the dog, intending to wait until she was ensconced in bed. He looked up at the night sky, at the stars, and felt nervous himself. Was he doing the right thing? She had not yet confided in him about what had happened in Croydon, but then he had kept the facts he had learned about that time to himself too.

She closed her eyes while he changed into his nightshirt. He washed and cleaned his teeth, for this was a very special occasion. He nipped the candle out and slid into bed beside her. There was silence; perhaps she really was asleep. He sighed, and at that moment she moved closer and murmured, 'Aren't you going to kiss me, Sam?' His arms closed round her warm and pliant body.

'I can do better than that, but only if you want me to,' he whispered.

Kathleen twisted the ring on her finger. Soon, she thought exultantly, soon I'll be entitled to wear it – and I'll be Kathleen Mason, not Kitty Clancy. I'll really belong here then.

ELEVEN

Doc was settling in well, and although he kept mostly to his own quarters, when Jessie was on her own some evenings she invited him to supper. Afterwards they would sit on the sofa drawn up close to the crackling fire, with old Bob curled up by their feet, getting to know one another better. Jessie told him how she'd coped with her grief after losing first her husband and not long after, her only daughter. 'Now,' she confided, 'I miss dear Kathleen and the baby I call my granddaughter.'

'But you are happy that she and Sam are together with little Heather?'

'Yes, and I know I am old-fashioned, but I wish they would tie the knot!'

'Perhaps it is difficult for them to decide where to marry. I believe Kathleen was brought up as a Catholic in Ireland, and Sam – does he attend church with you?'

'Both boys did when they were younger, but now . . . Still, I was happy when Danny and Marion chose to be married there.' She hesitated and then asked, 'Are you a believer, Doc? Or did your experiences before you came here affect you too much?'

'I am not an Orthodox Jew,' he said slowly. 'In fact my mother was from a Gentile family. I went to church with her. I was an only child. When the scourge began, she was a widow, but she had been married to a Jew, and like me, my wife and child, she ended up in the Catorga prison camp in Siberia. I suppose you would like to know what happened to us?'

'Only if you want to confide in me,' Jessie said patiently.

'I was newly qualified as a doctor. It made no difference to how I was treated, but I was useful to them in that terrible place. Because of the crowded conditions, many people became ill. These included members of my own family. My mother contracted tuberculosis and died; my dear wife cared for her until she also passed away . . . my young son, too. He was only five years old. It was a terrible time. Young women were beaten, like Kathleen, and violated. Along with a friend, I planned to escape. One day perhaps I will tell you about that part of my life, but even after all these years it is still a wound that will not heal.'

Jessie took hold of his hand and squeezed it. 'Doc, you have a family again, all of us.'

'Thank you, Jessie,' he said. 'Then you must call me by my name, I think: Abraham.'

*

Mrs Amos looked keenly at her daughter's midriff. 'No glad tidings yet, I see,' she commented. She turned to Danny. 'Could be your fault,' she said. 'Not on my side of the family. Mind you, I never wanted more than one child, so my husband had to toe the line.'

'Mother!' Marion said, shocked. 'Our private life is our own affair. We are in no hurry,' she added, but she knew her mother would guess this was untrue. She wasn't really sure why she had changed her mind and wanted a baby so much, but she supposed it would help to make their marriage stronger. She wouldn't admit to herself that she still worried about the effect Kathleen had on her husband. It was a relief to hear that Sam and Kathleen were now together with Kathleen's baby.

As if she could read her daughter's thoughts, Mrs Amos asked, 'What about your brother, Danny? No glad tidings there?'

Danny spoke before Marion could stop him. 'That's their business! Sam will make a good husband.'

'Oh well, you make your bed and you lie in it, eh?' Mrs Amos replied. 'But who knows what that girl was up to before she came here.'

'Mother!' Marion interrupted. 'We came over today to find out if you were coming to the farm as usual this Christmas – oh, and to ask if we can have a dozen eggs. Jessie is wanting to make the puddings and cake.'

'You can have the eggs, but tell Mrs Mason I am thinking of staying at home this year. Bert, my assistant, will be here and the fowl must be fed, Christmas or no Christmas. I had hoped you two might condescend to keep me company on Christmas Day.'

'We'll think about it,' Marion told her. She could sense Danny's relief, and remembering last Christmas, she thought it might be a good solution. Jessie would have a houseful anyway, for Sam, Kathleen and little Heather would be at the farm for a few days.

'Time to get up,' Kathleen yawned, prodding Sam, who lay beside her in bed. He yawned and then hugged her to him.

'Ten more minutes,' he whispered, 'while Heather is asleep . . .' He was proving an ardent lover, and usually she didn't mind at all.

'Not just now,' she said. 'We are usually eating in the kitchen by eight o'clock.'

Later, at breakfast time, he said casually, 'I'm taking the day off, and so are you. I thought we might visit your friend the minister's wife. We have something to ask her.'

'Have we?' she said, smiling.

'You know very well what I am getting at. I don't want to wait until spring to marry you, because if we carry on as we are, Heather could soon have a little brother or sister, and I think it would be good to be husband and wife before then. What about you?'

'You know I want that as much as you do, Sam. What about the new year?'

'How about Boxing Day?'

'Sam! How could we possibly arrange to be married so soon?'

'Well, it's three weeks away – let's see what Min says.'

'Her husband will need to be consulted,' Kathleen said. 'I know Jessie will be thrilled.'

She wondered how she would feel going back to the village below the Pilgrims' Way. However, bowling along in the buggy borrowed from Jessie was very different from stumbling along in a blizzard, not knowing where she was going. Heather, in a warm coat, leggings and bonnet, jigged up and down on her lap with excitement. Froggie was tucked in her pocket; the soft toy was her favourite and went everywhere with her. She could almost say his name; her best attempt was 'Foggie'.

They parked outside the manse beyond the little chapel. Sam noticed that Kathleen looked pale and swayed a trifle as he lifted them together to the ground. He took Heather from her and said quietly, 'Are you feeling unwell, Kathleen? Was it too bumpy a ride?'

She managed a smile. 'I feel a bit sick,' she whispered. 'Please don't say anything.'

Min opened the door. 'What a lovely surprise!' Just then, Kathleen felt herself falling, as she had the first time Min had called to see her at the farm. There had been a couple of visits since.

Sam handed Heather to Min and bent over Kathleen in the hallway of the house. Her eyes were already flickering open. 'We seem to be making a habit of this,' he said ruefully, as he lifted her up into his arms. Min pushed open an inner door. 'Bring her in here, Sam, there's a good fire going. You'll meet my husband Joshua, too; he's looking over his sermon for Sunday.

'Josh, this is Kathleen, who you have heard so much about. And this is Sam, and here is dear little Heather.'

Sam divested Kathleen of her plaid coat, and Joshua smiled and said, 'I seem to remember that cape . . . Min wore it, didn't you, my dear? When we were walking on the moors in Scotland and I picked you that sprig of heather.'

Kathleen found her voice. 'It's still in the pocket – it brought me luck, and I met Sam.'

Sam helped her into a comfortable chair. 'I'm so sorry to have alarmed you all,' she said. He picked up Heather, who was peering at a little Jack Russell dog hiding under his master's chair.

'It's not Ollie, Heather. Sit on Mummy's lap, eh?'

A little while later Min suggested, 'You have colour back in your cheeks, Kathleen – shall you, Heather and I go into the kitchen and make the tea? I have a batch of scones in the oven, too; I don't want to overcook those! We'll leave the men to have a chat. I imagine that's why you came today . . .'

It was an old-fashioned kitchen with a big pine table in the centre and eight chairs around it. 'Yes,' Min said, 'we are still a houseful! The two oldest are pursuing further studies; one wants to be a doctor, the other a lawyer. The four younger boys – aged ten to sixteen – are at school. They all have tremendous appetites; it is like feeding the five thousand, Joshua says.

'Now, here is the little chair we keep for visiting children, so pop Heather in it and I'll find a toy or two to keep her amused. She can have a scone when they cool down. And while the tea brews, we can have a chat.'

'I want you to know, Min, how happy I am with Sam and my baby, and I hope Sam is asking your husband at this moment if we can be married on Boxing Day in your chapel, because – oh, you must disapprove of our present situation, and—'

'My dear, I never presume to judge others, nor does Joshua. It will be a joy to us to be involved in your wedding. Is there something else you wish to confide to me?'

'Well, I have only just realised it myself, after fainting and feeling sick, that I might be expecting another baby. Sam obviously doesn't know yet, but we only . . .

you know, for the first time six weeks ago – could it be possible?'

Min smiled. 'I'm sure it could, Kathleen. Has this upset you?'

'No, because . . . well, as Jessie said when Heather was born, babies are always a blessing. But it could be a shock to Sam.'

'He loves you, he will soon get used to the idea. Now, does Sam take sugar in his tea?'

The two men were smiling when Min, Kathleen and Heather re-entered the study, and Heather toddled over to Sam. 'Up, Dada,' she told him. He swung her up and then sat her on his lap.

'What are you worrying about?' Min whispered in Kathleen's ear. 'He adores Heather; he will be a wonderful father.'

'It's all arranged,' Sam said. 'The banns will called here on Sunday, and for the third time on the Sunday before Christmas – we must arrange to be there each time.'

'A private ceremony,' Joshua put in, 'just family. Min, I'm sure, will play the harmonium and choose the hymns. We have decided on ten in the morning so that you won't have to travel home in the dark.'

Sam said, 'I asked the minister's advice on another important matter, Kathleen. He agrees with me that I should apply to the Church of England Adoption Society as soon as possible to formally adopt Heather, then she will take my surname and I will be her father.'

'Oh Sam!' Kathleen was crying tears of joy. 'You have made me so happy!'

That night, she plucked up courage to tell him that there was a definite possibility she might be pregnant again.

'Does that mean we can't . . .?' he asked tentatively.

'Not until the new year, because you never know with the first three months, but after that – well, things should have settled down. I want this to be a joyful time for both of us, so tell me, Sam, are you happy about it?'

'Of course I am! All those ridiculous ideas I had about marriage and children, well, those have been thrown out of the window. We have been together such a short time, though, it has come as a surprise! When do you think we . . .?'

'On what I think of as our honeymoon night,' she told him demurely.

At the farm that night, Marion had planned a surprise for Danny. She undressed quickly, stuffed her voluminous nightgown under her pillow and covered herself up to the chin with the sheet.

Danny was whistling as usual as he took off his clothes, which was a signal for Marion to shut her eyes. Tonight, however, she kept them wide open and couldn't help giggling because he was unaware that she was gazing at his body. As he reached for his nightshirt, she said, 'Don't bother with that, Danny, come as you are! It's time we had a revelation.'

'Whatever are you suggesting?' He came anyway and was about to snuff the candle out when she threw off the sheet. She was not behaving coyly as usual. He averted his eyes despite the excitement generated by seeing her unclothed and climbed hastily in bed next to her. He tried to pull the sheet up, but she resisted.

'Isn't this the most natural thing in the world?' she asked.

'Your mother would certainly not approve.'

'I don't care any more what Mother thinks; she's a bit of a tyrant, isn't she? And what she doesn't see, she can't worry about. Well, are you shocked, Danny?'

'You have . . . a womanly shape, Marion.'

'Is that all you can say? Who do I remind you of?'

'No one, believe me.' But that was not quite true. He remembered an older boy who had discovered a secret cache of rather risqué photographs under a loose floorboard and had brought them to school to show the other boys. Danny had blushed then, being fair-skinned, as he did now.

'Let's make the most of me not being in the family way!' Marion whispered. Desperate measures, she thought, but

I suppose I am playing a part. Danny had kept his word, avoiding Kathleen, but Marion was aware that he still thought of her; he had been dreaming the other night and had called out her name . . .

It was Christmas Day and they were celebrating Heather's first birthday at the farm. Heather was entranced by all the decorations. The cuckoo clock – Jessie's special gift from her two sons and their wives, for she already thought of Kathleen as that – amused the little girl too; she put her thumb in her mouth the first time she saw the cuckoo popping in and out of the clock door, but after that she had her eye on it, waiting for the next 'Cuckoo!' She opened her Christmas stocking first thing, and later, several birthday presents, which were round the tree with the family's Christmas gifts. She loved the humming top from Jessie, and Sam had to set it spinning whenever it stopped.

Sam and Kathleen had still not revealed that they were to marry on Boxing Day, or told anyone about the new baby. Sam promised Kathleen he would mention the wedding in his after-dinner speech. Maybe Jessie had guessed their secret, though, as Kathleen appeared to have lost her appetite, and disappeared now and then to the privy outside.

Danny and Marion were spending the day with Mrs Amos after they had finished their morning chores at the stables, so it was just Jessie, Sam and Kathleen with young Heather and Doc Wiseman at this year's festive table, under which Ollie lurked waiting for scraps. It was a more modest dinner – just one roast chicken – but accompanied by all the usual vegetables and sauces. They were lacking the elderberry wine that Mrs Amos always provided, but Jessie had made delicious lemonade, which was served in tall green glasses with a slice of lemon in each.

'You're staying tonight aren't you?' she asked. 'Sorry, it's still a single bed in Heather's room, but I'm sure you won't mind. Ollie can sleep in my peg basket, after I've removed the pegs!'

Sam grinned at her. 'I'll have to squeeze Kathleen in: I'm a big lad, remember!'

Later, as they pulled their home-made crackers, Doc stood up to thank Jessie for the lovely dinner and good cheer, then raised his glass of lemonade.

'To Jessie,' they chorused.

It was Sam's turn. He cleared his throat. 'What can I add to Doc's wise words . . .?' A pause for laughter at the pun, then, 'I am issuing an invitation from Kathleen and myself to our wedding tomorrow at half past ten in the morning. Doc, will you come along with Mother? We'd like you to give the bride away, and Mother to hold the baby while we tie the knot. We are to be married at the chapel where Kathleen stayed the night before she came here.'

'Have you asked Danny and Marion already?' Jessie asked anxiously.

'I spoke to Danny this morning at the stables. He will be my best man.'

'What did he say?'

'He wished me good luck, and when I slipped up on a patch of manure, he laughed and said, "There you are, you've got lucky already."'

Doc Wiseman rose again, glass in hand. 'Good news indeed. We can all travel together, eh? I've got my buggy here too.'

'What will you wear?' Jessie asked Kathleen.

'The lovely red velvet dress you gave me last Christmas,' Kathleen replied. She had a sudden thought: will it fit me?

'And you, Sam?'

'The suit I wore to Danny and Marion's wedding.'

'Heather will, of course, wear the lovely smocked frock you made for her,' Kathleen told Jessie.

Jessie had the final word. 'No Christmas cake for tea today; it's a wedding cake now! You have actually chosen a good time, because I made far too much food as usual, so your wedding breakfast will be here, of course. Oh, and I must iron Doc's best shirt . . .'

'Mother always rises to the occasion,' Sam said in the narrow bed that night. 'But we must decline to stay tomorrow night and go home to our own bed!'

At midnight, Jessie and Doc were still in the living room, with old Bob, who had been sulking all day because of the intrusive pup. They were talking over the day's events and surprises. 'Everything has changed this year,' Jessie said. 'Last Christmas, the boys were, well, just boys still. Then Danny decided to marry Marion, and now Sam is about to marry Kathleen; oh why are they in such a hurry?'

'I think you can guess why. Falling in love is like being consumed by a fever,' Doc said slowly, 'but eventually lovers cool down and family life begins for the next generation.'

'Do you mean there are babies already on the way?' She already had her suspicions.

'One baby, perhaps . . .'

'Marion or Kathleen?'

He smiled. 'We will have to wait and see, Jessie.'

'I can remember that fever, can you?' She sounded wistful. 'My husband used to say, "Let your hair down, Jessie", but it all seems so long ago.' He used to take the pins out of her bun, and her hair would tumble down round her bare shoulders, preserving her modesty. But she couldn't tell Doc that.

'It was a long time ago for me too, but you are still hopeful it will recur, perhaps?'

Jessie didn't answer that. She said instead, 'Time to retire, Doc, eh? We must make an early start.'

TWELVE

It was a cold and frosty morning on Boxing Day, so wedding finery was covered up with warm coats, while bonnets and stovepipe hats flattened hair but prevented it tangling in the wind. The ponies had red ribbons tied to their harness to match the bride's dress, and the guests huddled together under blankets. Danny was in the driver's seat of the first buggy and Marion sat beside him. Those behind only saw their back view and heard snatches of their conversation. Sam had a protective arm round Kathleen. He felt anxious because she had been very sick first thing and had refused to eat breakfast. Doc followed in his buggy with Jessie and little Heather, who was cuddled up on her grandma's lap.

They all braced themselves as they entered the chapel; it was almost as cold inside as out. Kathleen pointed out to Sam the settle where she had spent that fateful night. Today, lamps were lit, casting a golden glow, oak pews polished, and they were greeted by music, for Min was at the harmonium as promised. There were tall candles round the altar, Christmas greenery decorating the windowsills; it was a simple interior, but there were lovely biblical pictures on the walls, a wooden Nativity scene set out on a table, and the atmosphere was welcoming. There was a high domed ceiling, for there was a gallery above. No one sat up there today. On Christmas Day, every pew had been taken.

'I must take my cape off,' Kathleen whispered to Sam.

'Are you sure? It doesn't matter if you keep it on,' he said.

'It won't be for too long, and I want to look like a bride, Sam.'

Danny came alongside and indicated that he and Sam should go to the altar steps and wait for the bride there. Doc Wiseman took his cue and linked arms with Kathleen. 'Don't hurry,' he advised her. 'We don't want you to faint today . . .'

Jessie sat in the front pew with Marion, who took Heather from her. 'She can sit on my lap.'

Heather stretched out her arms to Jessie. 'Gamma!'

'She might need her bottle, Marion; I have it wrapped to keep it warm, in my bag . . .'

As Joshua, in his plain flowing robes, waited with the groom and best man for the bride and Doc to come down the aisle, they sang the inspiring hymn 'Jerusalem'. They might have been small in number, but this was something they all knew and loved, and they did it justice.

The bride's small hands were cold and almost numb, so Doc took them in his own large ones and rubbed them to warm them. Kathleen gave him a grateful look. Am I really standing here, she thought, about to make solemn vows? She felt a surge of joy within herself. How fortunate I am!

Sam looked down on her from his considerable height. He was clean-shaven again, after growing a beard for winter, and it made him look younger. He knew she didn't like the beard, and although she had never divulged why, he could guess.

The ceremony began; it was a simple service, but with meaningful words. Kathleen's mother's ring went back onto her finger, and this time she was entitled to wear it. They made their solemn promises and were pronounced man and wife. There were prayers, a short homily from the minister, then the harmonium swelled again and they sang the 23rd Psalm, followed by the final hymn, 'O Blessed Home Where Man and Wife'.

No bells, but the bridegroom put the warm cape back round the bride's shoulders, then they filed out of the chapel and there were hugs and congratulations for all concerned. Min and her husband waved goodbye until they had driven out of sight.

'I didn't kiss you properly when the minister said, "Now you may kiss the bride",' Sam whispered ruefully to Kathleen.

Jessie overheard, and told them, 'Well why not do it now!' As they obliged, a cheer went up from the others.

'I love you,' Sam murmured.

'I'm so happy,' Kathleen replied.

'You're crying again,' he said. 'Here, take my handkerchief, have a good blow.'

Marion said to Danny, 'I know you can't kiss me at the moment as you are holding the reins, but I shall expect you to do the same for me the minute we arrive at the farm!'

'You're not using my best handkerchief!' he teased.

Back at the farm, Ollie the pup was wondering where his family had disappeared to, while old Bob was snoozing as usual by the living room fire. Ollie crept over and insinuated himself between the big dog's splayed front paws, then rolled over submissively. Bob opened one eye and put one paw firmly over the pup's tummy to keep him in his place.

The wedding celebration was followed by the three birthdays in January, when Kathleen and Sam made their announcement, only to learn that the family had already guessed their secret.

Three months later, in March, Sam, having just finished reading the newspaper, was about to roll it up to use for lighting the fire when Kathleen snatched it from his hands. 'Why can't I know what's going on in the world?' she cried. 'If it's not suitable for my eyes, you shouldn't read it either!'

There had been no news about the mystery in Croydon since the coroner gave his verdict on the woman found dead at the house. Sam capitulated. 'Well, there's no good news, and I'm not sure you should be reading about the suffragettes, who are causing a great deal of trouble, or the bootmakers striking and marching in protest on Parliament – but go on, read it if you must.'

'I can't do much else except look after Heather and the dog and cook your meals.' She was still ruffled. 'Look how big I am for five months gone – very different to last time. I feel frustrated at not doing my bit, Sam.'

He looked at her pale face and her swollen belly, and said gently, 'I know it's my fault; perhaps it's too soon for you to have another baby after Heather – I should have waited until you were ready.'

'I *am* ready!' she sobbed. 'I needed to be loved and you have loved me and made me happy again . . . Still, the next few months seem like forever.'

'Well at least you'll have the paper to read every day now!' He smiled at her, and she smiled back. 'Don't go on strike like the bootmakers, will you?'

'I'll try not to!' she said, thinking how inspiring Emmeline Pankhurst was: Votes for Women – *yes*! She wondered what Jessie thought about that. Kathleen missed her so much now that she didn't see her every day – and the farmhouse, which she still thought of as home. She wouldn't be working in the strawberry fields this summer, nor helping Danny in the stables. Marion had taken her place.

By April, with three months still to go, Kathleen already felt very uncomfortable, for she had put on more weight this time, and her ankles were swollen. She hoped they wouldn't have a heatwave in the summer.

Sam tried to cheer her up. 'I'm going to fence off a piece of land at the back of the barn, which will eventually be the garden belonging to the house. Now that it's better weather, you and Heather need to be outside in the fresh air.'

Kathleen sighed. 'How can I keep her amused out there?'

'I'm thinking of making a seesaw and a swing, as there are two trees I can fix that between,' Sam replied. 'It will be a safe place away from the brickyard, away from the dust and bricks being fired. I've cut some chestnut spiles ready to attach to stout poles. The wood really is our most valuable asset, eh?'

When he mentioned the house, Kathleen realised there had been no bricks added to it since she had come to live there. I shouldn't be grumbling, she thought, but I feel so lonely during the day while Sam is busy trying to make a living here. I miss Jessie and Danny – even Marion, who is proving to be nicer than I imagined. I miss the horses at the farm . . . If I didn't have my little Heather, I'd be even lonelier.

'You're in a reverie.' Sam kissed the top of her head. 'Did you hear what I said about making you a garden? I'll buy you a parasol and you'll be a lady of leisure.'

'Thank you, dear Sam. I'm sorry I'm crotchety, it's just that . . .'

'I know, but it's not long till July now, is it? Then maybe we'll have our pigeon pair – a girl and a boy.'

'It could be another girl. Would you mind?'

'If it is, can we call her Kathleen after you? Or Kitty, maybe?' He watched for a reaction.

He was surprised when she said, 'Oh, my dada called me Kitty so that would be perfect in memory of him. And if it's a little boy, he can be Sam after you!'

'You deserve another hug for that,' he told her, 'but then I must get back to work.'

It was the start of a long, hot, dry summer. Tatsfield school was closed for much of April and May due to an epidemic of whooping cough. Jessie warned Kathleen that it wouldn't be wise to make her usual visits with Heather, as both of them would be vulnerable to the distressing illness. 'One whoop from an affected child, even if you are some distance away, is likely to infect you.' Kathleen understood, but she missed the family at the farm.

One afternoon in June, Kathleen was sitting in a basket chair with a footrest under a leafy tree in the garden. Nearby, little Heather called out as she tried to swing herself while fastened into the special seat that Sam had made her. 'Mumma! My want you push!'

Kathleen rose with difficulty and went over to the swing. There were delighted cries from the toddler as she swung back and forth. At that moment, Kathleen became aware that visitors were coming through the garden gate. Sam was with them in his long apron and heavy gloves. He lifted Heather from the swing and turned to Jessie, Marion and Doc behind him, who had arrived in the buggy. Kathleen was fretting already. 'It's lovely to see you, I must make a pot of tea – Sam, what about more chairs?'

Sam looked at his mother and shook his head, but he was smiling. 'Sit down, do, Kathleen, and I'll bring out that jug of lemonade you made this morning – it's just the afternoon for a cold drink, eh? A couple of rugs will be all right to sit on, won't they?'

'I'll help you,' Doc said. 'The ladies will want to chat, I think.'

Jessie embraced her daughter-in-law. 'You look well, Kathleen. The garden is coming along, isn't it? We brought some pots and plants in the buggy, and if you have a trowel, Marion and I will put them in the border.' Ollie, excited at the arrival of the visitors, jumped up at Jessie, and his claws caught in her skirt. 'Down!' she scolded him as she disentangled herself. 'Let me give my granddaughter a kiss first. I'm glad to see she is wearing a sun bonnet, Kathleen, and you . . .'

'The donkey's old straw hat,' Kathleen said ruefully.

Jessie wore a fetching new muslin gown, and Kathleen saw that she had released her pretty hair from its usual severe knot at the nape of her neck and tied it back with a blue ribbon. She didn't appear matronly today.

'You both look so smart,' Kathleen said to Jessie and Marion.

Marion was walking over to the swing, Heather holding her hand. She turned and said, 'I was sweltering in my breeches today. Danny likes me in skirts; he is looking forward to watching me pick the strawberries! He says I shouldn't hide my shapely ankles.'

The rugs arrived and were spread under the shade of the trees. As Jessie sat down beside Kathleen, she asked, 'Not long now, is it?'

'Still a month to go. By then you'll be busy with the strawberries.'

'My dear, you're more important than those. You'll come over to the farm to have the new baby won't you? Sam has promised to help with the strawberries, and he and Danny can do my job; it will be the usual workforce and they don't need much supervision. I can spoil my little Heather too, can't I? And after the baby arrives, Daisy, my help, can look after you. She's very competent.'

'But will you have room for us?'

'You and Sam can have my room, and I will share with Heather. Abraham will be around too in an emergency, and dear Nurse Buss is looking forward to the event.'

Abraham? Kathleen thought. We only ever call him Doc.

Sam hadn't yet returned with the lemonade, and Marion was out of earshot. Kathleen bent towards Jessie. 'I wish we still lived at Home Farm with you,' she said quietly. 'Oh, I know it's not possible now, and Sam has made the barn comfortable, but until the house is finished – if it ever is – I feel so cut off from you. The farm will always be home to me.'

Jessie reached up and squeezed her hand. 'I used to say to Sam that this wasn't somewhere I could live – in the middle of a wood – so I know how you must feel. But you *are* happy with him, aren't you?'

'He's the love of my life, you must know that.' Kathleen's lips trembled and she brushed away a stray tear.

'I do know it, but you should tell him what you have told me. You are always welcome to be with us, but it's not for me to say . . . Oh, here they come; mind you are smiling when they see you.'

After the visitors had departed, Kathleen looked in dismay at the chocolate stains on the front of Heather's dress. 'I wish Marion wouldn't give her sweets without asking me first, Sam.'

'She enjoys spoiling her. I expect she'd like a baby of her own, but she is very involved in the stables now. Doc told me she is entering Red Ruby and Grasshopper in a horse show later this month.'

I could have done that, Kathleen thought, if . . . She glanced down at her baby bulge and burst into tears. Heather looked at her in bewilderment and began to cry herself.

'You girls!' Sam said helplessly. Then he grinned. 'I'll get Heather to bed, and you put your feet up, Kathleen. It'll all come out in the wash.'

'I don't think the chocolate marks will,' said Kathleen, smiling now. 'You always know how to get round me, Sam.'

THIRTEEN

'I'm taking you to the farm today,' Sam told Kathleen as she lay in bed, drowsy after a restless night spent suffering intermittent pains.

'I feel much better this morning,' she said defensively. 'The baby isn't due until the end of the month, Sam. Anyway, I'm not ready to go, nothing is packed.'

'I can do that, and you know Mother, she is all prepared for the baby's arrival.'

Just then her face screwed up and she clutched at the covers. 'Sam, help me!'

When the spasm ceased, he lifted her from the bed and wrapped her in the top blanket. 'We'll have to go right away. I think Heather is awake, but we can't wait to dress her. I'll put a blanket round her and you must mind her while I bring the buggy round – it was good that Doc said we could borrow it in case of an emergency, eh? I'll be as quick as I can!'

It was already warm, very different, he thought, from the day young Heather had been born. This is the first time for me, he realised, but my second child is on the way . . .

Doc, Danny and Marion had just arrived back for breakfast after the early morning stable duties and milking had been done. It was Doc who opened the door and held out his arms for Heather, who was clinging to her mother. 'You go on up to Jessie's room, it's all ready for you. She's been sleeping in Heather's bedroom. I'll take Heather into the kitchen and they'll look after her there, don't worry. Then Jessie will come upstairs with me and we'll see what's what.'

The bed was all prepared for the birth. Sam laid his wife gently down and covered her with the sheet.

Jessie came bustling in. 'My dear, don't worry about a thing – young Daisy will cope downstairs, and Marion is looking after Heather. Danny is going to fetch the nurse, and Doc is cleaning himself up and will then come and see how things are progressing.'

'The baby isn't due for three weeks,' Kathleen said faintly.

'Well, Heather was early too, wasn't she? So don't worry.'

'I ought to fetch her things,' Sam remembered.

'Not now, Sam, there might not be time. You need to be here with Kathleen now.'

Doc leaned over the bed; he smelled of soap and his hands were red from scrubbing.

Sam stepped back next to Jessie. Doc finished his brief examination and then smiled at Kathleen. 'Everything is going well. Did you realise that your waters have broken? Sam, hold her hand and rub her back when the pains come. I'll go and wait for the nurse; she won't want me interfering unless it's necessary.'

'I must see that Marion is giving Heather breakfast and remind her no sweets until afterwards,' Jessie said.

For a few precious moments, Sam and Kathleen were alone. 'I love you, Kathleen,' he whispered. 'I can't bear to see you suffer.'

She managed a smile. 'It will soon be over,' she said, hoping this was true. 'Sam, I know I've been fractious, but I couldn't help it—' She gave a sudden gasp.

'What is it?' he asked anxiously.

'Time for you to . . . rub my back . . . Don't go . . .'

'I'm not going,' he assured her. 'I will always be here for you, my darling, I promise.' He thought of her as that, but it was the first time he'd said it aloud.

'I wish you had been with me last time,' she managed.

'But I was, Kathleen, I was! At the bottom of the stairs. I saw that Danny was outside your bedroom door, and I could hear a panic going on in the room.'

'Heather had the cord round her neck, but Nurse saw to it – I have every faith in her, Sam. So you cared about me even then and I never knew! But this time you— Oh dear!

You will be with me all the time, won't you?' She was panting with a new wave of pain.

'Shush,' he said. 'I won't leave your side, even if they want to throw me out.'

Nurse Buss was panting too, coming up the stairs, because Jessie had urged her to be quick. They came into the room just in time to see the baby emerging and Sam ready to catch the slippery little body in his hands.

Nurse turned to Jessie. 'Sam must move over until I've done what I have to do. It's a messy business, but he didn't pass out like some men I've had to deal with. He's done well, Jessie, you can be proud of him.'

A knock on the door. Jessie opened it to see Danny with the big jug of hot water. His eyes widened at the sight before him. 'He didn't . . .?'

'He did, Danny. Put the jug on the washstand and make yourself scarce.'

'It's another girl; all is well,' Nurse announced. 'Has she a name?'

'Kitty,' Sam and Kathleen said together.

'I'll go and spread the good news,' Danny said. He turned away so they wouldn't see how affected he was.

Later, they all crowded round the bed to welcome Kitty into the family. 'She's got a look of you about her,' Sam said to Jessie proudly. 'Not much hair, but the same colour as yours and Danny's, it seems . . . She's not dark like Kathleen, Heather or me, but she's lovely, isn't she?'

Heather, in Marion's arms, wriggled to be put down. 'Mumma,' she said uncertainly.

'Let her sit beside me, then she can see the baby properly,' Kathleen said. She was cuddling Kitty in what Sam thought was a maternal way, not awkward as she had been with Heather, but then this baby was the result of an act of love, unlike . . . He banished such thoughts firmly.

'This is your little sister, Heather. Her name is Kitty,' Kathleen smiled.

'Nice,' Heather said. She put her thumb in her mouth as if she was uncertain.

'Now off you go, all of you,' Nurse said. 'My patient needs to rest. Later you can bring her a bowl of bread and milk. Yes, you too, Sam,' she added.

'Where's Doc? He's not here,' Kathleen realised.

Jessie turned at the door. 'Nurse told us just family.'

'But he *is* family! I want to see him; he was so kind and helpful.'

'I'll bring him with me when I come up with the bread and milk,' Sam said. He was wondering if he would be allowed to share her bed tonight. There was so much he wanted to say to her, about how happy she'd made him. 'I must go home for a while, to fetch yours and Heather's things. I will ask the men to carry on as usual with their work, and also to see to the horse. I hope Ollie isn't making havoc downstairs, but old Bob seems to tolerate him, doesn't he?'

'Bob is like a grumpy old grandfather sometimes,' Jessie said with a smile. 'But Ollie won't require my peg basket this time; I suspect they both sleep on the sofa at night.'

Marion put Heather down for a nap in her bedroom, looking down at the sleepy little girl. 'Be good now. No calling out to your mumma, she's too tired to come.' She tucked a stray curl back from Heather's eyes. 'You need a haircut, Heather. I wish they hadn't said the baby looks like Danny – I know what my mother will say about that . . .'

She knew, of course, that such a situation was not possible, but she suspected that her husband still had fond feelings for Kathleen, hence his disappointment when he was summarily dismissed from the room when he brought the water to bathe the new baby.

She wasn't wrong about her mother's reaction. Mrs Amos, who hadn't been round to the farm since she fell out with Jessie last year, apart from sharing the wedding breakfast, appeared the next afternoon with a bunch of roses from her garden. Jessie hid her surprise.

'Thank you, Mrs Amos. You heard the baby had arrived, I imagine? Are the roses for Kathleen – how kind of you to think of her, she will be pleased. Sit down and I'll make a cup of tea.'

'Enough for two vases; one for you and one for her,' Mrs Amos returned. 'A cup of tea is just what I was looking forward to. I hear the baby looks like our Danny,' she added bluntly.

'Oh no, everyone says she's the image of me! Of course Danny does have my colour hair, as you know.'

'That's a relief then,' Mrs Amos said.

Jessie replaced the teapot on the stove. 'I think you owe me – us – an apology.'

Mrs Amos was flustered now. 'Oh, I didn't believe it, of course . . .'

'Who told you, your Marion?'

'Well . . .'

'I hope she said no such thing. I hear rumours too – about your assistant, Bert. Someone said he'd got his feet under your table, but you'll know if that's true or not . . .'

Sam came into the kitchen at that moment. 'Everything all right?' he asked.

'Yes,' Jessie replied, not very convincingly. 'Nurse is seeing to Kathleen and the baby at the moment, so don't go in the bedroom yet. Marion has taken Heather down to the stables to see the horses. They'll be back later with Danny, I suppose. Oh, and Mrs Amos brought this bouquet for Kathleen; excuse me while I put the flowers in a jug of water.' She went through to the scullery.

Mrs Amos was delving into her large handbag. She beckoned Sam to come nearer.

'I cut this piece from the *Times* newspaper – I thought you would be interested. I spotted it because I always look at the column about wills and whatnot; you never know, do you?' She passed him the slip of paper.

Sam read it in silence.

Any person knowing of the whereabouts of Miss Kathleen Clancy is asked to contact the solicitors named below. Should Miss Clancy choose to contact us personally, she will learn of something to her advantage.

Sam looked up. 'Thank you, Mrs Amos. I would prefer it if you didn't gossip about this, but I appreciate you bringing it to me. I will show it to Kathleen when things are back to normal again. Now is not the time, I feel.'

'Gossip!' Mrs Amos cried, just as Jessie returned with the flowers. She rose from her chair. 'I can't stay. I've been insulted by you, Jessie, and now by your son. Bert may have his feet under my table when he has his dinner, but he certainly isn't welcome in my bed!' She swept out and slammed the front door.

Sam looked helplessly at his mother. 'Whatever was she implying, Mother?'

Jessie dabbed at her eyes. 'I think she was referring to my friendship with Doc, but I assure you—'

'You don't need to, Mother,' Sam raged. 'What a mother-in-law Danny has!'

Nurse Buss bustled about the room while Kathleen put the baby to her breast. Best not to comment, she thought, but what a change from last time, when the girl refused to nurse her baby herself. She was thin and undernourished then, bewildered after a terrible beating that had made her flee her previous abode. Now she has some flesh on her bones, but she will always be small and slender.

'Well done,' the nurse said. 'I'll change her and then she can go in the Moses basket while you both have a nice nap, eh?' A polite knock on the door and she called out, 'Who is it?'

'Marion,' came the answer.

'Come in,' Nurse said.

'Heather went to sleep in the pram so I wheeled her into the kitchen,' Marion said. She sat down on the bedside chair. 'Daisy is keeping an eye on her; Jessie has gone along to the strawberry field to decide if it's time to start picking.'

'I wish I could be out there with you all,' Kathleen said. 'I had such fun last year.'

'You've another week to lie in,' Nurse told her firmly. 'I'm off now, but I'll look in on you this evening.'

'It's fortunate Daisy is so competent,' Marion observed. 'It means Jessie can be in charge as usual in the strawberry field next week.'

'I'm glad. I am very grateful to you, Marion, for helping out as you do with Heather.'

'Good practice for when we have a family of our own.' Marion sounded wistful. 'Mother keeps on and on about it all the time. I want to wait until next spring so as not to miss any horse events this year.'

*

Mrs Amos determined to confide in her daughter next time she came round. 'I'm sorry, Marion, if you are fed up with me asking if you have any news about you-know-what, but I feel lonely here without you. We always did everything together, didn't we? I can't help feeling it was rather unfair of Jessie to expect you and Danny to live with her at the farm after you married. It's hard for me to be without you. I wish you would think about coming back, with Danny of course, and make an old woman happy!'

'Mother, you aren't old; you're not fifty yet! Do you really want children running all over the house in a few years' time?'

'I suppose I do. I'd keep Bert on; I wouldn't expect you to work here again. I know you work alongside your husband. I just hope you'll keep me company . . .'

'I'll talk to Danny about it, but I can't promise anything,' Marion said firmly.

It was almost time for Kathleen, Sam and their two little girls to return to the Barn House. When they heard that Marion and Danny were moving shortly to the Amos smallholding, Sam wondered if Kathleen would ask him if they could stay at the farm until their new house was built. He brought the subject up one night when they were in bed.

'Kathleen, has this news made you change your mind about going home? I know how much you love it here, but

I feel, well, we need to bring our family up in our own way in our own place.'

She whispered instantly, 'As long as we are together, Sam, then I'm happy. Yes, the farm will always be special to me, but I know the barn is just a stepping stone to the Brickyard House. Also, Jessie could do with some peace and quiet, couldn't she? We will visit her and she can come to see us.'

He gave her a hug. 'Mother will find it strange at first, with none of us around at supper time, but Doc will still be in the attic, eh? So she won't be too lonely.'

Danny and Marion moved out the following weekend. Sam and Doc helped to stack their possessions into the cart and later put them in place at the Amos homestead. 'You will still see us every day of course, Jessie,' Marion told her as she gave her mother-in-law a farewell embrace.

Then it was Sam's turn to take his family home. More kisses, and Jessie's farewell gift was a large basket of strawberries and a pot of cream. 'See you soon,' she called as they drove away.

That evening she sat in the living room, sharing the couch with Bob. He was already missing Ollie and whimpered now and then. A polite knock on the door, before Doc came in.

'I'm glad to see you,' Jessie told him. 'I've something I want to say to you. Sit down, Doc—'

'Abraham, please,' he said with a smile. 'You are not about to give me notice, I hope?'

'Of course not! But I think you would be more comfortable here, especially in the winter, if you moved down to the two rooms that are now vacant. I wouldn't be nervous then, all on my own on that floor.'

'I accept your kind offer, Jessie. It makes good sense. But I will need Danny to help me move my things.'

'I will ask him tomorrow when he brings the milk,' Jessie said, yawning. 'Excuse me, but the goings-on these past days have been exhausting. I must get to bed.'

'I understand. May I bring you up a cup of cocoa later?' he asked. 'I will take the dog for a short walk meanwhile.'

'Thank you. Bob will be missing Danny, too. I would be grateful for a hot drink. I always read for a while, so don't hurry.' She was weary, she thought, because she had stripped and changed her bed earlier, and put things back in place in her bedroom.

A little later, another knock, this time on her bedroom door. 'Come in,' she called. She closed her book and took the cup from Doc. Sipping at it, she said, 'Sit down, Abraham, let's have a chat. I see you are ready for bed too.' She smiled as a sudden thought struck her.

'What is funny?' he enquired.

'Mrs Amos seems to think we share a bed,' she said.

To her surprise, he replied, 'Would it be so terrible if we did?'

'Do you mean that?'

'I do. I imagine you think I am past such things, but—'

'You are not *that* old! My husband, if he had lived, would have been older than you.' She patted the other side of the big bed. 'I'll be glad of the company, and the chance to talk,' she said softly. 'I miss putting the world to rights every night.'

'You understand I have never . . . since my wife died all those years ago . . .'

'There's no hurry. Will you snuff the candle out when I have finished drinking my cocoa, please?' We are both clad in flannel, she thought, despite it being midsummer . . .

'Good companions,' he said. 'That's all, isn't it?'

They were still talking when he saw her eyes close and realised she was asleep. It was just on midnight. He tiptoed out of the room and upstairs to the attic. Maybe it was just as well, he thought sadly.

Jessie didn't get a chance to talk to Doc until after the evening meal because Danny and Marion were with them at breakfast, after the early morning chores, and Daisy, the maid, was dealing with washing-up after supper.

'I'm sorry about last night,' she said when they moved into the living room.

'Please – there is nothing to be sorry for, Jessie. We are friends, good companions, as I said. It was good to talk, wasn't it?'

'I went to sleep,' she said ruefully.

'You were tired, you work so hard.'

'So do you, Abraham.'

'I think I will stay on in the attic, if you don't mind. May I make a suggestion? Why not ask Daisy to live in? I happen to know that her grandmother, who brought her up, has to move from her tied cottage; she is off to Bromley to live with her daughter. Daisy doesn't wish to go, as she says she loves working here and you are so kind to her.'

'Well, I must admit I enjoy female company, especially Kathleen, but dear Sam is set on providing a home of their own. Daisy was well brought up by her grandmother and I appreciate all her hard work – but where would I put her?'

He smiled. 'You have three spare rooms to choose from, Jessie!'

'I'll ask her today!' she decided. Daisy wasn't a waif like Kathleen, who, she thought, was still unpredictable at times. The maid was a homemaker, who'd learned Jessie's ways quickly, and a good plain cook.

Doc gave her an unexpected hug and kissed the top of her head. 'I care for you very much, you know. I hope you weren't too disappointed in me last night.'

'You were right. Good companions, Abraham; neither of us is ready for more.'

FOURTEEN

Jessie raised the subject the next morning, when she and Daisy were sitting at the kitchen table peeling potatoes for a fish pie. 'Doc tells me your grandmother is moving away, and he wondered if I might be glad to have your company living in here; what do you think of that idea? You already seem part of the family,' she added.

Daisy didn't hesitate; she sliced the potato she had just peeled and popped it into the pot. 'I'd really like that, Mrs Mason.' A smile lit up her rather plain face. She had sandy hair braided round her head; hence the freckles, Jessie thought.

'You'd have your time off as usual, of course,' she said.

'But what if Mr Danny and his wife decide to come back?'

'There are three spare bedrooms, don't worry about that. I think Mrs Amos needs them more than I do at the moment. Marion is her only daughter, after all.'

Daisy hesitated, her round face flushed, and then said slowly, 'You know how I was brought up, do you, Mrs Mason?'

'Your grandmother took you on, I presume when your mother passed away when you were just a little girl?'

'I must tell you this so you can make your mind up about me . . . My grandmother never married, and nor did my mother, but they were decent folk. Grandma had another daughter, my aunt Maggie, who has asked her to live with her family. I am welcome to go there too, but I was born and bred here and don't want to move away.'

'Well as far as I'm concerned you don't need to,' Jessie said. She put down her paring knife. 'Onions to chop next, eh? And parsley. I picked a big bunch of it this morning.'

'Just one thing, Mrs Mason. I hope you don't think I'm silly, but I've never slept in a room of my own before – I'm not sure about it.'

'Well when Kathleen joined us,' Jessie sounded wistful, 'she had a bed at the other end of my big room. You could do the same; I have an old screen I could put up for you, so you and I both have our privacy. What d'you think?'

'When can I come?' Daisy dabbed her eyes with the hem of her apron.

'As soon as you like, my dear! Oh, don't cry . . .'

'I always gets tearful when I'm happy!' Daisy said.

The good weather continued into autumn. The men were busier than ever in the brickyard; the red-hot kiln and the fumes from the brick baking were becoming intolerable. The garden was Kathleen's only refuge, but the air was tainted there too. Nursing little Kitty while Heather sat in her swing, she felt trapped. The Brick House seemed to look down on them reproachfully from the ridge. Would it ever be finished?

After the baby was napped up, as Jessie referred to it, Kathleen put her in the pram for her sleep and wheeled it into the shade. Heather was grizzling; she had been like that all morning following a restless night. Kathleen lifted her from the swing to give her a cuddle and discovered that the little girl was wheezing and breathless. She felt Heather's head; it was hot and clammy. Spotting Sam about to go into the Barn House for a cooling drink, she called out, 'Sam, quick, can you come? Heather is unwell.'

'I must wash my hands before I touch her,' he said instantly. 'I'll take off my overalls then get the horse and cart. Doc will come over to the farm to examine her, I'm sure. Pack a few things quickly, as she may have to stay with Mother again.'

'If Heather needs nursing, I must stay there too, with Kitty,' she told him.

'I realise that, my dear girl,' he replied, sounding weary and sad.

In case Heather was brewing something infectious, she was isolated in her own bedroom, and Jessie and Daisy took turns keeping a vigilant eye on her at night. 'It might be measles,' Doc said. 'We must watch out for a rash.'

As Kathleen was a nursing mother, she was isolated too, in the bedroom next door to her elder daughter. Sam came over after work the first day and found her tearful and depressed. He rocked her in his arms as if she were a baby too, and comforted her. 'Oh Sam,' she said. 'I can't take the children back to the barn. It's not the place to bring up a family.'

'You want to stay here where you feel safe, I know,' he said gently.

'It's always seemed like home, ever since I came here.'

'I know that too.' He came to a decision. 'If Mother agrees, we'll take over the rooms Danny and Marion had – we'll pay rent for them, of course. I'll be here with you at night, but I'll go to work at the brickyard as usual. Our future depends on it, Kathleen.'

'Oh Sam, how good you are – how understanding! But what about the barn – all our things there?'

'My foreman was hinting that when we moved to the Brick House, he and his wife would like to live on the job. We only need to move our personal possessions over here; we can leave the rest. I'll speak to Mother now.'

Kathleen caught at his arm. 'Sam, when the Brick House is ready and the children are bigger, I promise you we'll live there!'

'Best to take each day as it comes . . . What does Doc say about Heather?'

'He says she is much better today. He thinks she may have developed asthma; he suggests we ask the local doctor to confirm it.'

'Is that because of the fumes? That decides it: you can't go back there.'

After supper, Doc retired tactfully to his attic and Daisy tackled the washing-up while Sam and Jessie went to the living room. The evenings were drawing in, and were cooler. The fire was lit and Bob moved from the sofa to the hearthrug, followed by Ollie.

Sam cleared his throat. Jessie looked at him closely; he seemed tired, and the black stubble on his face indicated that he was growing his beard again. She knew instinctively what he was about to ask her. 'Mother, thank you for looking after Kathleen and the children. It sounds as if Heather has turned the corner, doesn't it? Would it be too much to ask—'

'You want to come back here to live, is that it? Of course you can. Danny and Marion will stay on with Mrs Amos now, that's obvious, and I don't like all those empty rooms. But you can't sleep in a single bed for ever.'

'I don't really mind, we just cuddle up.'

Jessie smiled. 'That's good, but you ought to buy that double bed you've been promising Kathleen ever since you married.'

'I'll go to town tomorrow. And I'll take Ollie with me to the brickyard every day; he's a bit of a handful still, isn't he?'

'Well, our old Bob can only tolerate so much fur-tugging and playfulness, so he'll probably be relieved. My dear boy, I've missed you more than I can say.' She gave him a little push. 'Go and give Kathleen the good news. I suppose Heather's room will become the girls' room now, eh?'

Kathleen was lying on the bed nursing the baby. 'Kitty's dropped off to sleep. Can you put her back in her cot, Sam?'

'Yes, of course,' he replied, lifting her up in his arms. Kitty was growing fast, he thought; she was bigger than Heather at that age, who would probably be petite like her mother. 'She's a contented baby,' he observed. 'She's smiling even though she's asleep.'

'Let's get an early night – I'll just look in on Heather and tuck her in, then I'll be back.'

He noticed that she hadn't rebuttoned her blouse. Dare he take this as a good sign? 'Mother agrees: we're welcome to move back home,' he said. 'I hope you're pleased?'

She turned at the door. 'Oh Sam darling, I am, I am! But you will take me back home one day to County Clare, where I was born, won't you?'

'I promised you that on our wedding night, remember? I'll take you home again, Kathleen . . .'

'My dada used to sing that song to my mother and me,' she said.

He was already in bed when she returned. 'Hurry up,' he urged. There had been no intimate moments since Kitty's birth three months ago, but tonight they would again throw caution to the wind, despite the hard, narrow bed.

After breakfast the next day, Kathleen took her babies into the sitting room while Daisy and Jessie tidied up the kitchen. Sam had left for work, taking the packed lunch Jessie had made for him. 'Thank you, Mother. I can make cups of tea in the barn, but I guess the soda bread we left behind won't be edible. Though Ollie might like to chew it.'

'Don't forget,' she reminded him.

'I won't – I'll take an hour off this afternoon and go shopping for that bed!' he said.

He went off whistling, looking happy – it was easy to guess why – and Jessie smiled to herself, recalling his father.

Kathleen was nursing Kitty again – the second feed of the day – and Heather had spread her toys out on the hearthrug. She lay on her tummy while she played with them, and Bob moved away as she began to build a little house from coloured bricks. He was wary because these pyramids were precarious and Heather enjoyed demolishing as much as building.

Jessie joined them and Kathleen held out the baby for her morning cuddle with Grandma. 'You are doing so well with feeding her yourself this time,' Jessie approved.

Kathleen's lips trembled. Jessie glanced at her, concerned. 'What's up, dear? You know you can tell me.'

'I might have to wean her soon, Jessie.'

'Oh, why, when she is so satisfied?'

'Last night – well, we couldn't help ourselves . . .'

'If you mean what I think you do, it's obviously time to resume, well, normal relations. It doesn't mean you have to deprive little Kitty, though.'

Kathleen gulped. 'But supposing I . . .'

'Supposing you fall again, is that what you're worried about?'

'Yes.' Kathleen was crying now.

Jessie laid the baby in her basket. She put her arms round Kathleen and hugged her tight. 'I should have realised you need a little advice and reassurance from time to time. This is the time you need your mother. Sadly, you lost her before she could talk to you about grown-up things. Kathleen dear, I never had that chance either with my Mary.'

'You are like a mother to me,' Kathleen sobbed.

'I'm glad, because I think of you as another daughter, and you are so young to be a mother of two, at only twenty. Now, let me tell you something you seem unaware of. Nursing mothers are protected when they are producing milk. Most mothers learn this quickly, and it helps them to space out their pregnancies. That's why some go on nursing their babies until they are toddlers. Nature's way! I have to say, sometimes this method lets you down, but I am guessing you are not experiencing your monthly problems yet, which is a good sign. Is that right?'

'Yes,' Kathleen agreed. She wiped her eyes. 'So what must I do now?'

'You should stop worrying and . . .' Jessie felt herself go hot under the collar, because she had not talked like this before to her daughter-in-law, 'carry on with the good work.'

'Nursing Kitty, you mean?'

'Yes – and make good use of that new bed when it comes!'

Then they were both laughing, and Kathleen said, 'Oh I do love you, dear Jessie!'

FIFTEEN

It was a year later, June 1906, and Marion was spending some of her Saturday afternoon off with her mother, while Danny continued working with the horses. Red Ruby was expecting another foal, while Grasshopper, the young colt, had been sold to a breeder, along with the one-time skittish gelding, who, after being well schooled by Marion, was now racing point-to-point. Doc and Danny were on the lookout for another brood mare. Things were going to plan at the stables.

'Why are you still wearing your breeches?' Mrs Amos demanded when Marion joined her in the garden; she preferred to see her daughter wearing one of her new summer frocks when they were relaxing. Breeches were for mannish women, and Marion was certainly not that.

Ankles were now a familiar sight, as fashion decreed shorter skirts. The more daring women wore bloomers when they went out on their bicycles, a mode of transport that was becoming a more familiar sight than riders on horseback these days, though there was still excitement at the sight of a motorcar on these back roads. Marion had mentioned casually only the other evening that she would like to ride a bicycle. 'I wouldn't have to wait for you to drive me about then, Danny; I'd be able to come and go as I please.'

Marion sipped her lemonade and sighed. 'I'm taking young Heather for her first ride on the old donkey today – I thought we'd go by the strawberry fields and see how the fruit is ripening. Also, Neddy isn't shod for the road. You can come along if you like.'

'No thank you. It's too hot for walking in the sun. There's always a shady spot in the garden. And why can't her mother do it?' Mrs Amos never used Kathleen's Christian name.

'She's got Kitty to look after as well, and anyway, I enjoy being with my niece!'

'So that's what you call her, is it?'

'Mother!' Marion was exasperated. 'I'm off now. I'll be back with Danny later on.'

'I must admit I'm fond of Danny, but he needs to buck up his ideas and get you in the family way! Mind you, I recall he had mumps badly when he was a young lad, and your grandma, who was interested in home remedies – folk used to go to her rather than the doctor – said he might never be a father.' She paused. Maybe I've said too much, she thought.

Fortunately, she kept her next thought to herself: in which case, Danny couldn't have fathered that girl's second baby, even if it does look rather like him . . .

'Do you know, Mother, we've stopped worrying about all that. I really enjoy being involved with training horses, and riding them too,' Marion retorted. She turned her head; she didn't want her mother to see the tears in her eyes. Who is at fault? she wondered. Is it Danny or is it me?

Neddy was not too happy to be caught when happily grazing on the pasture, or to have the bit inserted between his teeth. When the felt saddle was placed on his back, he responded with a loud *hee-haw*. His companions made their way in haste towards the far fence. Tails flicked as flies settled on sleek rumps and heads were tossed.

Danny lifted Heather up onto the donkey's broad back and kept his arm round her as Marion led Neddy to the track leading down to the strawberry fields. 'I'll walk with you as it's the first time,' he told his wife. 'She'll be more confident in a week or two.'

Jessie and Kathleen were already looking over the strawberries and picking the first few red ones for a teatime treat. Kitty, now eleven months old, bounced in her pram, rattling the small wooden beads fringing the canopy. She was crawling now, but she wasn't as forward as her sister had been in attempting to walk.

Danny's heart missed a beat when he saw Kathleen, in a blue dress with a bonnet protecting her from the sun, having returned to the donkey his ancient straw hat with the holes for his ears to poke through. She and Jessie waved as Neddy plodded towards them. The heat was relentless this afternoon. It was proving the hottest summer for decades. Marion's fair skin was reddened by the sun and her brow glistened with perspiration.

'Let's rest up under the oak tree before we go back to the stables,' Danny suggested. He lifted Heather down. 'Did you enjoy your ride?' She nodded, thumb in mouth. 'Here's Mummy,' he said.

'An' Gamma,' Heather said, before spotting the bowl of strawberries. 'Mine!' she cried joyfully.

'For all of us,' Jessie reminded her gently with a smile. 'Sit with Mummy under the tree and we'll share them out. I've a carrot in my pocket for you to give Ned.' It was obvious to her that Danny would love a little one of his own.

Later, back at the stables, after they had led the donkey to the water trough and removed the harness and saddle, Danny said diffidently to Marion, 'Do you fancy . . .'

'A roll in the hayloft?' she teased him.

'Well, I mean, it's a chance to talk to each other. Your mother is always listening in at home. The walls are too thin there, and we *would* have the bedroom next to hers.'

Marion said, 'She likes to know we're near, I think. In case she's taken ill in the night.'

'Not much chance of that,' he said, and he sounded bitter.

'Danny!' She was shocked at his response. However, she turned and climbed the ladder into the cool space above their heads. It was a regular bolthole for them.

He felt in his pocket for a cigarette, but she stopped him from lighting it. 'Not safe among all these bales of hay, Danny. Anyway, I thought you had a better idea . . .'

Some time later they sat up, brushing straw from their hair. They exchanged a long, lingering kiss. 'Feel better now? Not that we did much talking,' he whispered.

'Oh Danny, I saw the way you looked at Kathleen – please say it's *me you* love.'

'You know I do, Marion. But I can't help myself, I'm sorry . . . She obviously went through so much trouble before she came here. She seems like one of our family now.'

'At least she doesn't seem to realise how you feel,' Marion said sadly.

'You look as if you need a good bath,' Mrs Amos said, looking keenly at her daughter.

'Well Danny can bring the tub into the scullery, but I don't want the water too hot. You're not going to the pub tonight, are you, Danny?'

He shook his head. 'Thought we'd have an early night.' He didn't look at Mrs Amos.

'You can give my back a good wash for me, I feel all itchy in this heat.'

'I can guess why,' her mother said huffily, reaching out and pulling a piece of straw from her daughter's hair. 'I thought we might have a game of cards tonight.'

'Ask Bert, he's lurking around somewhere,' Marion said, surprising her mother. She turned to Danny. 'You can have the water after me.'

'Cleanse away your sins,' her mother muttered. She had the last word, as usual.

Sam was back from the brickworks. The men had Saturday afternoons off. He was gradually building up one side of the house, but there was still a long way to go. Sometimes he wondered if it would ever be finished. Would Kathleen come back there when it was habitable?

'Did Danny say anything about meeting up with me at the pub?' he asked. 'You wouldn't mind, would you, Kathleen?' She handed him a clean towel; he had just sluiced himself with cold water at the pump, rather than bother with a bath. They were in the scullery together.

'No – he said he thought they'd have an early night. Heather loved riding the donkey, and she ate most of the strawberries Jessie picked for our tea! Daisy is waiting to help me get the babies to bed – she likes playing nursemaid, I think.'

'How old is Daisy?' he asked. 'She doesn't appear to have a young man in tow.'

'I believe she's thirty – I don't think she wants to be married; she says women in her family prefer it that way.'

'What shall we do this evening, then?' he asked, pulling his freshly ironed shirt over his head. 'Doc and Mother are playing chess in the living room, so I suppose we'll go in our little sitting room and read a book – what do you say?'

'Marion gave me this week's copies of the *Times*; you haven't brought your paper back for me for days and I want to catch up on all the news.'

'I haven't bothered to go out and buy the *Daily Mirror* lately; too busy. I'll look through those papers with you,' he said.

'And tell me what I shouldn't read, no doubt,' she said, but she was only half joking. It was the only bone of contention between them, she thought.

He encircled her narrow waist with his arms, 'I'm glad you don't wear a suit of armour to ward off advances, like fashionable women in town.'

'If you mean a corset, I don't need it,' she murmured ruefully. 'Marion agrees with me, but I wish I had a figure like she has.'

'She's not a will-o'-the-wisp like you,' he teased.

The carrier called unexpectedly at the farmhouse one morning. Daisy answered the door, drying her hands on her apron, for she'd been giving the sink a good scour round.

'Miss Daisy Jennings?' the man asked, looking at her rather doubtfully.

'Yes, but I expect you want Mrs Mason – I'll fetch her while you sort out the parcel.'

'No, it's much bigger than a parcel and it's addressed to you!'

Who would send her something by carrier? she wondered. The man lifted down an unwieldy object swathed in brown paper and fastened with rope. 'Here you are then,' he said, and he was off before she could ask him to show her what was inside.

'Whatever is that?' Jessie said, coming downstairs with Heather wriggling in her arms; Kathleen was feeding the baby in the bedroom.

'May I use your big scissors, Mrs Mason? And then we'll find out.'

Minutes later, surrounded by paper and string, the mystery object was revealed.

'A bicycle!' Daisy cried in amazement, taking in the gleaming black enamelled frame with embellishments of gold leaf, the shiny aluminium wheels, rubber pedals and leather saddle mounted on coiled springs. 'Whoever . . .?'

'There's an envelope tied to the handlebars,' Jessie said, restraining Heather with difficulty, for she was intent on investigating what she obviously thought was a new toy.

The scissors released the envelope, which fell to the ground. The bicycle was propped carefully against the wall and they went into the living room so Heather could play with her own toys while Daisy took the letter out of the envelope.

'From my Aunt Maggie,' she said. 'Would you like to read it?' She passed the sheet of paper to Jessie.

Dear Daisy,

Your grandma sold some of her possessions, as you know, when she came to us, and she wanted to buy you something special for your birthday. We sent for the bicycle from my catalogue. It is the latest model – a Rudge. She hopes you will be pleased and will send us a picture of you riding it!

Grandma is well and happy and hopes you are the same. Jack and I bought the bicycle bell as our present to you.

Do write to us again soon. Grandma has some spectacles now and can read letters herself, she says, but she finds writing too much.

Happy birthday, with love from us all,
Aunt Maggie

'When is your birthday?' Jessie asked.

'It's today, Mrs Mason. My twenty-first,' Daisy said shyly. In her family, birthdays had never been treated as anything special, until now. She was not much older than Kathleen, Jessie realised.

'You should have said, Daisy – but now we know, we'll celebrate! You must have the day off.'

'Oh no, thank you, Mrs Mason. I want to carry on as usual, if you don't mind. But I must spend an hour or two learning to ride the bicycle. Just think, I can ride to the village and get any shopping you need. It's got a lovely big basket, hasn't it? And I can ride to Westerham sometimes – it's a bit far to walk.'

Jessie nodded, sharing her excitement. 'If the strawberries do well, I might join you on a bicycle of my own!'

'The only thing that worries me, Mrs Mason, is it's called a lady's bicycle and folk might think I'm getting ideas above my station.'

'Nonsense!' Jessie said firmly. 'We are all sisters under the skin.'

'You sound like one of them suffragettes, Mrs Mason.' Daisy admired her employer and listened avidly to her views on life.

'I'm going to save up for a bicycle too,' Marion told her mother. 'And I've said I'll make Daisy some bloomers!'

'Bloomers! Flagrant, Marion, that's what they are.'

'Oh Mother, they're not meant to titillate, if that's the expression; they're baggy, ugly garments, and you wear a short skirt over them. Besides, it's better to reveal bloomers than normal underwear, and you still need to wear stockings and boots, so you won't be showing too much leg!'

'Just as well, when cycling is likely to cause you to develop muscular limbs. Women will soon look like men!'

'Some of them do already,' Marion said daringly. 'Especially if they're brought up on a farm!' She held up a length of printed cotton material. 'Better get on with my first order – I believe all the women round here will soon want a pair!'

'You've got a peculiar sense of humour, Marion.'

'Now I wonder who I inherited that from?' Marion said, trying not to laugh.

Sam was yawning over his supper. 'Who's the cake in honour of?'

'It's Daisy's birthday; I told you earlier but you never listen.'

'I've had a busy day.'

'So have I. Heather is a little scamp nowadays; she tied a ribbon on Bob's tail and he looked very fed up about it.'

'I'm not surprised . . . So I guess that splendid machine in the hall has something to do with Daisy's birthday as well, eh?'

'Her grandma sent it to her – what a wonderful surprise! Marion is going to make her some bloomers and a short skirt to cover 'em.'

'Ask her to make you a pair too. I'd love to see you riding a bicycle in them!'

'Well I need my own bicycle first,' she said plaintively.

'You'll have to wait for your special birthday next January – are you looking forward to being twenty-one?' Perhaps then, he thought, she'd be free from what had happened in the past . . .

SIXTEEN

The winter that followed that hot summer and autumn was bitterly cold. It wasn't a time for bicycle rides for the young women in the family, and children couldn't play outdoors. It was hard, Kathleen thought, to keep Heather amused, and baby Kitty looked like one of the Egyptian mummies pictured in Sam's books, wrapped up in layers of flannel, plus bonnet and mitts. The men were busier than ever. The ground was hard and frosted white, and the horses were kept in the stables. Milk came home frozen in the pail, and the hens were not laying any eggs.

Following an austere Christmas, it was still freezing in the new year, when another notice appeared in the newspaper. Sam cut the piece out and then burned the paper before Kathleen could read it and ask what was missing.

> *Miss Kathleen Clancy, formerly of Dublin, believed to be in Surrey or Kent, having attained her majority, is again urgently requested to get in touch with the solicitors named above to learn something to her*

advantage. There are no conditions attached to this request. Confidentiality is assured.

Sam agonised over what he knew he must do. He was at the brickyard on Thursday, the second day of January, when he felt compelled to speak to someone impartial about the dilemma. He called over his foreman, who had moved into the Barn House with his wife a few weeks before Christmas, and said quietly, 'I have to pay a visit to a friend; I won't be back here again today. And remember I am having Saturday morning off – my wife insists as it is my birthday tomorrow – and Monday, too, when she will be celebrating her twenty-first.' I'm gabbling, he thought, I didn't need to tell him all that.

The man nodded his head. 'Yes, of course, Sam. I'll finish loading the wood in the cart and it will be ready to deliver to customers tomorrow. They are all anxious to get their supplies before the weather changes. Are you going back home to tidy yourself, or would you rather do that here?'

'Thanks,' Sam said, 'that would save time . . . Oh, and here are your wage packets, due today.' He took two envelopes from his jacket pocket and handed them over.

Now that Sam had a bicycle – a sturdy model without embellishments, bought second-hand from the foreman, who didn't need it any more – he could get to and from the farm without borrowing Doc's buggy and pony. Ollie hadn't taken to running alongside the bike, and had decided to move back into the Barn House. He had an important job to do guarding the brickyard, but he was still a friendly fellow. His absence was perhaps a relief to Bob, who sadly was losing the use of his back legs and didn't tolerate the young dog as before.

Although he knew he had the newspaper cuttings safe in his wallet, he checked they were there before he set off on his journey. Around four o'clock, he was knocking on the door of the manse, which was opened by Min, rubbing floury hands on her apron. She beamed. 'Just in time for a hot cake! Didn't expect to see you today, Sam. Are the family well?'

'Yes thanks. Min, is Josh at home? I need to speak to him – it's important.'

'Yes, he is, come through; he's in his study as usual. Oh, its Kathleen's birthday soon, isn't it? I have a card and a little present. I was hoping to visit her tomorrow, depending on the weather; by the look of the sky, those could be snow clouds . . .'

'I know she'd like that,' he said as she ushered him into the study and closed the door behind him.

Joshua was at his desk. He pushed his spectacles up on to his forehead. 'Ah, Sam, good to see you.'

'I need your advice, Josh,' Sam stated.

'Sit down, I'm ready to listen.'

'It's . . . difficult to know where to start,' he began. 'I've kept this secret for three years now, since the day we found Kathleen lost in the snow and took her in. After Kitty was born, I meant to tell her what I am about to reveal to you, but I didn't know how she would take the news. I couldn't find the right words, I suppose. We have a happy marriage, two lovely daughters, and Kathleen is settled and content; I was fearful, I suppose, of spoiling all that.'

He didn't have the original cuttings about her disappearance from Croydon to show Josh, having burnt them before Kathleen could see them, but he knew the wording by heart. Then he produced the latest cutting, together with the one given him by Mrs Amos eighteen months earlier – the messages from the solicitors in London.

Joshua listened to the rambling story without commenting, but when Sam had told him everything, he said quietly, 'You must be relieved to get this off your chest. I am not going to judge you in this matter because I am positive you did what you felt you must in order to safeguard Kathleen, both before and after she became your wife. However . . .' he paused, weighing up his words, 'I think the time has come to tell her what you have confided to me. She may be angry, she may well be upset, thinking of what she went through before you met, but she will realise sooner or later that you concealed these facts to save her from further pain. The latest message seems to me to be unconnected with what happened in Croydon; rather a bequest of some sort by one who cared for her – a close relative, perhaps?'

'Kathleen only told me that her father died when she was seven, and her mother when she was fifteen. I have gathered some facts from the newspaper articles but have not heard the full story. I can only guess why she ran away from the house in Croydon; she still bears the scars of what must have happened there . . .'

'And the man who fathered her baby?' Joshua prompted him gently.

'I don't want to think about that, and nor does she. She was taken by force, I'm sure.'

A knock on the study door; Min came in with mugs of tea. 'You need a hot drink before you venture home; it's dark already. I hope you have a light to show you the way.' She looked at Sam with concern. 'Be careful, Sam, and don't make any hasty decisions.'

'How did you know?'

'I guessed you were in some trouble. I hope Josh was able to help and advise you.'

'Yes, he was. Thank you both,' he said.

Sam gulped the hot tea down and said goodbye. As he left, Min tucked Kathleen's gifts into his pocket. 'There's a card for you for tomorrow, too,' she told him.

He arrived back at the farm around his usual time, and Kathleen opened the door with the little girls clinging to her skirts. 'Dada's home!' she cried. 'The carrier came this afternoon, Sam, as he said we might have snow by Monday, but I haven't unwrapped your present to me, even though I was very tempted!'

He scooped up a little girl under each arm and kissed them.

'What about me?' Kathleen joked. She touched his cheek. 'It must be freezing outside! Let's go in the kitchen where it's warm . . .'

Jessie gave him a searching look, guessing something was up, but she said only, 'Dinner's on the table.'

By midnight the house was quiet and the family were all in bed. Kathleen snuggled up to Sam, but for once he lay there not responding. Disappointed, she whispered, 'What's wrong, Sam? Have I upset you in some way?'

'No, no! I have a confession to make, Kathleen, and I don't know how to begin . . .'

When he had finished telling her about concealing the articles in the newspapers over the past three years, she didn't immediately respond.

'You have kept your past a secret from me, Kathleen,' he blurted out.

'I thought it would spoil everything – and look, I was right, it has!'

'Can't you tell me about it now that I have confessed my mistake?'

'You would be shocked! I felt . . . defiled by what happened.'

'Kathleen,' he pleaded, 'please let me hold you close, don't turn away from me.'

'Leave me alone! You are asking too much of me, you must know that!'

Without another word, Sam lit a single candle on the washstand and hastily dressed, then snuffed the candle out and left the bedroom. He hesitated for a moment before cautiously opening the children's bedroom door. There was a night light in there, out of reach of small hands, and he could see that they were both asleep. Tears coursed down his face, running into his beard, trickling down his neck.

I have always loved Heather as if she was my own flesh and blood, he thought sadly. They are both my daughters. What can I do to make everything all right again?

Later, Jessie bent over Kathleen's bed saying softly, 'Why don't you tell me about it?'

'I should have told Sam, but I couldn't,' Kathleen sobbed. 'Now he's gone off and I can't tell him I'm sorry.'

'He did something to make you feel like this, obviously. But knowing my Sam, he acted as he did because he wanted to protect you.'

Kathleen took a deep breath. 'This is what I could never tell, Jessie. It wasn't true that I couldn't remember what happened in Croydon, but I tried to blot it out of my mind.'

'You were sent there by your stepfather?' Jessie prompted her.

'Yes, I was glad at first to escape his unwelcome attentions after my mother passed away. He said I needed to be taught a lesson. He said his sister, Mrs D'Estrange, needed help in the home and I would be her servant and not be allowed to question my duties. It was a terrible journey; the sea was so rough and I only had the clothes I was wearing when he threw me out, so I must have reeked when he met me . . .'

'Who was "he", Kathleen?'

'My employer's paramour, that's what she called him. He didn't approve of her behaviour towards me, and I suppose I thought of him as a friend. But . . .'

'But what?' Jessie prompted her. 'It's all right, Kathleen, you can tell me – you are doing well, keep going, my dear.' She put her arms around Kathleen and held her close.

'One night, I was crying in my room because Mrs D'Estrange had used the whip on me for the first time. She used to ride in Rotten Row when she lived in London; there were pictures on the walls of her when she was younger, all dressed up and sitting side-saddle. I think she attacked me because she was jealous and he made it worse by showing he liked me. That was when it happened, when he came to . . . comfort me after that thrashing. I didn't realise what he intended to do; I was only seventeen and unworldly. I couldn't escape, and he held me down. He could be violent too, like Mrs d'Estrange. I avoided him thereafter, but I was afraid to tell anyone.

'When she saw I was pregnant, she attacked me again and accused me of enticing her lover away from her. The thrashings went on, and then one night he tried to get between us. She suddenly gasped and fell to the ground as if she was having a fit. He was standing over her, holding her down, and I grabbed a few things from my room and ran off down the street. He chased after me, shouting, but I managed to get away . . . and you know the rest.'

'I know the rest, my dear. Don't worry, Sam won't have gone far, I'm sure.'

'It's his birthday . . . today – oh Jessie, what have I done?'

'It's what you *must* do that matters now. First we must get the little girls up, washed, dressed and fed. Then Danny will be back with the milk. He may be able to help.'

Danny had already milked the goats before he noticed the bicycle outside the stable. He was alone this morning because Marion had a headache and wanted an extra hour or two in bed. He put the churns down and went to investigate. The animals looked at him curiously; it was too early for feeding. Danny climbed the ladder to the loft and spotted a figure lying in the hay. 'Sam . . .?' he said tentatively.

'Go away,' Sam muttered. 'I'll be gone when you come back. Don't tell Kathleen where I am.'

'Stay where you are. I'll bring you some food before you go wherever you're intending to go.'

Danny slung the yoke over his shoulders and began the walk back to the farmhouse, wondering what on earth had happened. As he entered the hall and put down his burden, the kitchen door burst open and Kathleen came rushing out. 'Oh Danny, Sam has left me – please help!' Her face was white as chalk, her hair uncombed. She was still in her night attire.

Jessie, not far behind after leaving the children with Daisy and closing the kitchen door, saw Kathleen clasped in Danny's arms. She was shocked by the sight. Danny's embrace was not a brotherly one. He was stroking her hair, and then, unexpectedly, he kissed away a tear that was rolling down her cheek.

She found her voice and realised she was shaking. 'Danny, that's not helping. Sam has gone off, goodness knows where.'

He released Kathleen and gave her a gentle push towards Jessie. 'I know where he is; he slept the night in the hay-loft. I need you to make sandwiches and a bottle of tea, for both of us; I promised to go back, and I will try to talk him round. Tell Doc not to come down there for a while.'

'Marion?'

'She's feeling unwell. Having the morning off.'

'Tell him . . .' Kathleen said, 'tell him I love him.'

'I will,' Danny told her, knowing it was true.

Mrs Amos took a cup of tea into her daughter's room; Marion waved away the biscuit.

'You've got something to tell me at last, I reckon,' her mother said.

'I haven't even told Danny yet.'

'You'll have to stop all that careering round country lanes on horses,' Mrs Amos said firmly.

'I didn't think I would feel so poorly, Mother. I didn't realise it would be like this, you never said . . .'

'Why do you think I only had one child? But I was so lucky to have you,' she admitted.

'I don't want an only child; I missed having a brother or sister,' Marion said. She took a deep breath. 'Quick – the chamber pot! I'm going to be sick!'

'You'll change your mind, you'll see,' said Mrs Amos, passing the receptacle. 'When are you going to pass on the good news to young Danny?'

'He's not so young now – he'll be twenty-two in a couple of days!'

'That girl, she'll be twenty-one, I understand . . .'

'Don't speak of my friend like that!' Marion said sharply. 'I want to get up now, Mother, I don't feel like talking at the moment.'

'I know when I'm not wanted,' her mother said huffily.

Danny had his arms round his brother, comforting him. 'Come on, Sam, Kathleen is very upset; she's frightened you're leaving her for good.'

'It would be difficult,' Sam managed. 'I have responsibilities, a business to run.'

'The biggest responsibilities are your wife and children. Please tell me what all this is about. You love Kathleen, don't you?'

'Isn't that obvious? I can't tell you anything without her say-so. But sometimes I wonder if I can cope.'

'Go back right now and you'll be welcomed with open arms. I won't come with you because I have jobs to do here, and Doc will be arriving any minute now. I believe Kathleen has confided in Mother . . .'

Kathleen rushed to the door when she heard him arrive outside. 'Sam, oh Sam, I'm so sorry – I was the one who should have said . . . I feel better now it's out in the open.'

Jessie called out, 'Go upstairs and talk there. Everything will be all right, I promise.'

'Would it be too awful to go back to bed?' Sam asked tentatively. 'I'll have a good wash first, I promise.'

'Well I'm still not dressed myself, and I was awake all night too.' Kathleen took off her wrapper and tidied the bed. 'Won't they wonder where we are?'

'Oh, Mother will know, she always does . . .'

When Danny arrived home, still feeling guilty about embracing Kathleen as he had earlier, Marion rushed to hug him and whisper in his ear. 'Danny, it's happened – we're going to have a baby at last! Are you pleased?'

He let out a whoop and cried, 'I'm the happiest chap in the world!'

'I won't be riding a bicycle for some time, so I can put my savings towards things we'll need for the baby,' she said. 'Oh Danny, you do love me like I love you, don't you? Sometimes I wonder—'

'Shush,' he said, 'stop talking rubbish and let me kiss you.'

'Until I'm breathless?' she asked.

'Come here and I'll show you . . .'

They were standing outside the front door, and Mrs Amos could see them from the side window. She let the curtain fall back into place with a satisfied smile.

Danny squeezed Marion's waist. 'Are you sure?'

'I'm sure,' she said fondly. 'It will be mid-August by my reckoning. Kathleen will be so pleased for us when I tell her the news. Do you want a boy or a girl?'

'I don't mind at all. If it's a girl, I hope she has golden hair like you.'

My headache's gone, Marion realised. Danny's thrilled about the baby and all's well.

'Are you going to the pub tonight to celebrate Sam's birthday?' she asked.

'No – I think we would both rather be at home with our wives tonight,' he said. You have to grow up sometime, he thought, and it's happened to my brother and me today.

SEVENTEEN

The weather worsened during January, with more snow, and there was not much they could do about the solicitors' message except write a letter to Messrs Bartholomew and Hartley-Jones in Chancery Lane in London. Doc was asked to advise Kathleen on what she should say.

'I can spell, you know,' she said rather indignantly to Jessie when she heard he was willing to help. 'I had a good convent education back home in Ireland.'

Jessie said soothingly, 'But this is a business letter, Kathleen dear, and I really think that Doc is the best person to help.'

'What about Sam?'

'He's emotionally involved. Doc isn't.'

Kathleen went up to the attic, taking the newspaper clippings to show him. They sat side by side at Doc's desk, and he took notes. When they were both satisfied with the draft, Kathleen dipped her pen in the inkwell and Doc moved aside and took up a ledger. 'I should get our accounts up to date,' he said tactfully as she began to write.

Dear Sirs,

Regarding your recent notice in the *Times* newspaper, I wish to inform you that I am the person you are seeking. I was formerly Miss Kathleen Clancy from County Clare and Dublin, after which I spent a short period in Croydon. I am now married to Mr Samuel Mason; we have two young daughters and reside at the above address in Kent.

I understand there is an important matter you wish to discuss with me. If you could suggest a date that would be convenient for my husband and me to meet with you at your office, I would be grateful. I can provide proof of my identity.

Yours faithfully,
(Mrs) Kathleen Mason

Although it was still cold in February, Sam decided it was time to travel to London to meet Mr Thomas Bartholomew, the senior partner in the firm. When the date and time were confirmed, Mr Bartholomew offered to take them out for lunch after discussing business. To Sam, this appeared unusual, but he kept his thoughts to himself, as Kathleen was already worrying about the journey, which would involve catching the steam train from Westerham station to the main line station at Dunton Green, where they would link up with the London train. When they arrived in the city, they would need to catch a double-decker bus, or a cab, to Chancery Lane.

'You haven't been to Westerham village yet, have you?' Jessie said now, as they watched the children playing on the lawn in the back garden. Sam had brought the swing over from the Barn House and had also made a box on wheels for little Kitty to push along the paths, though she sometimes veered off course and ran over the flower beds. Then the cry would come, 'Gamma! I's falled over!' old Bob sometimes staggered out and sat by the back door. His eyes were clouded over now and he couldn't see much, but his ears twitched as he carried out his duties of watching over the girls.

'Sam said the other day that I should go with Daisy next time she's cycling to the shops. I want to buy a hat to wear to London to match the costume I've ordered from your catalogue. I wonder – would you let me borrow your shoulder cape, please, Jessie?'

'Of course, with pleasure! It will go nicely with the costume. You might go to Westerham this afternoon perhaps, while the girls are having a nap. I can doze alongside them, eh? I'll ask Daisy if she'll take you and I'll write a shopping list! Do you think you could get me some more two-ply white wool? I want to knit little bootees to match the matinee jacket I am making for Marion's layette.'

'I'm sure I can. August will be here before we know it. It's good that you and Mrs Amos are talking again; she's so much nicer now she's got her heart's desire!'

Jessie hesitated and then said, 'She was worried for Marion, you know; they could see that Danny had feelings for you.'

'I can't help that!' Kathleen told her. 'At the start I was confused because I thought it was Danny I liked best, then I realised Sam was the one for me. Marion and I are good friends now; Danny has a soft spot for me, that's all.' She didn't add, 'As I have for him.'

'I hope you're right,' Jessie said with a sigh.

'Have they seen bloomers in Westerham before?' Kathleen asked Daisy as they pedalled away from the farm.

'Course they have! I go there reg'lar, don't I? Some of the ladies look down their noses, but I reckon the men think we're suffragettes, don't you?'

'I don't mind at all. Votes for women, eh? When I get my chance, I'll vote for the Liberals – I hope Lloyd George will become prime minister!'

Daisy grinned. 'Watch out for the puddles; go round those, else we'll arrive all muddy.'

As Kathleen swerved round a water-filled hole in the road, she thought, I feel like a young girl again, not an old married woman!

Westerham seemed more like a country town than a village. Daisy pointed out places of interest and they had a tour around before going to the shops in the high street. Kathleen learned that there would be a fair on the green in the summer, which was something to look forward to. The grand houses were awesome: Quebec House, the childhood home of Major General James Wolfe, and Farley Croft.

Sam had already told her about the famous people connected with Westerham. In addition to General Wolfe, there was also Charles Darwin, whose writings Sam studied avidly, and William Pitt the Younger. He hadn't noticed that she was suppressing a yawn as she listened.

Kathleen's tour with Daisy included St Mary's Church, though they didn't have time to go inside; the statue of Queen Victoria to mark her Diamond Jubilee; and Westerham railway station. There wasn't a train in sight, so no clouds of steam to alarm Kathleen. She was relieved to see it was a modest station. They pushed their bicycles up Vicarage Hill and past the almshouses. At the west end of the village, Croydon Road joined the high street, where a sharp bend led to the old smithy.

'I know where the places are, but you know more about them, Mrs Sam,' Daisy said ruefully.

'Only because Sam gave me one of his history lessons,' Kathleen admitted. She added on impulse, 'Why don't you call me Kathleen? We're friends, after all.'

'But Mrs Mason . . .'

'She was Jessie to me when she didn't know me from Adam! She won't mind.'

'Here's the draper's, Mrs . . . Kathleen; I think we ought to buy the wool before we forget.'

They propped their bicycles against the wall and went inside the shop.

When they emerged a few minutes later, they had to wait for a crocodile of schoolgirls, accompanied by a mistress, to pass. The girls were smartly dressed in short tunics with wide sleeves to the elbow, and carried hockey sticks.

'They come from that private school for girls,' Daisy told Kathleen. 'They should have worn coats, not capes, in this cold weather . . .'

They looked rosy and healthy, anyway, Kathleen thought.

They had arrived at the milliner's and stood for a minute or two looking at the display of hats on stands in the window. Daisy gave Kathleen a nudge. 'Someone's looking out at us, see? Wond'ring if we're customers. Let's go in.'

The shop assistant was disappointed. Judging from their attire, and the bicycles outside, they didn't appear to be the sort who would appreciate the lavish confections on offer. She had a sudden brainwave. There was that hat that had been under the counter for several years. 'I think I have something you might like, madam,' she said. 'Very popular with marching women.'

'What colour?' Kathleen asked. Her legs were aching from turning the pedals all afternoon on her bicycle.

'Dark blue, madam. I'll fetch it for you.' The shop assistant moved some boxes around behind the counter. 'This one is half price.' She discreetly brushed the dust off on her sleeve. 'As you can see, it is a small felt bowler with turned-up brim; made with the marching woman in mind, I reckon.'

'The colour would be right with the costume,' Kathleen said to Daisy. The hat was placed on her head. 'I'll take it!' she said. 'And a matching ribbon, please.'

'I hope Mrs Mason likes it,' Daisy said doubtfully as they pedalled home.

When Sam came in, he burst out laughing. Kathleen turned her back on him and said, 'If you don't stop that, I'll . . . I'll . . .'

'Kiss me?' he said. 'It will be fine as long as you don't put your hair up!'

'I like Mummy's hat,' Heather said loyally. Kitty sucked her thumb and didn't give her opinion.

Kathleen left them abruptly and went upstairs. Jessie looked reprovingly at her son. 'Sam, stop teasing her. You know she's sensitive. Go after her and reassure her, otherwise you won't be going to London at all, I reckon.'

Kathleen was lying face down on the bed, and refused to look up when Sam touched her shoulder. 'I'm sorry,

Kathleen, I didn't mean to poke fun at the hat, but it does look like the ones ladies wore in the 1890s.'

She turned then. 'Don't you realise I've never bought a hat from a posh shop before?'

'Oh, my darling, I know you didn't have your mother around to take you shopping and advise you what to buy . . . Actually, that saucy little hat suits you – honestly. Let's kiss and make up, eh?'

'Oh Sam,' she sighed. 'Where would I be if you hadn't kissed me at the brickworks that day?'

'I knew you were special right away,' he said.

'I'll kiss you now,' she said, sitting up and drying her eyes. 'But I may decide to wear my tam o'shanter when we go to London.'

EIGHTEEN

It was just after 7 a.m., and Sam and Doc were enjoying their breakfast while Jessie and Daisy were busy feeding the little girls. Jessie glanced at the kitchen clock. 'Where is Kathleen, Sam? She'll need to eat something before you leave for the station.'

'Still getting dressed, I hope,' Sam said with his mouth full. He didn't appear anxious. He was all ready for the journey: clean-shaven, smart in his wedding suit. Jessie had tucked a serviette round his neck to protect his collar and tie. His hat and overcoat were on the hallstand, brushed and ready to wear, along with the cape for Kathleen.

Danny came through with the churns of milk. 'The big day,' he observed to his brother. 'Where is Kathleen?'

'What are you all fussing about?' Kathleen said, walking into the room. She was wearing her smart costume, but on her head was the tam o'shanter. Sam was crossing his fingers that no one would comment.

Jessie tossed her apron to Kathleen. 'Cover your good clothes while you eat your breakfast.'

'I don't want anything,' she said mutinously.

A pause, then Danny appeared from the pantry. 'Well if you don't want it, I could do with a nice plate of eggs and bacon!'

'I thought Marion would be cooking your breakfast later at home,' Jessie said, 'now she's given up work.'

'She hasn't given up work, Mother; she's feeling too poorly at the moment, so I told her Doc and I can manage.'

Doc cleared his throat. 'Well I think it's time I fetched the buggy. I'll take you down to the station to catch the train. Please excuse me. When I return, I will come straight back to the stables to help you, Danny.'

'Just a piece of toast, Kathleen, you must have something,' Jessie said, worried.

Kathleen turned to Daisy. 'Could you take the girls into the living room, please? Then they won't see me go.' She nibbled on the toast, leaving the crusts.

We pander to her as if she is still a child too, Jessie thought, for once feeling exasperated. She looked at Danny. He was unshaven and in his working clothes; he looked tired, and was obviously hungry. His eyes were on Kathleen, her long glossy hair tied back with ribbon, the tam o'shanter at a jaunty angle on her head.

Danny was thinking how smart Kathleen looked. Marion seemed to spend most of her time complaining these days because she had put on so much weight despite being only three months pregnant. He suspected Mrs Amos was responsible for advising her daughter not to allow normal relations with her husband; although, he thought bitterly, I shouldn't be surprised if she called it carnal relations . . .

Sam broke into Danny's reverie. 'I'm not sure how long everything will take today; we might perhaps need to stay overnight.'

'No need to worry,' Jessie reassured him. 'You can always telephone us.' She was very proud to have the telephone installed; it was needed for business mainly, but was proving a good investment all round.

'What about the children?' Kathleen asked. She had packed a valise in case, and had tucked away in her purse the sprig of heather from the pocket of the cape she had been given by Min on the last lap of her journey here.

'They will be fine; after all, we look after them for you when necessary, don't we?' Jessie reminded her. 'If you do stay in London overnight, Daisy, I'm sure, will sleep in their room with them.'

The train arrived, belching steam, and Kathleen clung to Sam's arm. They had arrived at the station with ten minutes to spare. Doc wished them farewell and good luck; he had a busy day ahead in the stables, and also two appointments later in his role of horse doctor. He was still much in demand with the local horse breeders. These were thoroughbred mares and their progeny were destined for the world of racing and hunting.

There was a clanging of carriage doors as passengers disembarked or climbed aboard. Sam guided Kathleen to an empty carriage near the guard's van. She settled herself with her back to the engine and told him, 'Hold my hand! The guard is waving us off.'

'Now we begin our big adventure.' As he removed his stovepipe hat, he saw her bottom lip tremble. 'Anyone would think you'd never seen a train before.'

The train was jolting forward, getting up steam, and would soon be well on its way to the main line station. No one joined them in the carriage. On the platform, people were walking about, some waving as they spotted friends and relatives through the train windows. Sam put his arms round Kathleen and hugged her tight. He gave her a long, lingering kiss. 'There, you didn't kiss me this morning!'

'Well, you weren't off to work, were you?' She actually giggled. 'I do love you, Sam.'

'I know you do, darling.' He released her and sat back.

'Sam, I'm worried about Danny,' she ventured.

'Whatever for? I don't suppose he likes being at the Amos place and probably regrets leaving the farm, but it gave us the chance to return there, and I know how happy you were to do so,' he said.

I'm not going to say what I really think, she thought, but I know Danny still cares for me.

They were in good time for the London train, but the platform was crowded. Kathleen clung to Sam, trying to ignore the noise and bustle. 'Would you like a paper?' he asked.

'Yes, and a magazine – for ladies!' she decided.

They were aboard at last, and this time the carriage was full. Two men had a spirited exchange over opening and shutting the window. 'D'you really want a smut in your eye?' one demanded of the other. Sam and Kathleen pretended to be engrossed in reading.

Kathleen actually found herself nodding off; after all, it had been an early start to the day. She let her head rest on Sam's broad shoulder and he gently tilted her hat away from his neck because he could see the lethal-looking hatpin. A girl's best friend, so it was said.

London was bewildering to them both. The roads were busy with motorcars, some with chauffeurs honking horns, as well as horse-drawn and motor buses, the latter with crowded top decks open to the elements and eye-catching advertisements on their sides. Dodging between these were donkey carts and bicycles, and pedestrians taking a chance by dashing across the road to the other side.

Taking advice from a well-dressed businessman, also waiting to cross over at his peril, they boarded a motor bus, which would take them close to their destination.

They were relieved to arrive in Chancery Lane, though when they located the correct building, they discovered it was occupied by several different businesses. Fortunately there was a sign on the wall indicating where they needed to go. They had to climb several flights of stairs before they arrived at the solicitors' office.

'This is it,' Sam said, pressing the doorbell. 'We are just on time.'

The door opened and a young clerk ushered them into the outer office, where a lady typewriter, as they were called, was pounding away on a machine with a long carriage necessary for legal documents. She looked up and said politely, 'Good morning.'

Kathleen plucked up courage to whisper to her, 'Is there a . . . a cloakroom, please?'

'The door on the left. No need to hurry, Mr Bartholomew knows you're here.'

Kathleen surveyed her image in the mirror over the basins. Her face was pale, so she pinched her cheeks to give them a little colour. Her hair was tidy, thank goodness.

Sam emerged at the same time from the cubicle on the other side. The clerk beckoned to them. 'Mr Bartholomew says that when you are ready, would you please tap on his office door.'

'Come in,' they were told as they knocked. They entered the room and closed the door behind them. Mr Bartholomew was a man of indeterminate age, possibly in his early sixties. He was not tall and imposing, but rather tubby and bald, with a watch chain straining across his waistcoat. He stood up and held out his hand to them in turn. He had a deep, pleasant voice. 'Please sit down. I am happy to see you at last.'

Noting her pallor, Sam thought for a moment that Kathleen was about to pass out, as she still did occasionally in stressful moments. He made sure she was comfortable and then reached for her hand.

Mr Bartholomew took all this in but didn't comment. Then he cleared his throat and said, 'If you are ready, Kitty, I will tell you the good news.'

Kathleen gave a start. No one had called her that since . . . She tried to put the thought to the back of her mind. 'Have we . . .' she managed, 'met before, Mr Bartholomew?'

'We have indeed. I was going to tell you that after the official part.'

'Please tell me now,' she said.

'I was a close friend of your father's. We grew up together in Ireland. I went off to college and he stayed to look after the family farm. I married his sister, your aunt, and when we moved to England, I joined this same firm as a lowly clerk.' He smiled. 'Your parents were overjoyed when you arrived, as they were both past forty. I stood as godfather at your baptism, as well as being your uncle by marriage. Unfortunately, my wife and I were unable to have children of our own, and we were both very fond of you. When you were almost seven, your father wrote that he was very ill, and wished to see us urgently.

'When we arrived at the farm, he told me that he wished to set up a trust fund for you to inherit when you were twenty-one. I had already helped with the wording of his will, which he had lodged with local solicitors some time before. That was straightforward; his estate would be passed on to your mother.

'He required me to keep the trust fund for you in England, because if his wife remarried, her estate would go to her new husband; he wanted to be sure that you were provided for. This would remain a private matter between the two of us. He died a month or two later, and your mother did indeed remarry within a year. I didn't trust the man she chose. We were told we were no longer welcome to visit. This is the first time I have been able to speak with you in all these years.'

Kathleen seemed unable to speak, so Sam stepped into the breach. 'How did you discover that Kathleen was missing?'

'Like you, I read the reports of the terrible happenings in Croydon, and the rumours of her ill-treatment. I hoped to hear that she was safe and well. We – my wife Dora and I – were distraught to hear that she was pregnant at the time. Eventually, as Kitty was approaching her majority, I decided to advertise in the *Times*.'

Kathleen found her voice. 'I came over the Pilgrims' Way and somehow found my way to a safe haven. Sam's mother Jessie nursed me back to health. Sam and I fell in love and married. He adopted my first baby, Heather, and she has a little sister, who is called Kitty.'

The men were both silent for a few minutes, then Mr Bartholomew said briskly, 'I must tell you about your inheritance, then we will go upstairs for our lunch. I will just say, Kitty, your parents would be very proud of you.'

'Upstairs?' Kathleen was puzzled.

'We live above the shop, as it were; we have lovely views of London from our front windows. Dora is so anxious to see you again at last. Now, down to business . . .'

The sum that Kathleen would receive was £5,000, plus interest accrued over the years. Mr Bartholomew – she couldn't yet bring herself to call him Uncle – wrote the cheque while they watched, dipping his pen in and out of the inkwell, then blotting the cheque with care. He tucked it inside a long manila envelope, 'Now, if you will please sign these forms, Kitty? You will want to examine the cheque before you seal the envelope and take it to your bank. You have an account already?'

Kathleen shook her head. 'No, Sam has a business account; we could pay it into that.'

Sam spoke up immediately. 'No, Kathleen, this is your legacy from your father; you should have your own account.'

'The money will benefit us all, Sam, don't argue about it!' Kathleen asserted.

Sam asked, 'What about the police? Do we tell them she is safe and well?'

Kathleen immediately became agitated. 'I don't want to talk about it to the police or the newspapers. I don't want to reveal my present address and circumstances – please.'

'The case is closed,' Mr Bartholomew told her. 'The man concerned confessed what had gone on in the house in Croydon; he is not considered mentally stable enough to attend any court hearing. I will, however, inform the police that I have seen you; that you are well, and settled in your new home. The press must be told to respect your privacy.'

'My stepfather . . .'

'He had a stroke. He is not fit either to defend himself for his part in all this.'

'I can't say I am sorry,' Kathleen said.

'No one would expect that, Kitty. Put it all out of your mind. Are you ready for lunch? Dora will be wondering where we are.'

The apartment was not what they had expected. It was rather claustrophobic, with heavy old-fashioned furniture, highly polished; the chairs were upright, with flat cushions, and weren't comfortable to sit on for too long. However, the view from the drawing room window was spectacular, and Kathleen spotted pigeons fluttering on the roof in the warm air from the chimneys.

Dora was of a similar height and rotundity as her husband; Kathleen had a sudden memory of the little weather house on the mantelpiece in the kitchen of the family farm, when she was fascinated to see if the old woman or the old man had come out, to indicate whether it would be a fine day or a cold one. She wondered what had happened to that favourite ornament; she didn't recall it in the Dublin house.

'We would have taken you in,' she became aware that Dora was talking to her, 'when your poor mother passed away, but the wretched man she married said you were going to live with his sister in Croydon. I would have been a mother to you, Kitty.'

'I have someone I think of as my mother now,' Kathleen said. 'Jessie, my mother-in-law. After Sam and my children, Jessie is the most important person in my life.'

There was an uncomfortable pause, then Dora said abruptly, 'Lunch is ready. What time do you plan to leave?'

Sam had been about to ask if he might use the telephone, and if the Bartholomews could recommend a local boarding house, but before he could do so, Kathleen gave her answer: 'We are travelling home tonight.'

'I have a timetable for the trains,' Mr Bartholomew said. 'Please sit down. Ah, fish.' He sniffed the aroma. 'Good for the brain, so they say . . .'

Everything was white, Kathleen thought; the fish, coated in white sauce without the addition of chopped parsley, was served with lumpy mashed potato, followed by rice pudding, pallid without the usual topping of grated nutmeg. It was with relief that she and Sam sat down after the meal and were given an old photograph album to study, with sepia pictures of herself as a small child with her parents.

'You may keep it and take it home with you. The pictures were taken by me,' Mr Bartholomew said, sounding sad.

I could have said I would keep in touch with him, Kathleen thought, but although Dora is my father's sister, too much has happened in the past to make that possible. I just want to go home to my family.

NINETEEN

'Aren't you getting up today?' Mrs Amos demanded of her daughter. She pursed her lips. 'You'll have to be livelier when the baby arrives, I can tell you. Look after Danny, too – why should I have to cook him bacon and eggs every morning, and do his washing?'

Marion turned her face to the pillow and muttered, 'I'm too tired to do anything – you don't seem to understand.'

'Understand? Of course I do! Childbirth is something to be endured, but women must look after their husbands or they are likely to stray.'

'That wasn't your advice earlier on,' Marion reminded her. 'I had to keep Danny at arm's length, you said.'

'I was only thinking of you – men just want what they want,' her mother asserted.

'Well all Danny wanted was to be loved – like me. Please leave me alone!'

'I'll ask Nurse Buss to call in this morning to talk to you; I must say, the telephone saves a lot of running about.' Mrs Amos was exasperated when she saw Marion's eyes close.

She's pretending to be asleep, she thought. She dabbed fiercely at her own eyes.

Later, Nurse Buss bustled into the bedroom, pulling the curtains open on her way to the bed, and said briskly, 'Now, Marion, what's all this I hear? You should be up and about . . .' She broke off as she saw how pale her patient was, that she was literally gasping with pain. Nurse felt her pulse, then her forehead, which was cold and clammy despite the warm weather outdoors. She pulled back the covers gently and said quietly, 'Oh, you poor girl! You're in labour, my dear. How long have the pains been coming?'

'All night,' Marion said faintly, gripping the nurse's hand. After a pause, she managed, 'The baby is coming too early . . . will it be all right?'

Nurse Buss didn't answer that, said instead, 'We must telephone the local doctor and get his opinion. You may have to be taken to hospital. Where is Danny?'

'He's at the stables – he came back earlier for his breakfast, but Mother sent him off with a flea in his ear. All he said was "I'll see you later."'

'He must be contacted too. I'll be back shortly, after I speak to Mrs Amos; she can deal with the telephone calls while I make you more comfortable.'

Danny had actually returned to Home Farm before going on to the stables. 'Sorry,' he said to Jessie, who had just cleared the breakfast table, 'but the dragon said she hadn't the time to cook me anything, and Mother, I'm starving!'

'Don't exaggerate, Danny, and don't call Mrs Amos the dragon,' Jessie reproved him, but she added, 'How about bread and milk? I just made a bowl of it for little Kitty; she's cutting teeth and needs something soft to eat.'

Just then the phone shrilled in the hall. Jessie answered it. There was an agitated voice at the other end: 'Mrs Mason, it's Mrs Amos. Big trouble here – I need to get in touch with Danny immediately.'

'He's here, I'll fetch him – just a minute.' She took a deep breath. Marion, she thought. What was wrong? 'Danny, your mother-in-law needs to speak to you!' she called.

When Danny replaced the receiver on the telephone, he turned to his mother. 'Marion's in labour – Nurse Buss is there and the doctor is expected. She said that Marion will probably have to go into hospital. I'll have to go over there, Mother. Can Daisy let Doc know I won't be working again today – oh, and Mrs Amos said Marion is asking for Kathleen . . .'

Jessie nodded. 'Just go, Danny! Good luck.' Six weeks early, she thought, poor Marion. I'd better tell Daisy and Kathleen what's up.

The doctor agreed with the nurse. 'Twins, did no one suspect that before?'

Nurse Buss took him to one side. She whispered, 'I can only detect one heartbeat . . .'

'It's vital that the patient is delivered as soon as possible then, before we lose them both.'

Danny, despite Mrs Amos telling him to knock on the door first, burst into the room and rushed to the bedside. Marion, moaning, eyes closed, appeared not to be aware he was there. The pain was constant; she couldn't speak. Danny knelt beside the bed, attempting to hold her hand, but she thrust him aside. He asked the nurse, 'Will she be all right?'

'The ambulance is on its way to take her to hospital; Mrs Amos should pack a bag for her with a few things.'

'Can I go with her?' he pleaded.

'The doctor came in his motor car; he'll take you there. I'll be looking after her in the ambulance.'

Mrs Amos was in the kitchen. She turned and said, 'Thank goodness you are here, Danny!' The next thing he knew, she was sobbing. He put his arms round her and held her close as he would have done if she were his own mother.

The back door opened and Kathleen rushed in. She hadn't bothered with her bicycle bloomers, but had hitched her skirt up and ridden there the moment Jessie told her about Marion.

'Nurse is getting her ready to go to hospital,' Danny told her. 'I'm going too.'

Mrs Amos said, 'I'll wait here for news. I must pack her bag – excuse me.' She dried her eyes firmly and went back to the bedroom.

Danny sat down abruptly on a kitchen chair. 'Jessie said I was to make sure you ate something,' Kathleen said. 'She made ham sandwiches. They are in my bicycle basket.'

As she gave him the packet, he caught at her arm. 'Kathleen, do you think Marion will come through this?'

'Oh Danny, I can't answer that,' she said sadly. She looked out of the window. 'The ambulance is here . . . the doctor's there too. Mrs Amos is giving him the bag.'

Mrs Amos came into the kitchen. 'Danny, Doctor asked if you would you carry Marion out to the ambulance. Kathleen, you can see her for a minute when Danny brings her out. Then go home and wait for news with Jessie.' She added unexpectedly, 'Thank you for coming.'

Danny gathered his wife into his arms; the nurse adjusted the blanket round her. Marion was sweating profusely and her breathing was shallow. He tried not to stagger under her weight. No wonder she hasn't been able to get around this past month or so, he thought.

The ambulance was like a horsebox on wheels, with a large cross painted on both sides. It was pulled by two sturdy chestnut horses, and the young male driver was already on his seat, ready to urge them on.

Kathleen was allowed to step up and watch her friend being transferred to the long leather-covered bunk, where she was gently covered with the blanket from her bed. She spoke her name quietly and saw Marion's eyes flicker. 'Don't be afraid, you're in good hands.'

'I'm following the ambulance in the doctor's car,' Danny promised.

'Look after Mother, Danny. Please . . .'

'I will.'

'Let me help you down, Kathleen,' he said, and the next thing she knew, she was in his arms for a brief moment before he jumped into the doctor's car. She stood by the door, waving to them, and then became aware that Mrs Amos was beside her.

'You'd best get off home to your little girls,' Mrs Amos said.

'Will you be all right?' Kathleen asked.

'I will telephone you with any news,' Mrs Amos told her. 'Now I must get on, I've a bed to change.'

'I could help you with that.'

Mrs Amos shook her head. 'Bert will help me when he comes back from feeding the poultry. Please pray for Marion, Kathleen.'

'I will.' And Danny too, she thought. She mounted her bicycle and made sure her skirt wouldn't catch in the wheels. Another wave, then she was pedalling fast to Home Farm.

Bert had observed all the comings and goings but had tactfully kept out of the way. He followed his usual busy morning routine among the henhouses. It was getting on for lunchtime when he ventured into the kitchen. There were no pans bubbling on the stove, no cooking smells; the kettle was boiling dry, so he shifted that off the hotplate. He was hungry, because like the rest of them, he had not had his usual hearty breakfast. Mrs Amos seemed to have disappeared. He called out, 'Missus?'

She emerged from the scullery, sleeves rolled up, hands red from pounding the soiled linen from Marion and Danny's bed, scrubbing the stains fiercely in the sink full of soapy hot water. 'What do you want?' she asked. Bert noticed that her eyes were red-rimmed too.

He hesitated. He had known from his first day working on the poultry farm that it was not wise to question anything she said, because she believed she was always right.

'It's dinner time, missus. Can I get something for you – us – to eat? I guess you've been real busy this morning . . .'

Mrs Amos sat down on a kitchen chair, which creaked under her weight. 'Help yourself, Bert, I'm not hungry.' She didn't sound at all like her usual self, Bert thought. She indicated a paper bag on the table. 'Mrs Mason sent some ham sandwiches.'

'I'll fill the kettle first, missus, I need a cuppa tea, and I 'spect you do too.'

'There's cheese and pickles in the pantry, and some lettuce from the garden. Plenty of bread; I was baking yesterday . . .'

'I'll see to it, missus,' he said. He took down two plates from the dresser. 'You got to eat.'

'You're pretty handy for an old bachelor,' Mrs Amos remarked.

'I was married once,' he said, surprising her.

'I didn't know that. All you told me was that you'd been in the army and fought in the Boer War.'

'I was younger then, not an old codger. I was born in the East End of London in 1860, and was married when I was twenty. My wife was only eighteen years old and she died a year later.' He didn't add 'in childbirth'.

'You're about the same age as me,' Mrs Amos exclaimed. Although he was short and stocky in stature, he had a ramrod-straight back as befitted an old soldier, but his face was seamed and brown from working outdoors and his hair was sparse and grey. She thought, I hope I don't look as well worn as that. I haven't got any grey hairs yet, thanks to using henna.

'I feel older'n that, missus.' He had a wry smile. 'But we're both widdered.'

She said, 'Well I am now, but if you must know, my husband ran off with the girl I employed to collect and sort the eggs when Marion was young. I'd inherited this business from my parents, and he resented that he was just . . .'

'The hired man, like me?'

'I suppose so – but I never intended it to be like that.' She gulped down the hot tea. 'I reckon you think I'm a hard woman, Bert.'

'I respect you,' he said honestly. 'You're not as bad as my old sergeant major.'

Bert started work at 6 a.m. each day, and was busy until 1 p.m. Then he had three hours off until the evening shift from 4 p.m. until 7. He seemed tireless. He could see that Mrs Amos was exhausted from dealing with the laundry this morning. 'You have a rest on your bed, missus. I'll listen for the telephone and call you if it's the hospital,' he offered.

'Thank you, Bert, I will. I have to believe no news is good news.'

Marion only had a hazy recollection later of the ride to the hospital in the bustling town of Bromley, some five miles away, and then of being wheeled down a long corridor to a small side ward, where a doctor waited to examine her. She didn't realise that the local doctor and Nurse Buss had relinquished her care to these white-clad strangers, and she was unaware that Danny was slumped on a hard chair in the outpatient reception area, with his head in his hands, trying to stem the tears.

He felt a hand on his shoulder and looked up. 'Sam!'

'I came to keep you company. Mother and Kathleen said I should, or else how were you going to get home tonight? This is a splendid hospital, Danny; it was originally the Phillips Homeopathic Hospital, and they raised money during the Jubilee in 1897 to enlarge it—'

'I don't want one of your history lessons just now, Sam. I know it's a good place – the Matron spoke to me to reassure me. She said they have a modern operating theatre and specialise in difficult cases. I won't leave until I know everything is all right. They won't let me see Marion, though.'

A nurse had spotted them and said briskly, 'Let me take you to the waiting room; there are some comfortable chairs there. Would you like a cup of tea and a biscuit?'

'Please,' Sam answered for them both.

'Your hair is dripping on your collar, Sam,' Danny said as they followed the nurse.

'Mother said I had to wash and brush up before I came here,' Sam said. He hoped Kathleen wasn't still crying; it upset the little girls when they saw her like that. It had been made worse because Jessie had whispered that poor old Bob had passed away that morning, and unfortunately it was Kathleen who had discovered him lying on the fireside mat. He added, 'Mother is carrying on as usual. She said Mrs Amos telephoned but told her she'd heard nothing from the hospital yet.'

Marion was wheeled to the delivery room. The first baby was struggling to be born and it was hoped it could be delivered with the help of forceps. The problem was that after a prolonged labour and one delivery, contractions would cease, but it was vital that the second child be delivered as soon as possible, even though it had not survived. If a normal birth was not possible or the mother's health was endangered, she might need an emergency Caesarean section, and that would involve chloroform.

Time was of the essence and the decision was taken: a frame was attached to Marion's face, holding a pad in place onto which chloroform was dripped. Mercifully, the patient was unaware of what was happening. Within a few minutes the first baby was lifted clear and handed to a waiting theatre nurse, and then the second baby was removed. The surgeon told his assistants that this foetus had not been viable for some time, and had impeded the progress of the stronger child. This was what had caused Marion to feel so bloated and in pain for the last couple of months.

The surviving baby boy was small, though he weighed more than most premature babies, and was taken straight away to the nursery for intensive care. Marion was stitched up while she was still sedated, and returned to a side room off the ward, for she would need vigilance too.

It was some time before a nurse came to find Danny and Sam. Danny clutched at his brother's arm. 'Is she . . .?'

'Your wife has undergone an emergency operation and is now recovering, so you can see her for a few minutes only. Another nurse will fetch you. We suggest you then go home. She is in good hands.'

'The baby?' Sam asked, for Danny was obviously in shock.

'A little boy. He has every chance of surviving. However, he will be here for some weeks before he can go home. Hopefully Mrs Mason will make a speedier recovery. Have you a name? It's important we have one, as he is premature . . .'

'We were talking about Wilfred – that was my father's name,' Danny managed.

Sam followed the nurse out of the room and asked in a low voice, 'Was there another baby?'

The nurse shook her head. 'It would never have survived . . . it hadn't developed properly. They have the joy of one baby, though, who stands a good chance of survival. We will inform your brother, and he can judge the best time to tell his wife.'

Danny bent over the narrow hospital bed and kissed Marion. She was still sleepy. He told her, 'You will see the baby tomorrow. I told them he was to be called Wilfred. I will visit you soon. I'll tell Mrs Amos all is well. I love you so much, you must believe me . . .'

Her voice was husky. 'I do, Danny, I do . . .'

Jessie had been watching out for them. She opened the front door and greeted Danny with a hug. 'How are things at the hospital? Did you telephone Mrs Amos?'

'I made the call for him,' Sam said. He looked up. Kathleen was coming down the steps, clasping her wrapper around her. Her feet were bare; she hadn't bothered with slippers.

'Is everything all right?' she asked breathlessly. 'Oh Danny, you must have been so worried.' She had her arms outstretched as if to hug him, and the chemise she was wearing under her wrapper was revealed.

Danny didn't answer. Jessie looked at Sam. 'Go upstairs with Kathleen, then you can give her the news. Danny will be staying the night here; he can be in my room, and Daisy will go in with the girls. We can talk together tomorrow.'

'Get back into bed, Kathleen,' Sam said once they were in their bedroom. He sounded weary rather than angry. 'Danny is in a state of shock. You are my wife, remember that.'

'Oh Sam, I didn't mean . . .'

'I know, you couldn't help yourself. How do you think that makes me feel? Was I your second choice? Poor Marion almost didn't make it today – don't step into her shoes.'

'Sam, come to bed and I'll show you how much I love you,' she cried.

'That's not the answer I want. If I lost you, I don't know what I'd do . . . Oh Kathleen, I need to be hugged now.'

'I felt so sorry for him, that's all . . .'

'Well you needn't. There are other ways of showing your support. Pray for that tiny baby, and for Marion and Danny too.'

He climbed into bed and held her tight. 'There, is that better? I'm too tired for any more talking, but . . .' He gave her a long, lingering kiss, then snuffed the candle out.

PART TWO

1912–1918

The summer's gone, and all the roses falling,
'Tis you, 'tis you must go, and I must bide.
But come you back, when summer's in the meadow,
Or when the valley's hushed and white with snow,
'Tis I'll be here in sunshine or in shadow,
Oh Danny boy, oh Danny boy, I love you so.

'Danny Boy', Frederic Weatherly, 1913

TWENTY

During the ensuing five years from 1907 to 1912, Sam had at last laid the final bricks of the Brickyard House and crowned it with shiny new roof slates. He had had the time to finish the house because, like many businesses in these troubled times, his industry was in decline.

Kathleen remembered the promise she had made to him, that they, along with eight-year-old Heather and six-year-old Kitty, would move into the Brickyard House once it was ready, and she knew she would be expected to do so shortly. Heather appeared to have outgrown the asthma attacks that had once plagued her, and which had precipitated their return to Home Farm in the first place, and due to the halt in firing bricks, the pungent smell that came from this process was no longer a problem.

The house might look splendid from the outside, but the inside did not live up to Kathleen's dreams. The Home Farm attic had yielded up stored furniture dating back to late Victorian times, and though the new bathroom, which Kathleen had so looked forward to, had plumbing in place, there was not yet a bath, basin or WC. Jessie was more fortunate in that respect, as Sam had built an extension to her scullery, and she now had a proper bathroom and a laundry room. The family kitchen remained much the same, though, and was the hub of Home Farm. The kitchen in the Brickyard House had a second-hand range installed; there was no gas supply, so Kathleen couldn't have the latest gas stove and boiler she would have liked.

She had put the past behind her at last, and had saved the money she had inherited for a rainy day. She didn't know if Sam would agree, for he always said firmly that it was his duty to provide for his family, but she'd suggest when the time was right that they should use the interest accrued on her capital to fit out the bathroom. For now, they still shared the outside privy with the family in the Barn House. Herbie, the foreman, was still working at the brickyard; though his future employment was not guaranteed, he planned to stay on in the house, and Sam and Kathleen were glad of the rent. His assistant had departed some time ago and enlisted in the army. Rumours of a war in Europe were becoming all too familiar.

With Danny and Doc having recently invested in a Humber motor car – mainly driven by the younger man – the old pony and buggy were now kept in the brickyard stable along with the carthorse, which was put between the shafts of a wagon when deliveries were made. Kathleen used the buggy to take the children to school each day. She still had her bicycle, but Sam said the girls would have to wait until their tenth birthdays before they had wheels of their own.

Kathleen was aware that Sam had always wanted a son, but now that women were free from unplanned pregnancies – if they had a co-operative husband – this had become a man's responsibility. If she broached the subject, he would say, 'This is not a good time. We can't afford another child, Kathleen.'

As Jessie remarked to Kathleen one day when she confided these longings to her mother-in-law, 'It's a topsy-turvy old world.' She hugged Kathleen to her and whispered, 'Be happy with your lot, Kathleen. Your marriage is a solid one. I am not so sure about Danny and Marion. Money isn't everything, you know.'

Jessie asked Danny if he was willing to take over the reins at Home Farm now rather than later, as Sam and Kathleen were moving out. Now that the poultry farm was jointly owned by Mrs Amos and Bert – who'd revealed that he'd accumulated money to invest, as he'd never spent his army pension – Danny and Marion agreed. Bert, having bided his time, had indeed got more than his feet under the table. Mrs Amos suspected that he had enjoyed a full life, as she put it, in the army, but surprisingly, she was as keen as he was to rekindle youthful passion. After all, she thought, no need for restraint at our age!

Marion was the disapproving one now. 'Aren't you going to marry him, Mother?' she demanded.

'One husband was more than enough for me,' Mrs Amos replied. 'I'm a lady of leisure now. We struck a bargain: he sees to the poultry and I look after the accounts.' She added, 'He checks those too!'

When Marion asked her mother's advice about moving over to Home Farm, Mrs Amos said drily, 'You will get your wish, Marion. You and Danny will be set up, you can return to your job in the stables with the horses, and my only grandson will be handed over to his other grandmother. He will no doubt soon be running wild with his cousins.' She looked hard at Danny.

'They are just high-spirited,' Danny said in their defence, 'like Sam and I were as boys.'

'Ah, but they are girls, Danny. Still, my Marion was high-spirited too, as you put it. Wilf's a good little boy. I will miss him,' she sighed. Wilf was due to join the village school with the girls come September, and Mrs Amos was worried how he would cope in the energetic rough-and-tumbles with other boys in the playground, being small for his age and not keen on sports. He was reading already, and writing stories.

'A scholar like his uncle Sam,' Danny said somewhat ruefully. It was unlikely they would add to their family after Marion's experience delivering Wilf. He accepted that his honeymoon days were long over. Despite his own success in business, he envied his brother's obvious married bliss. Whenever Danny saw Kathleen, he had to suppress his feelings, but he couldn't help thinking: if only . . .

'Mother has made up her mind at last,' he said to Sam. 'Not only about the farm, but to marry Doc.'

'They took their time! Kathleen thinks it's really romantic.'

'Nothing will really change; Mother will still be in charge of the kitchen, which we don't mind because Marion is not the best cook in the world, and Doc will move down from the attic – that will make a good playroom for the youngsters, eh?'

'What about Daisy? Does Mother need her now?'

'Oh, Daisy will look after Wilf while we are working. Mother says we can have the parlour opened up for our private use, and the sitting room upstairs will become Wilf's bedroom. Daisy will move in with him; she doesn't like being on her own at night. Mary's room will remain the spare room.'

Home Farm was now all about the horse stud. There was a big modern stable block for the newcomers, while the aged donkey, the shire horse and the goats shared the old quarters. Only one strawberry field remained, together with the orchard and the vegetable garden.

Jessie was actually relieved to be semi-retired. The horse breeding was much more profitable than the strawberry fields, and she wouldn't need to hire labour now. She could take the fruit from the single field to the local market to sell. 'The girls can help me,' she said to Sam. She included Kathleen in that description, for she still seemed so young, although she was now twenty-six years old. Marion was much more mature and capable, although she wasn't really maternal. Jessie suspected that the faithful Daisy would have more to do with Wilf's upbringing than his mother. Still, she thought, Marion and I get on well, and she will be an asset to the new business, which is flourishing thanks to Doc and Danny.

She had realised that it was time to put a seal on her relationship with Doc. Don't I deserve some happiness after all my hard toil over the years? she thought. Doc too was looking forward to not working so hard; he would become more of an adviser to Danny and Marion, but still available to all when needed.

It was a simple wedding, held in the local church in April. The bride wore a new dove-grey jacket and skirt, with a ruffled pink blouse. She was fifty-one years old, and her bridegroom some fifteen years older. Jessie ruefully recalled the time when she had contemplated a more romantic coming-together. Were such moments possible now? she wondered. She walked down the aisle on Sam's arm, while Abraham waited with his best man, Danny, at the altar steps.

Kathleen had wanted her daughters to be bridesmaids, but Jessie had demurred. 'I am too old for that, but they could be flower girls, and Wilf could walk between them, though I expect Marion will want him to be dressed as a page boy – he has the long hair for that,' she added fondly. Marion was loath to cut the golden curls that hung over his collar. I expect she was hoping for a little girl, Jessie mused. Poor Marion, she is afraid to give birth again. That must affect her relationship with Danny.

The parlour was opened up for the modest reception. Danny had whitewashed the walls, and Jessie and Daisy had polished the furniture and dusted off the piano keys, which Marion was coaxed to play. Two tables were placed together, covered with a snowy white cloth, with the wedding cake in the centre. It was an informal meal, and the guests filled their plates with sausage rolls, sandwiches and chicken drumsticks. They toasted the bride and groom with Mrs Amos's elderflower wine, the recipe for which she guarded zealously. Bert had not accompanied her, though invited, declining with, 'The chores don't do themselves,' though the real reason was that he didn't want to follow suit, and nor did Mrs Amos.

Sam cast off his worries for the occasion and led the tributes and good wishes for the bride and groom. Kathleen and her daughters enjoyed the singing and dancing and persuaded shy Wilf to join in; he held Daisy's hand as they whirled round to the music.

The party broke up around 10 p.m. Sam and Kathleen were the first to leave with their family and offered to take

Mrs Amos home. Daisy accompanied Wilf upstairs while Danny and Marion insisted they would clear up downstairs.

Jessie relaxed at last, and after all the hugging and congratulations, she and Abraham went up to their room. Daisy had turned back the covers on the bed invitingly, and pulled the curtains. Her bed had already been moved away and replaced with Doc's beloved desk and chair. He sat there with his back to Jessie while she undressed and brushed her hair. When he judged she was in bed, he turned around and saw that she was writing in her diary. He disrobed slowly and then climbed into bed beside her.

Jessie closed her book and asked, 'Shall I put out the light?'

He reached out a hand and touched her long hair. 'You are not grey like me, Jessie; such beautiful hair . . . Yes, see to the lamp, please.'

'Do you realise,' she whispered, 'that the only time we've kissed was in church?'

His arms went round her and he said softly, 'We are married and *now* it is permitted, Jessie. We will be more than good companions.'

'I'm glad,' she said with a happy sigh.

Back in their new house, Sam and Kathleen lay apart in bed. They had quarrelled at the end of what had been a very happy day. She was crying silently, knuckling the tears from her eyes. She had thought he would be pleased when she told him she'd spent some of her legacy at last and ordered a bathroom suite. Why did he fly off the handle like that and shout at me? she wondered.

'You make me feel less of a man, Kathleen. I should provide for *you*,' he had said earlier.

Now he turned and pulled her roughly into his arms. He was angry still, but with himself. 'I hurt you, Kathleen, I made you cry . . . Please forgive me,' he pleaded.

She would not give in just like that. 'I'm not sure I can. I saw another side to you, Sam. I thought we were equal partners in marriage, but you have belittled me – I don't understand . . .'

'Nor do I.'

'You have done so much for me over the years; I thought you would be pleased that I wanted to do something in return. I was broken-hearted when I came here, but you healed me, you made me so happy.'

'You need a fatherly kiss,' he said unevenly, 'like the one I gave you once before. That was when I realised I loved you, and you felt the same, didn't you?'

'You know I did. Oh Sam.' She was weeping again and didn't resist when he drew her to him again.

'Let me make it up to you,' he murmured.

It was only later, as she drifted off to sleep in his arms, that Kathleen realised they had not taken the usual precautions. She smiled to herself. No, it wasn't the time for bringing another child into the world, but then, was it ever?

TWENTY-ONE

Christmas 1912 was almost here, and Sam and his family were settled in their new home. They planned a quiet celebration for Heather's ninth birthday on Christmas Day, as Kathleen was now eight months pregnant. She would be twenty-seven in January on the birthday she shared with Danny, who would be twenty-eight, and Sam would be thiry-two two days before that. Jessie had sent over a hamper of food knowing they were experiencing hard times, so they were not short of festive fare. Heather and Kitty had fun, and squabbled a little, over where to hang the decorations, and who should dress a humble peg dolly in sparkly clothes as a fairy to top the Christmas tree.

Heather was growing up: her thick black hair was swept back at the sides, and like Kathleen she had a fringe over her forehead, but she didn't have the same fair complexion and Irish blue eyes as her mother. Her skin looked tanned even in the winter. Kitty topped her sister by two inches and was obviously the leader of the two. She resembled her grandmother in her colouring, determination and cheerful disposition.

Both girls were doing well at the local school, and Heather proudly brought home a composition at the end of term that had gained top marks and a gold star. Her father said he would find the time to frame it after Christmas.

'Read it aloud to us,' he suggested on Christmas Eve.

Heather demurred. 'Oh I'd rather not, Dad. I'll go all red and then you'll laugh.'

'Of course we won't,' Kathleen said quickly. 'But I'm sure Kitty will read it for you . . .'

'You know I will,' Kitty said eagerly, almost tearing the page as she snatched at it.

'Give it back! *I* will read it, *you* didn't write it!' Heather decided after all.

Exciting Events of 1912
By Heather Mary Mason, age nearly 9

There was a terrible disaster when a ship called *Titanic*, which means it was very big, hit an ice-berg on its way to America. It sank to the bottom of the sea. It was its first voyage. Lots of passengers perished. There were not enough lifeboats.

Another disaster was when brave Captain Scott and his men got to the South Pole after many struggles. Oh no! Another explorer called Amundsen got there first. They were not seen again but Miss said they must have all perished in the terrible weather. They were real heroes. In November a search party found them but it was too late. I don't like snow as I was born during a snowstorm on Christmas Day. There is a lot of wars going on, mostly in the Balkans. Not sure where that is. Something like Ottomans? Dad said it's not good that Italy, Austria and Germany have made what is called a Triple Alliance. Turkey is in the news a lot. They are at war with Greece and Serbia.

This December they found a bust of Queen ~~Nefur Nefirt~~ Queen Nef, in Egypt, and in this country they found Piltdown Man! Was he the first man on earth?

My mother said she wished she could be a suffragette but my dad won't allow her, I think. She is not big and strong like some of them. Last March the suffragettes smashed lots of windows in Oxford Street, a very posh place in London.

I would like to fly an aeroplane one day. The men are called pilots and very daring. They are not in the army or navy but in the Royal Flying Corps.

I shall be a Liberal like all my family. They think Lloyd George is the best. There are so many strikes and it is all they talk about.

The best thing this year was the Olympic Games in Sweden. We winned 10 gold medals,15 silver and 18 bronze. I would never make a athlete because I am too small, but I like riding a horse. My sister can run faster than me.

There may be another big event before the year ends. A new baby! Dad would like a boy. Us girls do not mind. Mum said she will be jolly glad when it comes, as she is like a roly-poly pudding! That is true.

PS I hope spellings are right. I used the dictionary Grandpa Doc gave me. He could only spell in Russian before he came here. He is very clever. The horses like him very much.

Sam had spent a fruitless day on 22 December calling on customers who owed him money for bricks delivered much earlier in the year. It probably didn't help that it was a Sunday. He arrived home to discover there was no supper keeping warm in the oven and that Kathleen had gone to bed soon after the girls. He stumbled up the stairs because he had done something he had not done in many months: he'd called in at the pub on his way home and drunk two pints of strong ale. Fortunately he had no more coins in his pocket to carry on drinking. Ollie had rushed out of the Barn House, barking, as if Sam was a stranger. He had to be restrained by Herbie the foreman. Uncharacteristically, Sam uttered a curse.

'No luck?' Herbie asked.

'No!' Sam said curtly.

Upstairs, a solitary candle flickered in the niche in the landing wall. Sam opened the bedroom door cautiously. He heard the sound of sobbing. He paused to light the lamp, then went into the room.

'Where have you been? I was so worried.'

'I'm bloody hungry,' he shouted. 'Nothing for supper.'

She was shocked. 'You've never sworn in front of me like that before!'

'I had no luck – no money – and you couldn't even make me a sandwich!'

'I was upset . . .'

'Why?' He sat on the edge of the bed and untied his boots.

'Because I won't be over at the farm with Jessie when I have this baby. I felt safe there, and Nurse Buss came, but she won't come out here because she feels nervous walking through the wood. Though I know Doc will come if the local doctor can't . . .'

Sam saw her blotched, tear-stained face and realised he was being too hard on his beloved Kathleen. He sat down on the bed and reached for her hand, saying soothingly, 'Shush, you mustn't get so agitated. The baby isn't due for two weeks.' He knew that if he kissed her, she would smell the alcohol on his breath.

'Remember, the girls were both early.'

'I'll be here from now on, so I can do what I did last time, can't I? Any of that pork pie left in the larder?'

'Yes, and some cold potato you could fry up . . . But don't open the hamper, that's our Christmas surprise from Jessie. I took the turkey out and put the cover over it, though.'

'I'll bring you a cup of tea after I've had my supper, eh? Warm up my side of the bed!'

She called after him, 'I love you Sam, you know I do, but this place will *never* feel like home, not like Home Farm does. You mustn't be so proud. I've got that money – that would see us through . . .'

He didn't answer; he felt choked up. He was the one crying now, silently, tears running down his face. I'm a fool, he thought, chasing a dream like my uncle, and now it's all turned to ashes.

When he returned with the tea, Kathleen was sitting up in bed, smiling. 'Sam, I've just realised. I'll invest that wretched money in the business, and you can make me a partner, like Mrs Amos did with Bert.'

'Hey! You *are* my partner, you're my wife, and I think the world of you, Kathleen.'

'As I do of you,' she said. 'But you have to realise I'm a woman and a mother, not the frightened girl Danny lifted from the snow!'

Sam interrupted. '*I* carried you upstairs that first night, remember? We'll talk about it after the baby arrives, and don't forget it's just two days to Christmas Eve and Heather's birthday on Christmas Day . . .'

'I haven't forgotten – *oh*!' She gave a gasp and clutched at her middle. 'Sam, it can't be, but it is . . .'

'Thank goodness for the telephone – is it too late to ring Doc?'

'It's only ten o'clock; they won't be in bed yet. Hurry, Sam, don't keep talking on the telephone – I need you here with me. And don't wake the girls up, please.'

Doc put the receiver back on its rest. 'Who is ringing at this late hour?' Jessie asked.

'Sam. Kathleen's in labour, he thinks. They need me, so I may be gone some time.'

'I'll come too,' she decided. 'Wait a minute while I tell Danny and Marion. They're in bed, I expect.' She snatched at the old plaid cape hanging on the hallstand. 'This will keep me warm.' She felt in the pocket. 'She must have taken the sprig of heather . . .'

Sam and Kathleen heard the motor car making its way down the track to the house. Ollie barked next door and whined at the unfamiliar noise. Sam opened the door to Doc and Jessie; he was still dressed, and when Jessie hugged him she smelled the alcohol on his breath but wisely refrained from comment.

Upstairs, Jessie bent over Kathleen. 'How is it, my dear?'

'Oh, I'm glad you could come too, Jessie. I'm afraid . . .' She paused as another wave of pain swept over her. 'The bed's soaked, but at least I'd covered the mattress with plenty of newspaper '

'Sam, can you lift her up and sit with her in the chair? Doc will help me get the bed sorted. Are you boiling up plenty of water?'

'Yes,' Sam said, struggling to sit down with Kathleen in his arms. Doc wrapped them around with a blanket.

This was not to be an easy birth for Kathleen as it had been with the girls. Doc straightened up after ascertaining the situation. 'A big baby,' he said briefly.

Jessie wrung out a cloth in cool water and gently blotted the perspiration from Kathleen's brow, then replaced it with a fresh cloth. Kathleen was moaning softly, but she didn't cry out. She murmured, 'Hold my hand, Jessie . . .'

Sam stood helplessly by. She doesn't need me like she did last time, he thought. It's my own fault, upsetting her like that . . .

But after the next spasm, she found her voice. 'Sam, Sam, where are you?'

He came out of the shadows and knelt beside the bed. 'Hold on, hold on,' he heard someone say, before he realised it was his own voice.

It was a long night; only Doc's reassurances kept them together. Jessie was tired, and even nodded off for a time, but she didn't lose her grip on Kathleen's hand. Sam's head remained bowed. Thank goodness the girls are unaware of all this, he thought.

At first light, when Doc was about to send Sam to fetch the doctor from the village, Kathleen struggled to sit up. At last the baby was about to be born.

'Keep calm,' Doc told Jessie and Sam.

'I can't . . .' Kathleen cried.

'You can, my dear, you're almost there,' Doc told her.

Sam was silently praying; he couldn't remember the last time he had done that.

Suddenly it was all over. Kathleen fell back on her pillows, and with one last heave, the baby emerged. 'Sam!' Doc commanded. 'Be ready to take the baby and wrap him in that flannel sheet when I've cut the cord . . . He's crying, that's a good sign, but I must see to his mother first. Poor girl, she is exhausted. Jessie will help me . . .'

As Sam took the baby into his arms, he saw to his joy that this was indeed a son, much bigger than the girls had been. As if he could read his thoughts, Doc said, 'He must weigh around ten pounds . . .'

'Like his father when he was born.' Jessie was wiping away tears of relief, rolling up her sleeves for action.

Kathleen said weakly, 'He is to be called Sam after his father.'

Doc looked at his watch. 'Well, he's arrived in time for Christmas, eh?'

Sam looked down at the baby's red face and kissed the fuzz of damp black hair on his head. A new life – a new hope for the future, he thought.

'He looks like you,' Jessie observed. 'Let's get Kathleen settled, then I'll make tea and tell the girls the good news!' She yawned. 'And after that, Abraham and I need to catch up on our sleep.'

TWENTY-TWO

Christmas Eve, and without Nurse Buss to decree she must stay in bed, Sam carried Kathleen downstairs and deposited her on the sofa by the fire. It was the sofa from the living room at Home Farm, with colourful new cushions made by Jessie. So many memories came with this familiar piece of furniture, including fond thoughts of old Bob comforting her after she was rescued from her ordeal in the freezing world outside. So different from today, for it was mild for the time of year, though the old farmers predicted a gale on the way.

Heather sat beside her mother and proudly held her little brother. 'He is the best birthday present ever!' she said.

'We'll celebrate your birthday a day early,' Kathleen told her. 'Grandma and Grandpa Doc, Daisy, Uncle Danny, Auntie Marion and Wilf are coming over for tea, and bringing the Christmas presents to put under the tree, as well as your birthday gifts, which you can open right away so you can thank them.'

'Are we having the turkey for dinner?' Kitty asked hopefully.

'No, your dad will cook it tomorrow, with some help from you two, I hope.'

'What are we having today? I'm hungry.' Kitty made a sad face. 'Dad said it would be bread and scrape.'

'Well, Grandma sent us some butter, so no scrape!'

'I'm not *that* helpless,' Sam said. 'I've got a cauldron of soup bubbling on the hob. I threw everything in like you do, Kathleen. And Heather baked some soda bread to make more of it.' The baby was stirring. 'Time for a feed, I think; he's a hungry lad.'

'I need to have my soup first, I'm starving!' Kathleen told him.

'Can we watch, Mum?' Heather asked after lunch, as the baby made mewling sounds.

'Of course you can, but don't ask so many questions.' What a difference this time, Kathleen mused. I couldn't nurse Heather because I wasn't well enough; I was able to feed Kitty, but I tried to do that in private. I'm more relaxed now that I'm a mother of three – and I've had a brainwave about how we can turn the business around . . .

'Good to see you smiling again!' Sam said in passing. He was smiling too, putting his cares firmly to one side before the visitors came. He was glad Jessie was bringing a chocolate cake for Heather's birthday, because he hadn't discovered a recipe for that.

'Kitty, don't tickle the baby's toes,' Kathleen said, but she didn't sound reproving.

'I can't resist it, Mum,' Kitty said with a grin. 'I think he likes it. Why hasn't he got any socks on?'

'I'm a very slow knitter, and I'm not good at turning heels,' Kathleen replied.

'Mum,' Heather said, 'I know you haven't had time to get me a birthday present yet, but I've been thinking what I would like – a puppy. One like dear old Bob. We've got Bob's couch here now, haven't we?'

'What about Ollie?'

'Oh he belongs next door, doesn't he?'

Sam, overhearing, put in, 'I met a fellow the other night who had a litter of black pups at home – didn't say what breed, mongrels probably – and asked would I like one? Shall I say yes?'

'As long as I can call it Bob!'

'It might be a bitch,' Kitty interrupted.

'That's a rude word – tell her, Mum!'

'Well, I am just about to change the baby and you won't want to watch *that*! Why don't you set the table for tea? Everyone will be here soon.'

'Nearly got blown away driving here in the trap!' exclaimed Jessie when she arrived. 'The wind is getting up, we're promised a gale tomorrow. The others are following in the car; hope they are all right. Goodness me, you're up, Kathleen!' She was obviously surprised.

'Up, but not about!' Sam said firmly.

'Doctor's orders?'

'No, mine! Though the doctor who came yesterday was amazed to see her so well.'

'And *happy*,' Kathleen said firmly. 'Well, what do you think of the baby now, Jessie?'

'He's a very handsome chap! May I hold him?'

'You may,' Kathleen said, handing her little bundle over. She drew her feet up so Jessie could sit on the sofa beside her.

The girls were busy arranging several promising packages round the base of the tree, which Doc produced one by one from his bag. 'New fairy?' he enquired. 'What's her name, I wonder?'

'Topsy,' Heather said proudly, 'though Dad said she looked more like Ragged Rose. I am not very good at sewing, you see.'

'Or knitting?' Jessie enquired. 'Open your birthday present, eh?'

Kitty joined her. 'What is it?'

Heather unwrapped a rush sewing basket, equipped with a pin cushion, needles and thread, a silver thimble, scissors and a little book: *Sewing for Girls*. There was another package – a skein of knitting wool in blue, a pair of bone needles and a simple pattern for baby bootees. 'Oh Grandma, thank you! Look, our baby needs something on his feet! Will you show me how to knit?'

'Of course I will. But not today. Your dad is calling you from the kitchen; I think he needs some help bringing in the tea things.'

'My turn, I think,' Doc said, holding his arms out to receive the baby. He sat down in the nursing chair, which had come from the attic at Home Farm. It creaked under his weight. The baby didn't cry, but seemed to regard him solemnly. Those watching became aware that Doc was saying something in Russian to him: '*Ya tvoy ded.*' He looked up and saw their puzzled faces. 'I am your grandfather,' he translated for them.

Jessie caught her breath, knowing that he must be remembering his own small son who had been lost long ago in the pogrom in Russia.

The rest of the family arrived and the baby was passed carefully to each in turn. Marion looked pensive as she held him. He was so much bigger and healthier-looking than her little Wilf had been. Why am I denying Danny his needs as a husband when I know he would love another child? she wondered.

When it was Danny's turn to be introduced, he smiled at Kathleen and said huskily to Sam, 'What's your secret?'

Daisy said quickly, 'What do you think of the baby, Wilf?' The little boy reached up and whispered something in her ear. ''Scuse us, may we use the bathroom? A little accident; Wilf is so excited . . .' Poor Wilf had developed this problem when he started school. Kathleen had counselled the girls not to mention it, because he couldn't help it.

After the chocolate cake was cut and only crumbs remained, the family gathered round the sofa and sang Christmas carols. They chose them in turn. 'Silent Night' was the favourite, but outdoors it was wet, noisy and windy.

The guests went home at eight o'clock, saying there were preparations for Christmas Day to be done before retiring for the night. After they left, Sam took the baby to the cradle beside their bed, and then returned to carry Kathleen upstairs.

The girls were in the bathroom and larking about, cleaning their teeth with the new Odol toothpaste. 'Tastes much nicer than salt,' Kitty said. 'Shall we try some of Dad's Eno's fruit salts?

'No,' Heather replied. 'Aren't they for constipation?' They both had a fit of the giggles.

Kitty asked suddenly, 'Do you know how babies are born?'

Heather didn't hesitate. 'They grow from a little seed in a mother's tummy, and when they are ready they pop out.'

'Who plants the seed?' Kitty wondered.

'You are an ignoramus, Kit! That's what dads are for. So Grandma said.'

Next door, Sam had tucked Kathleen up in bed. 'I'm sorry I haven't got you a Christmas present,' she said.

He bent over and kissed her. 'But you have – a most precious gift, our little son.'

'Sam, I've had an idea. We have clay, we have a large empty barn, as well as a smaller one, and I think we could become a pottery! It makes sense. People may not want bricks, but they always need household and garden pots. Our clay is superior and streaked with colour, and would make lovely jugs and kitchenware. I can help a bit; I could do some sketches to work from. We'd need a potter's wheel and a small kiln, but we already have plenty of wood for the firing, and as we can do that in the barn, the fumes won't affect Heather. We should buy a book or two to study, but if you can make bricks, you can throw pots!' She'd made that bit up on the spur of the moment.

'Will it cost a lot to set up, though?'

'No, because we have the clay to hand. Oh, I'm so glad you agree!'

'We'll call it Artisan Pots,' he decided. 'Shall I tell the girls?'

'You can tell the world if you like!' she said happily. It was going to be a good Christmas after all.

Marion was in bed when Danny came into their bedroom after seeing to Wilf's stocking. He glanced over at her before undressing. She was pretending to be asleep. Though she needn't worry; he wasn't intending to try again. Sam's lucky, he thought; they may have their ups and downs, but they have come through and the new baby is proof they are still a loving couple. He sighed and got into bed beside Marion, putting a tentative arm around her waist.

'Marion, are you awake? It's just on midnight. Happy Christmas.' He didn't expect an answer, so was startled when she turned towards him and kissed him. Her face was wet with tears and she was trembling. 'What's the matter? What has upset you?'

'You know what the matter is,' she said huskily. 'I saw the way you looked at Kathleen with her new baby.'

'Marion, please don't think—'

'I can't help it,' she wept. 'If only you felt like that about me!'

'But I *do* – I've loved you ever since we were sixteen years old. Can't you remember how it felt, kissing outside your front door with your mother spying on us!'

'That was young love – we had mixed feelings, wanted to do things we were told we shouldn't.'

'You made the first move then,' he reminded her.

'You didn't object!' she flashed back.

'Of course I didn't. And I wouldn't object now if you . . .' He held her close, kissing her closed eyes. 'Marion, I know you're afraid of having another baby, and I understand that because you had such a bad time of it with Wilf . . . but can't we be a loving couple?'

She gave a little groan. 'Oh Danny, I know I shouldn't be so jealous. I must have inherited that from Mother . . .'

'Shush,' he whispered. 'Let's make a new start and forget the past.'

They were both aware it would not be as easy as that.

Sam was having second thoughts about Kathleen's suggestion of a pottery. It couldn't be set up until spring, he mused. If it turned cold, folk would still want wood to keep the home fires burning. Kathleen wouldn't be able to play an active part until the baby was bigger, of course. Would Herbie want to be involved? They would probably have to employ experienced staff . . . He knew he'd have to keep all this to himself, or he would upset her again. He'd have to give in about the money side too, otherwise none of this would be possible.

He turned and gently stroked her hair as she slumbered. It would be some time, he realised, before they could resume their love life. Danny and Marion, he thought, should enjoy that side of marriage while they only had one child; it was a sobering thought that he and Kathleen were responsible now for *three* children.

Jessie and Doc were talking about family affairs as they lay side by side in bed. She said suddenly, 'Abraham, do you think Marion and Danny are happy? I wonder sometimes if she is still jealous of Kathleen . . .'

He murmured, 'It is not our business, Jessie. Marion is a natural with horses; I think her job at the stables compensates her for having only one child. Danny, I believe, is a good husband and father, so you have nothing to worry about there.'

'It's just that I am aware Danny has these feelings for Kathleen.'

'He doesn't give in to them, does he? I think he'll grow out of this fascination if he doesn't have any encouragement. Didn't *you* sometimes wish—'

'No! Never!' she said vehemently. She turned to him. 'Wilf was my rock, like you.'

'Thank you, dear Jessie, that means so much to me.'

Daisy was still awake in the room they now called the nursery, which she shared with Wilf. She sighed. This little chap, she thought fondly, is to me the son I will never have. He is a nervous child; I hope I will always be there for him.

She'd enjoyed her visit to the Brickyard House, but it made her realise how much she'd missed Kathleen's companionship since she moved away. She is like a younger sister to me, she thought. Dear Mrs Mason took us both to her heart. Kathleen and I had fun exploring the countryside on our bicycles. It's not the same with Mrs Danny . . . she's nice enough, but the only thing we have in common is young Wilf.

Wilf stirred and called out, 'Has Father Christmas come yet?'

'Not yet,' she answered. 'He won't come until we are sound asleep.'

TWENTY-THREE

In the spring of 1913, newspaper headlines warned the public of war clouds on the horizon. Kathleen asked Sam anxiously whether he believed this to be true, and he told her, 'It might well be . . .' adding, 'We have to carry on as normal and hope for the best, but also concentrate on our new venture, eh?'

Bobby, the puppy, was a cross between a spaniel and a collie. He had the floppy ears of the former and the long legs of the latter. His coat was black and curly, and he was already aware that he must keep an eye on the baby while the girls were at school each day. Little Sam was growing fast and it was obvious he would be tall like his father. The girls suggested calling him Jimmy, as his second name was James. 'He can change it back to Sam when you pop off, Dad!' Kitty said artlessly. When they came home from school in the afternoon, Bobby was waiting with his red ball, eager to play fetch. Ollie watched from next door, head on paws, grumbling to himself, ready to put the pup in his place if he crossed the invisible dividing line between house and barn.

Sam now had another employee, a lad called Dennis who was twelve years old; an orphan from the workhouse who'd just left school and was lodging with Herbie and his wife. Herbie was showing him the ropes and they were busy digging out clay from the new pit. This would be stored in the big barn for a while to dry out some of the moisture until it was ready to be moulded. However, there were other stages to go through first.

'You need an experienced potter to advise you,' Doc pronounced when he came over to the brickyard to see how things were progressing. He produced a parcel from Jessie. She had sewn four roomy smocks in dark blue canvas for the potters as her contribution to the enterprise.

'She says they need to be washed regularly, not with other clothing. Dust will be a problem so she suggests you buy some face masks. By the way,' he added, 'I know someone who once owned a pottery – like me, she sought asylum with those who were already established in the East End.'

'What is your friend's name – did she come from the same place as you?' Kathleen asked.

'Her name is Olga,' Doc replied. 'She did. She has been unable to contact her family ever since. Would you like to meet her? She is, I think, in her early sixties; she is an artist still, but sighs over her first love – throwing pots. She was quite famous then, I'm told.'

'Could she tell us what equipment is essential?' Sam asked. 'I have already inspected a second-hand pottery wheel with a treadle and a small kiln. *Webster's Dictionary* mentions pugged clay and a pug mill, which consists of sharp revolving knives set in motion by turning a handle. Then the clay is pressed between two rollers into sheets of a precise thickness.'

'Dad,' Heather interrupted, 'you sound like a dictionary yourself! Grandma has her old mangle out in the scullery; could you use that?'

'I will write to Olga today,' Doc promised. 'And I will ask Jessie about the mangle. It's another heavy object to lift about, but it still works. Jessie asked me if she could have a new one as my wedding present to her!'

'I expect she was excited to receive what she asked for!' Kitty grinned.

'What is pugged clay?' Dennis asked. He was showing plenty of interest in his new job, though he didn't get much chance to ask questions when the girls were around.

'Clay kneaded like dough and then sliced and mixed in the pug mill,' Sam answered. We have a bright lad here, he thought. He's big and strong for his age, too.

There was great excitement the following weekend when Doc, who'd driven with Danny to London after the early morning chores, leaving Marion in charge of the stables, alighted from the car and helped a stout lady out from the back seat.

The girls were waiting on the doorstep, with Bobby restrained on his lead, as he tended to jump up at visitors and give them licks of welcome. Inside the house, Kathleen took a batch of scones from the oven, put them to cool, and wondered whether to make tea or coffee.

Olga, who had been invited to stay for the weekend, waved to the girls and made her way along the path to the front door. Doc followed behind after seeing to her luggage. She had snowy white hair plaited round her head, and a round face creased in smiles. She was dressed in an ankle-skimming black skirt with a bright pink blouse, which was obviously hand-dyed as the colour was blotchy, and a matching head-scarf. The shawl round her shoulders gave her an old-fashioned air. 'Good morning, children,' she greeted them.

'Don't you speak Russian any more?' Kitty was disappointed.

'Yes, but it is polite to speak in the language of your hosts. I shall tell you that good morning in Russian is *dobroe utro*, and children is *rebyonok*. May I come in and meet your mother and father, please?'

The children moved aside immediately. 'Follow me, Olga,' Heather said, eager to show she was the elder of the two. Doc beckoned to Danny, who'd reappeared after parking the car round the corner of the house.

Kathleen, baby on hip, greeted the visitor. 'Come into the kitchen for a nice cup of tea – or coffee, if you prefer it. We also have scones and some of my mother-in-law's butter . . .'

'Thank you. I would like coffee, please. No milk or sugar. I have tea without, too, but I like a squeeze of lemon,' Olga said.

'Who wants to hold Jimmy while I make the coffee?' Kathleen asked.

'It's my turn!' Heather said, nudging Kitty aside. She lifted Jimmy up against her shoulder, because she didn't have hips yet to balance him on. She had a question to ask their guest. 'You have tea in a glass, don't you? We studied Russia in geography this term.'

'Tea in a glass? In Russia, yes, but here I have a mug! This scone is good, Kathleen, and the butter is delicious.'

Doc came into the kitchen having taken Olga's bags upstairs to the spare bedroom.

Kitty whispered to her sister, 'Do you think she'll like the jam jar full of dandelions I picked for her? I put them on the windowsill.'

'Not if she knows they make you wet the bed!' Heather whispered back.

'Something smells good.' Doc sniffed appreciatively.

'Take a seat, Doc; coffee for you too?' Kathleen asked. 'Where's Danny?'

'Talking to Sam, I think. Sam said he'll be in shortly for his elevenses.'

'I hope he washes his hands first,' Kathleen sighed.

'You've got flour in your hair, Mummy,' Kitty observed.

'Oh dear, my fringe is getting too long and I brushed it out of my eyes while I was mixing the scones,' Kathleen said with a smile. She sat down at the table between Olga and Doc. 'You'll have to excuse me when Sam arrives; Jimmy needs a feed before his morning nap. I must drink my tea first!'

Sam and Danny were removing their boots before coming into the kitchen. 'Have you got the papers ready to show Olga?' Danny asked.

'They're in the kitchen drawer,' Sam replied. 'You go on in and I'll wash my hands before joining you all.'

'I won't be too long,' Kathleen said to Olga. 'Let me just introduce you to my husband, Sam, who will be the chief potter and needs all the advice you can give him! Take my chair, Sam. Girls, you'd better come upstairs with Jimmy and me. You haven't made your beds yet, have you?'

Kitty pulled a face. '*We* want to know all about the pottery, too!'

'You shall not miss much; we discuss the business first, eh, Sam?' Olga assured them.

Doc rose too. 'I must get back to Home Farm. Danny will pass on the information to us later. We will see you tomorrow, I hope; Jessie has invited everyone to dinner. Goodbye for now, Olga.'

Later in the day, after Olga had explained the process to Sam, she came to a decision. 'You say you need someone with experience to guide and advise you. If you agree, I could be that person. I have told you all I know, but one weekend is not enough to learn; you have to find your way and it will not be easy. But now it is getting late and I can tell Kathleen is tired and needs to retire for the night.'

Kathleen suppressed a yawn. 'I must get some sleep before Jimmy wakes for a midnight feed; he doesn't go through the night without that yet. Thank you, Olga, we have a lot to think about, but we can talk again in the morning before we go over to Home Farm.'

Danny rose from his chair too. 'I must go home. Marion will be anxious if I don't turn up soon . . . Goodnight, all, I'll see you tomorrow.'

Kathleen went out with him into the hallway and paused before going upstairs.

'Oh Danny, it all seems so promising, but I'm not sure I can be much help at the moment.'

He saw that her eyes were brimming with tears and resisted the urge to hug her. 'What Olga said made sense. It sounds as though she might be willing to stay and train Sam and the others.'

'We might not be able to afford that, though.'

'There is always a way,' he said slowly. 'Off you go, and don't worry about it tonight.'

'Goodnight,' she said, and before he could open the front door, she put her hands on his shoulders and reached up to kiss his cheek. 'Thank you, Danny, for being here tonight. We will see you tomorrow. Give my love to Marion.'

He closed the door behind him and wondered why she'd kissed him. He faced a walk home because Doc had taken the car earlier, but he needed time to gather his thoughts.

By the time the family and their visitor arrived for lunch with Jessie and Doc, the plans for the pottery were set to go ahead. Olga's generous offer had been accepted; she would gladly give her services in return for her board and lodging in the Brickyard House.

'I don't need money at the moment; I will be happy to be in the country instead of the East End. I have never married or had children of my own, but I shall enjoy the company of your lively young daughters, I know.'

Now they sat down to roast chicken and all the trimmings, served by Daisy, and Bobby hid under the table ready to receive any scraps that might come his way.

Doc was beaming. He passed the redcurrant sauce and filled the wine glasses. 'You would like Danny and me to collect your belongings?' he asked Olga. 'Can you manage with what you have here until next weekend?'

Olga was smiling too. 'Yes, of course. What lovely tender meat; you carve so well, Doc. I like the pudding very much. It is from Yorkshire, yes?'

'The recipe, originally, I believe. I'm glad you like it,' Jessie said. 'Help yourself to more roast potatoes and cabbage.'

Heather and Kitty were drinking lemonade with slices of lemon floating in it. 'Wonder what's for pud?' Kitty whispered, while surreptitiously dropping a morsel of fatty bacon to the dog under cover of the tablecloth. Olga, observing this, winked at her.

Kathleen's meal was interrupted by a wailing from the Moses basket where Jimmy was supposed to be asleep. She pushed back her chair, 'Excuse me, the baby's hungry too!'

Heather said, 'We'll save your pudding for you, Mummy!'

'Some of the first strawberries and cream,' Jessie enlightened them. 'If you eat all your dinner, of course!' she added, glancing at Kitty. 'A little bit of fat never hurt anyone!'

Marion was not having anything special to eat over at her mother's house. She felt a bit uncomfortable in Bert's presence. When he greeted her, he put his arms round her and hugged her. She was all too aware that, because he was shorter than her, his face lined up with her generous bosom. She gave him a little push away. I hope Mother didn't notice, she thought, but I reckon she did. I wish I wasn't suspicious like her, but last night I thought Danny had a guilty air about him. What was he up to over at the Brickyard House? She expelled a sigh. 'Wilf, don't play with your food. Eat up.'

'There's a caterpillar in the lettuce and it's *alive*!' Wilf shuddered.

Danny leant over and removed the wriggling object with his fork. Then he squashed it. 'There, eat up as your mother says.'

'You *killed* it, Daddy.' Wilf was red in the face. 'You could have put it outside . . .'

'No he couldn't, not back on my vegetable garden,' Mrs Amos said loudly and firmly. 'You spoil that boy, Marion.'

'Nothin' wrong with caterpillars,' Bert put in. 'They're nourishment too.' He sniggered, but no one joined in.

'You can eat them, but I never shall!' They all looked up in surprise as Wilf actually shouted. He appealed to his father. 'Can't we go home?'

'Shush!' Danny warned him.

'I have something to say first,' Mrs Amos told them. 'I have to tell you that Bert and I are selling up. We have been lucky; someone wants to buy the place, but it won't be as it is now. Businesses are going down the drain all over the country. There'll be a world war, Bert says, and he knows the signs from his army days.'

'Where will you live, Mother?' Marion asked anxiously.

'We intend to travel. Enjoy ourselves while we can – go to Australia, which is so far away from Europe it seems unlikely it will be affected by war. There won't be any money coming your way, Marion, and Danny has already had *his* inheritance. I can't say when we'll be back, so enjoy your last meal in this house!'

They arrived back at Home Farm still in a state of shock. The girls took Wilf out in the garden with the dog, and Marion and Danny explained to Jessie what had happened. She said, 'If there is a war, the Commonwealth countries will be fighting alongside Great Britain.' She put her arms round Marion. 'I don't suppose your mother meant to upset you.'

'Yes she did!' Marion sobbed.

Danny kept quiet. At least we're happy and secure here, he thought. And my mother won't let Marion down.

TWENTY-FOUR

Despite all their efforts, the pottery was not proving to be a profitable business; in fact by early 1914 they were barely earning enough to cover the cost of running it. Enthusiasm was dwindling as the shelves in the big barn stayed filled with platters, mugs, jugs and preserving pots; the everyday things they had optimistically thought would provide their bread and butter. Chimney pots and garden urns did sell, but not in great quantities.

Kathleen and the girls seemed unaware that their dream was fading fast, due to the turmoil throughout the world. There was now a united workforce in the British Isles, who were employed in preparations for the inevitable conflict. Women were needed to work in the new munitions factories. London was on full alert and coastal towns were preparing to resist an invasion by sea. People had become complacent over the years following Napoleon's defeat a hundred years before. The old guns that had been lined up and trained on enemy ships then were still in place, but they were now landmarks rather than viable weapons.

Small towns like Westerham were also buzzing with activity. The town's population soared towards the end of the year with the arrival of a battalion from the 2nd West Lancashire Brigade, Royal Field Artillery. The townsfolk wondered if the arrival of their protectors signalled further trouble sooner rather than later.

Not only was the pottery in trouble; the stables at Home Farm had been visited by officials, for horsepower was vital to the army, despite mechanisation growing rapidly. Teams of shire horses were required urgently to pull the heavy artillery guns; only horses over sixteen years old were exempt. Fortunately, the big carthorse at the pottery was in that category. Riding horses too were needed for the cavalry; there would be further training for their new duties before they were taken to the battlefield. Contracts were given to the owners, with remuneration promised after the war, but many owners worried that their horses would be lost in battle. It would be a struggle for farmers who still relied on horsepower to farm their land, and some of the workforce were already being conscripted to care for the horses overseas. It was becoming clear that women would need to take over the farm work while the men were away.

At Home Farm, the horses they bred for showing and racing would become warhorses for the cavalry. Only the aged shire horse would remain at the Home Farm stables with the donkey, the Shetland pony, the foals and a couple of brood mares, which Doc would care for.

Seeing Danny's distress after he had insisted on loading his horses himself into the army vehicles, the chap in charge asked him, 'Why don't you join them? The army are recruiting experienced men like you; you would soon rise up the ranks to sergeant.'

After the horses were gone and Wilf had been taken off to bed by Daisy, Danny told Marion, Jessie and Doc that he had decided to enlist without waiting for conscription. 'I have the right qualifications, it seems.'

It seemed that Marion had come to a decision too: she informed the family that she planned to join the local Red Cross, hoping to train as a Voluntary Aid Detachment at Sevenoaks Hospital. 'As for Wilf,' she said confidently, 'I know he will continue to be cared for at Home Farm. I'll see him regularly, of course, when I have time off.'

Danny was as surprised as the rest of them, but he privately accepted that he and Marion were drifting apart. He said quietly, 'Now we will both be involved in the war. I am proud of you, Marion.' He suspected they both wished to be rid of their marriage ties.

They discussed it that night. 'We should tell Wilf about our decision together,' Marion said.

'He's seven years old now, and I believe he will understand,' Danny agreed.

They still shared a bed, but Danny accepted that there was an invisible division between them. For some time, he'd maintained the ritual of a goodnight kiss, but this was not reciprocated.

He said now, 'I hope we can remain friends for Wilf's sake, Marion.'

After a long pause, she said sadly, 'On good terms, yes, I do hope for that. We must try, anyway.'

He said quietly, 'Don't worry. I will be away and I would never betray my brother regarding Kathleen.'

Kathleen, worrying about the future, worked as much she could in the pottery. Daisy was always willing to collect Jimmy and take him over to Home Farm when called upon. Wilf, after all, was now at school all day like his cousins.

When the girls were around, they were eager to help. They were not involved with the potter's wheel, the pugging machine, the kiln or the process of preparing the clay for moulding small objects, but they enjoyed fashioning simple plates and bowls; these had to dry to a leather-like texture, but while they were still slightly pliable, handles could be applied if necessary. Then the article would be trimmed, sponged and dried. Eventually it would be decorated before or after firing.

Heather was proving dextrous at making quaint little animal ornaments. Small hands were ideal for the pinch-pot method shown to her by Olga. She poked her thumb and forefinger inside a ball of clay, stretching it out on each side to form a hollow and rounding the open end into a plump rump. This was the body of the pig, and a smaller ball of clay was then fashioned into a head and attached with a mixture of clay and water. Features were defined: a snout, tiny black beads for eyes, four sturdy legs with trotters, ears, a curly tail. Heather then marked a slit along the back, turning the pig into a money box as well as a little character, before glazing it or decorating it with paint. She also made ceramic owls, cheeky mice and egg cups.

'Can we make a grasshopper?' Kitty asked Olga.

'The legs might be difficult to get right,' Olga smiled. 'Why a grasshopper, I wonder?'

'Mummy will tell you the story, 'cos Daddy told her. Uncle Danny named one of his horses Grasshopper,' Kitty said. 'I'd like to use green paint, it's my favourite colour!'

So Kathleen, who was busy ironing at the other side of the kitchen, put down the flat iron and joined them. She had an attentive audience. She had meant to get on while Jimmy was out in his pram with Daisy, who had pedalled over with Wilf on her bicycle carrier.

Young Dennis tapped on the window. 'I'll be over with your elevenses soon!' Kathleen called back. 'That boy has got hollow legs.'

'Like the pottery pigs,' Heather said. Her mother looked at her reprovingly.

Olga was regarding Heather in a reflective way. Suddenly she said, 'Your young Heather, she has a definite Latin look.

That beautiful apricot-coloured skin, those almost black eyes . . . I would like to paint her, if you permit it?'

'Everyone says she is the image of *me*,' Kathleen said, sounding defensive.

'She is small and slight like you, and has inherited your black hair, but at her age she is – how do you say it? Emerging from the chrysalis, eh? Her artistic bent must be encouraged too – who does she take after in that respect?'

Heather was embarrassed. Why were they discussing her as if she couldn't hear?

Kathleen said abruptly, 'You have made her blush. Heather is herself – as we all are.' But she couldn't suppress the image that came to her mind. It was painful but true: Heather had a look of her real father now. A struggling Italian artist, at first he had been kind to Kathleen, protecting her from her mistress's violence, but he had also destroyed her innocence and she could never forgive him for that.

'If you really want to paint a picture of Heather, you must ask her permission, not mine,' she said, adding, 'Now, excuse me.'

She waited until bedtime to confide in Sam. 'Oh Sam, I suppose we will have to eventually tell Heather that you adopted her.'

'Shush, Kathleen. She is not ready for that yet. Think how it could upset her.'

'Now I have something else to haunt me . . . If only *you* were her birth father!'

'Kathleen, it might be better to say nothing at all. Those who know will never divulge it,' Sam said. He meant the family at Home Farm, of course. 'Besides, I *am* her father; I'm the man who raised her, with you.'

Another secret, Kathleen thought. Why can't I be free of the past?

The next morning, a letter came in the post from Min. Her husband was retired from his ministry now, the boys were all grown up and doing well, and the little chapel where Kathleen had found sanctuary ten years before was closed and deserted. The congregation had moved to the new brick-built chapel within the village itself, where they had a proper slate roof over their heads rather than a rattling tin roof. However, the minister and his family would always be remembered by those who had known them.

Min and Josh were now living in the East End of London, doing voluntary work among the poor parishes there. They had been given the old harmonium as a parting gift from the chapel. 'I miss her,' Kathleen sighed. 'She loved being in the country; it can't be the same in London . . . I wonder if we will ever see them again.'

During the lazy, hazy days of that summer, Heather, the proud owner of a bicycle now that she was ten years old, shared her steed with her sister, who had just celebrated her eighth birthday. They took turns standing on the pedals or sitting on the seat. They were aware that life as they knew it was changing; however, some of the activity was puzzling. They could understand why Uncle Danny wanted to join his horses at the training centre, but not why he had to wear a uniform. Auntie Marion's absence was a puzzle; they had seen her only once, in uniform too, with a red cross on the front. Her blonde hair was restrained in a tight knot. She had hugged Wilf and was obviously trying not to cry.

'Why can't she stay at home like our mum?' the girls whispered to each other.

One day they went further afield on the bicycle without permission. They were curious to see what had happened to the poultry farm after Mrs Amos and Bert had left.

The old house, mainly timber-built, was no more. The fencing around the property had been reinforced with barbed wire. The girls peered over the new double gate, taking turns to stand on the saddle of the bicycle, kept steady by the other. The gate was obviously locked. A new building had been erected, in the style of the Nissen huts, but much larger. There were bars on the windows and the place appeared deserted, but Kitty gave a shiver. 'I'm sure someone is spying on us from that window . . .'

The chickens and their coops were gone – their grandma had benefited from that, as she had been given a dozen pullets at point of lay – and the grounds surrounding the big hut were now covered in grass, on which a few sheep were grazing. There was a big notice: DANGER. KEEP OUT. GOVERNMENT PROPERTY.

Heather turned the bike around. 'Come on, Kitty, let's go home. Don't you dare tell Mum where we have been!'

The final crisis came on 28 June 1914, when Archduke Franz Ferdinand, heir to the throne of the dual monarchy of Austria-Hungary, was shot dead in Sarajevo along with his wife Sophie. All over the world there was shock at this terrible event. With Germany supporting them, Austria used the assassination as a chance to crush Serbia. Russia rushed to support Serbia.

On 1 August 1914, Germany declared war on Russia.

'Lights Out' was immediately in force. This was necessary because of the threat of attack by German Zeppelin planes at night, on their way to bomb London. No lights must be visible after 10 p.m. However, nothing happened immediately; no bombs rained down.

Olga promptly travelled back to the East End. The painting of Heather, unfinished, was left on its easel. The pottery was closed for the duration. 'I'll be back,' she said, 'but I need to be among the dockland families who have not found safe places like our refugees here.'

The first bombshell was dropped by Sam. He told Kathleen and the girls that Herbie was about to join up, even though he was over forty, and that his wife was taking young Dennis and the dog to her sister's farm in the West Country. 'They will be safe there,' he said. 'Dennis will help to replace one of the men who has gone to the Front.' In a quiet voice he added, 'I am enlisting too. If I don't do it now, they'll conscript me anyway. They are digging trenches all over Europe, and I know all about digging clay pits as well as making bricks. I can offer building skills too.'

'What about us?' Kathleen cried, rocking young Jimmy in her arms, while the girls clung to her skirts. 'We can't manage without you.'

'I'm taking you home, Kathleen,' Sam said solemnly. 'All of you.'

TWENTY-FIVE

One month after war was declared, Kathleen, Sam and the three children returned to Home Farm. Mary's room was available, so the two girls shared a single bed alongside their parents' double bed. Jimmy, now almost two years old and toddling around, slept on a truckle bed in Wilf's room, with Daisy looking after them both. Jessie hesitated when she viewed the sleeping arrangements and suggested, 'Danny and Marion's room – well, I don't suppose they'll mind, as they are away, if you and Sam—'

'Sam will be off shortly.' Kathleen could hardly believe it still. 'Danny will be back on leave from time to time, and what about Marion, too? When it comes to it, the girls and I can share the big bed.'

She was worrying about how they would pay for their keep until Sam was enrolled in the army and began initial training, and then it occurred to her that perhaps she could resume the early mornings at the stables, this time with Doc. After all, their own old carthorse and the buggy pony had joined the other horses, and there were two new nanny goats to milk; fortunately the billy goat had moved to another farm and only came back for a few days when his services were required. She'd ask Doc after she'd mentioned it to Jessie.

'We will discuss later whether it's best for you to work on the farm or look after the children, Kathleen,' Jessie said. 'Not that I'm really sure what is happening. Well, while you make the beds up and put your clothes away, I'll get on with some cooking. Daisy's made enough bread to feed an army – oh dear, I shouldn't have mentioned that when the boys . . .' She dabbed her eyes with her apron. Oh why did they both have to join up like that? she thought. Conscription was still voluntary and married men were exempt; also those in important roles. Whatever was Sam thinking when he decided to volunteer so quickly?

'Don't be sad, Grandma. The war will soon be over, Dad reckons,' Heather said.

'Where's Bobby?' Kitty asked.

'I put him on the long lead in the garden until one of you can see to him.'

Bobby was nibbling something: a postcard with a picture of Sydney harbour. 'He must have picked it up from the front doormat; it could be from some days ago,' Jessie sighed as Kitty took the damp card to her. The writing was blurred, but they managed to decipher it. The card was from Mrs Amos, addressed to Mrs Marion Mason.

Dear Marion,

I have both good and bad news for you – we were in Sydney hoping to settle there, as the Outback is not my cup of tea, when Bert was rushed to hospital after suffering a stroke. He died the following day. I decided to return to England – the climate in Australia did me no favours. I am in London at the moment seeing to my affairs and changing my will. I plan to stay with you on a temporary basis. I will be arriving shortly.

Your mother,

Ann Amos

Jessie was agitated. 'This will come as a shock to Marion; we must get in touch with her at the hospital. Mrs Amos can't stay *here*; I hope Marion will have her in the boarding house where she is staying . . . Oh dear, I must get on. Why is she vague about the date like that?'

'Because she likes to surprise people,' Kitty put in.

'More likely to worry them,' Heather said knowingly.

The following day, after taking the children to school, Daisy and Jimmy went to the shops. While they were there, Daisy decided to find out about a group of women who met in the village hall and were knitting for the troops. Money rattled in tins on shop counters as customers were asked to contribute towards the wool for the garments. Heather might be interested too, Daisy thought, now that she was a proficient knitter.

Sam had gone to the brickworks to make sure all was as it should be there, and to bring back some more things Kathleen needed from the house. He fastened a sack to the carrier on the bike. After locking up, he stood for a long moment looking up at the house that had taken years to build. It is something to be proud of, he told himself, but at some point we will have to let everything go. Well, I fulfilled my promise to my uncle . . . He sighed as he mounted his bicycle.

Sam had learned that his training in basic warfare would be carried out locally. He would be able to nip home on occasion to begin with, especially if he joined the men training in Knole Park, Sevenoaks. There had been such an influx of volunteers that there weren't yet many facilities for training, and so village halls, barns and big empty houses with grounds were commandeered. They read in the paper that in London, men drilled in the big parks, with broomsticks instead of rifles; these were in short supply, for the men at the Front must be equipped first.

Jessie, alone in the house for once, took the opportunity to ring Marion, who was not pleased at her mother's news, particularly as she was called from the hospital ward to take the phone call. Sister had told her to hurry back and not talk for too long.

'Where on earth is she at this moment?' Marion asked Jessie.

'I don't know. I presume she'll come here thinking you and Danny still live with us.'

'Well, let me know when she arrives and I'll get time off to collect her. She'll need to share my bed in the lodgings; most of the VADs stay here, as it's near the hospital. I hope she is grateful for your help!'

Jessie had just put the phone down when there was a loud rapping on the front door. 'It can't be, can it?' she exclaimed.

When she opened the door, Mrs Amos was standing there, surrounded by her luggage. 'Well, aren't you going to ask me in and make me a cup of tea?' she demanded. 'Where's Danny? I'll leave my things here for him to bring inside. Marion is working, I presume?'

How am I going to break the news that there have been big changes here? Jessie wondered.

'Your card didn't arrive until yesterday,' she said. 'Have you had breakfast? I can soon rustle up some eggs and bacon.'

Mrs Amos shook her head and sat down on one of the kitchen chairs. Jessie saw her trembling mouth and realised that she was blinking away tears. She has aged, she thought, her hair is white, her face wrinkled from too much sun . . . 'I have lost my appetite,' Mrs Amos said. She swallowed convulsively. 'My throat is dry; I'll be glad of the tea.'

'Oh my dear, I was sorry to hear about Bert.' Jessie put an extra spoonful of sugar in the cup. There were rumours that imported food might soon be rationed, but Mrs Amos needed a boost of energy, she thought.

'Things didn't work out as we'd believed they would. There was just as much warmongering there as there is here, with young men going off to join the army. In Sydney, we saw a huge new battleship in the harbour, ready to leave at short notice. It was well guarded; people were not allowed to take photographs. Then Bert had a stroke and was taken to hospital. We were married by then, as we had intended to stay in Australia until all this happened.

'Bert died within a few hours, which was a blessing really, as I don't know how I would have managed to leave the country with a sick husband. We had some trouble during the journey back with German U-boats; they lurk at the bottom of the sea. Luckily our ship evaded them, but when we finally arrived, we were kept on board for hours and questioned about our motives for returning here.'

'Drink your tea, Ann. You're home now, aren't you?' Jessie knew she must tell her the news. 'Danny has joined up, and Marion is training to be a nurse – neither of them is here.'

'Wilf, where is he?'

'At school. Don't worry, he'll stay with me. It seems for the best. Sam will be off soon too; Kathleen and the children have moved back here.'

'You're saying there's no room for me?' Mrs Amos didn't sound like herself at all. 'Where can I go?'

'Marion has lodgings near the hospital in Sevenoaks; she hopes to collect you shortly and take you there. Meanwhile, their room is empty at the moment, and you are welcome to stay here until she comes. You will want to see your grandson, of course.'

'I don't suppose he will remember me,' Mrs Amos said dolefully.

'I'm sure he will.' There were footsteps in the hall. 'Kathleen is back with the milk.'

'*She* turned out all right after all,' Mrs Amos said unexpectedly.

'Yes, she did. I am very fond of her, as I am of Marion.' Jessie bit her lip. How can I tell her that Marion and Danny have separated?

Kathleen came into the kitchen with the churns. She was wearing her old breeches, but since she'd filled out after bearing three children, they were now a tight fit. 'Where's Jimmy?' she asked first, with a sidelong glance at Mrs Amos, expecting a snub or a snide comment.

'He's shopping with Daisy in the village. They say there will be shortages soon, so we are stocking up – they could be a while yet,' Jessie replied. 'Did you see the luggage on the front step? We'll have to wait for Abraham to move it.'

'I nearly tripped over it with the yoke on my shoulders,' Kathleen said ruefully. She took the milk through to the pantry. When she returned, she sat opposite Mrs Amos at the table and asked hesitantly, 'Did you have a good journey?'

'I did not,' was the terse reply. Then Mrs Amos added, 'I apologise for my rudeness. You might as well call me Ann or Annie, as they all did in Australia. How are you, Kathleen? I hear there is trouble again in Ireland and that de Valera has declared neutrality . . . You are missing Sam, no doubt?'

'Sam is still here at the moment; he's making sure everything is secure over at the brickyard. I know I mustn't show him how much I worry about him going to France.' Kathleen decided to ignore the reference to her birthplace.

'Danny is already over there,' Jessie put in, 'He is involved in the military training of horses, not only ours, but from all parts of the country. The horses had their hides trimmed short because it is very muddy in the fields round the trenches. Danny worries that without their winter coats, they will be affected by the cold weather later on.'

'I have to get back to work,' Kathleen apologised. 'I will see you later, Ann. I'll tell Doc you've arrived; he may want to pop in and say hello.'

When they were on their own, Mrs Amos said rather tartly, 'I gather your marriage is turning out all right? I was worried about you at the time, but you certainly look well, Jessie, unlike me.' She supposed it would be difficult at her age to replace Bert, though some of his coarse habits had repelled her.

Jessie offered, 'I'll take you upstairs now if you like. You look as if you need to catch up on your sleep.'

Later on, when Sam was back, he took his mother to one side and confided, 'I've only got two more nights at home, so I was going to ask if Kathleen and I could use the spare room for that time; we can't . . . do anything while we share with the girls . . .'

'Oh dear, of course I should have realised that, but what could I do? She has nowhere to go until Marion fetches her.' She paused and then said, 'Sam, I don't like to interfere, but I really don't think we could cope with another baby in the house . . .'

'I'm aware of that, Mother, don't worry,' he reassured her. 'Let's hope we get at least one night to ourselves . . .'

Young Dr Gillespie was having his breakfast in the boarding house when Marion came downstairs, taking them two at a time and stumbling as she reached the bottom. He was on his feet immediately, steadying her. 'Whoa! Where are you off to in such a hurry? I was hoping it was your day off,' he grinned, 'and that you'd agree to spend it with me.'

'We'll probably see too much of each other when we go to France,' she replied. 'I didn't expect it to be so soon.' She had an opened letter in her hand. How could she explain to her mother that she couldn't bring her back here? she thought. She liked Bruce Gillespie, who came from Edinburgh and had just graduated from medical school; she supposed that meant he was around twenty-six. Just a boy, while she was still a married woman, and thirty years old.

'Put on a nice dress and let your hair down,' he urged her. 'You look so prim in that drab uniform, though I can tell you are a pretty girl underneath.'

Girl! Marion thought, glancing down at her left hand; she no longer wore her wedding ring. 'How would you like to drive me to Home Farm, Bruce, at the back of beyond between Tatsfield and Westerham? I am supposed to fetch my mother back here with me – she has just returned from Australia – and I could do with some moral support. It will be good to see my son before I leave for France too.' She had seen Dr Gillespie's motor car and thought it might be nice to bowl along with the top open, enjoying the wind in her hair.

'I didn't realise you were married,' he said slowly.

'It is all very amicable; we are separated but in the process of divorcing. We won't see my husband; he is already in France. My boy, Wilfred, is eight years old.'

'Who looks after him?' Bruce asked.

'His grandmother, Jessie. Well, will you take me there or not? I know Jessie will make you welcome, but my mother, I'm afraid, is rather . . . aloof.'

He made his mind up. 'Could we have a light lunch together on the way, before we go on to the back of beyond, as you call it?'

'Why not?' Marion said. 'I'll have some of this lumpy porridge first, and then I'll go and get changed as you suggest.' She added daringly, 'I'd like to get to know you better.'

She hadn't had occasion to wear the summery dress she had packed in her trunk on impulse, but now she shook it out. A bit crumpled, but the weather was warm for October. She unpinned the severe knot in the nape of her neck, and shook her hair free. She would have worn her straw boater, but she hadn't remembered a hatpin.

Did she need a jacket? she wondered. The dress, her own design, showed off her ankles, and she decided against the lace jabot she usually wore to fill in the low neckline. She was glad to be free for a while of the stiff starched collar of her nurse's dress, which made her chin sore. Gloves? Her hands, so often in water while she gave bed baths to patients, needed covering up. She snatched up a lacy shoulder shawl, and smiled at her reflection in the mirror, then went downstairs to join Bruce, pretending not to notice his admiring glances.

He was about the same height as Marion, with a sturdy, stocky build and a thatch of black hair. She fancied he would look even more handsome in a kilt with a sporran. Like all the men she encountered, he obviously appreciated her curvaceous figure, and for some reason she felt a tingle of excitement.

'Ready to go?' he asked, offering his arm to escort her to the motor car.

I shouldn't be doing this, she thought belatedly. Goodness knows how Mother will take it. I hope she won't say something tactless.

TWENTY-SIX

They sat opposite each other on hard wooden chairs at a small table near the bar in the local pub. 'I've never been inside a public house before,' Marion admitted. She wrinkled her nose, 'Or tasted beer! Mother made some rather potent elderflower wine, though.'

'I guessed you might not have imbibed beer, so that's why I got you a half-pint glass,' Bruce said. 'Eat your pork pie; we mustn't be too long, I suppose.'

'I wouldn't mind a pickled egg,' she admitted, 'as there isn't any salad, and I daren't eat those pickled onions like you, or Mother will know. She's bound to notice my breath.'

He went to the counter, where a pickled egg was duly scooped out of the jar and served on a plate. 'Thanks!' she said, and jabbed it with her fork. It slithered about on the plate and they both laughed. 'Got it!' she cried.

'Marion,' he said suddenly, out of the blue, 'do you still love your husband? I gather it was a childhood romance and you married young.'

'Do I love Danny? Of course I do, I'm fond of all his family. But I'm not *in* love with him any more. When I had Wilf, it was a very difficult labour, and although I knew Danny wanted more children, I couldn't . . . you know . . . I couldn't go through that again.'

'I understand. It obviously made both of you unhappy,' Bruce said.

'There was another reason,' she said slowly. 'Danny and his brother Sam both fell in love with Kathleen, the girl Sam eventually married. Danny swore to me it was just an infatuation, but . . .' She broke off. 'Why am I telling you all this?'

'Because I'm a good listener?' he said. 'I know if it was me, I wouldn't dream of being unfaithful.'

'Danny wasn't unfaithful physically, but I suppose he was in his thoughts,' Marion said. 'Well, we'd better go and face my mother, but I warn you, she'll give you a grilling!'

It was actually Jessie who was disgruntled, because she had planned a good lunch for them all. She'd cooked a ham hock with a couple of bay leaves, and had picked lots of fresh salad stuff from the garden. There were jacket potatoes, her special recipe mayonnaise, cottage cheese with chives for Doc, and crusty bread, plus apple tart to follow, with whipped cream. They drank elderflower cordial rather than wine, as none of the latter had been brewed since Mrs Amos went to Australia. They waited until 2 p.m. and then decided they must eat. 'She is obviously not coming,' Mrs Amos said. 'How impolite of my daughter not to let us know.'

They were having the usual cup of tea out in the garden after washing up, while Daisy went to fetch the children home from school, when Jimmy fell and grazed his knee on the crazy paving path and yelled so hard they didn't hear the motor car arriving, or the knock on the front door.

'Shush!' Kathleen said to her red-faced son. 'I'll get the box of ointment . . .' So it was she who heard the repeated knocking, when she went indoors. Ointment in hand, together with a roll of bandage, she opened the front door. Her eyes widened as she saw that Marion had a companion. Now she wished she had changed out of stable clothes before lunch!

'Come in,' she said. 'Everyone is in the garden, and you're just in time, Marion, to do a bit of first aid on an injured knee!'

'This is Dr Gillespie, who is our first aid instructor,' Marion explained. 'Give me the remedies and I'll see to the injured party!' She left the other two in the hall.

Flustered, Kathleen held out her hand to Bruce. 'I'm Kathleen, Marion's sister-in-law.'

'She told me about you,' he said, as he shook her hand.

'Oh . . .' Kathleen said uncertainly. She bit her lip. 'Only nice things, I hope?'

'Naturally,' he replied. 'Well, aren't you going to take me outside to introduce me to your family?'

They joined the group in the garden and introductions were made.

'Well, Marion, you have deigned to visit me, but I have a feeling you are reluctant to take me back with you,' Mrs Amos said, ignoring the unexpected visitor.

'Actually, Mother, it's just been confirmed that our set of VAD nurses will be going over to France next week – you won't want to be in Sevenoaks alone without me, will you? The hostel,' she added tactlessly, 'is really for young people training at the hospital. I was wondering,' she looked appealingly at Jessie, 'if you might stay on in our room here until you find somewhere else, as neither of us will be back for some time.'

'Well, Jessie?' Mrs Amos demanded.

What could Jessie say except 'Of course you can, Ann. I'm afraid I shall have to ask you to help with things here, inside and out, but you'd be earning your keep, of course.'

The girls and Wilf returned and rushed straight outside to see what was going on. When Kitty heard that Marion's friend was Scottish, she asked him immediately, 'Have you brought your bagpipes?' And Doc, who'd come home at the same time, was heard to say, 'Bagpipes! Instruments of torture! Can't stand the noise!'

Fortunately, Bruce saw the funny side. 'I can play the pipes, but I prefer to hurl the caber at the Highland Games!'

Shy Wilf hung back, seeing Grandma Amos's disapproving look.

'What's a caber?' Heather asked, before Daisy rounded them up to go and change out of their school clothes.'

Jimmy plucked at Doc's coat. 'Look Gran'pa, I is an injured soldier!'

Doc replied, 'A brave one, I see; no tears, that's good.'

Sam was back too. Kathleen rushed to impart the news. 'She's staying on! We won't have the room tonight after all.'

Sam lifted her up and hugged her tight. 'There's always the old sofa,' he whispered. 'It's back in the living room.'

'I never thought of that! Of course you always know what to do, Sam – that's why I love you so much, and will do for ever and ever,' Kathleen told him solemnly.

After Bruce and Marion had driven away, while young Wilf stood waving with his left hand because he had the florin Marion had given him clutched in his right, they settled down in the living room. It was cooler now in the evenings and Sam lit the fire with the bundle of wood he'd brought home. The girls were playing patience at the table, while Bobby eyed the sofa and then settled on the rag rug nearer the blaze.

'Bedtime, Wilf,' Daisy told him. 'Kathleen has just settled Jimmy down.'

'I think I'll go up too, if you don't mind,' Mrs Amos said. 'I'm glad I'm staying with you, Jessie, as Marion was obviously flirting with that young doctor.' She had managed a short private conversation with her daughter earlier, but fortunately had refrained from saying this to her face. In fact, she had actually drawn her daughter close to her and whispered, 'Marion, I know it's partly my fault that you and Danny have parted. I was too keen to have you married off, and really, you were both too young, weren't you? But don't do anything rash just because you feel lonely, will you?'

'Now, now, Ann,' Jessie admonished her. 'They are just friends, I'm sure. I'll go shortly and get ready for bed myself. It's been a long day . . .' After Mrs Amos left the room, Jessie told Abraham, 'You won't be up yet, I know, but girls, you can take your cocoa upstairs at the same time as me. Done your homework?'

Kitty said airily, 'I've a composition to write. I might call it "A visit from a crotchety grandmother".'

'Write something nice about her too, mind,' kind Heather reminded her sister.

'We might not be up until later,' Kathleen put in. 'Good-night, girls.'

Sam gave them both a hug. 'I'll be gone early in the morning, but I hope to be home now and again before—'

'Before you sail the seven seas, Dad!' Kitty told him.

It was not long before Abraham followed them upstairs. Kathleen plumped up the cushions, took off her shoes and stretched out on the sofa. 'Pass me that rug, please,' she said to Sam.

He was making the fire up. 'We don't need the lamp; it's nice to talk in the firelight. Mind you, I've got other things on my mind while we're unlikely to be interrupted,' he added.

'Wait until I've taken my trousers off.'

'Kathleen – honestly!' he laughed.

'I meant to change them earlier but didn't get a chance – Mrs Amos was looking very disapproving.'

'I must get you a new pair – Mary wore those when she was twelve, you know.'

'I wish I'd met Mary. I would have had a sister then.'

'You had Marion.'

'I know, but I felt quite envious when I saw her with that nice Bruce. They will be going to war together . . . Though I do feel sorry for poor Danny.'

'Well don't. I suppose I am relieved he will be away from home like me.'

'Sam, you're not still jealous of your brother, are you?'

'No, like you, I feel sorry that he and Marion are ending their marriage.'

Kathleen threw the offending garment on to the mat. Bobby sniffed, scuffed it with his paws, and then settled down on it.

'Oh Sam.' Kathleen cuddled up to him. 'I love you more every single day!'

'Prove it,' he teased. 'No stuffy petticoats or stays, Kathleen,' he added approvingly.

'No room in the trousers, or they would split!'

'Saves time,' he said daringly, looking down at her shapely bare legs.

'Turn the key in the door first.'

'That reminds me of the saying about bolting the stable door after the horse has gone,' he mused, but he did as she suggested.

The fire had dwindled when she yawned and said, 'We'd better go to bed. The girls will wonder where we are.'

'Before we go up, I wanted to let you know that I have signed a document with the bank so that if you wish to let either the Brickyard House or the Barn House, you have my permission to do so. Also, if anything should happen to me . . . well, you'd be able to sell the property, because you would be left with three children to bring up, my darling.'

He had expected tears, but she said quietly, 'Thank you, Sam, I knew you would provide for me, but I pray it never happens. You'll have my rosary to take with you when you go to the battlefield.'

'Thank you. Having something with me that you treasure means a lot to me,' he said.

Marion and Bruce went upstairs in the hostel; their rooms were on the same floor. She paused at her door to thank him for taking her over to Home Farm, and also for lunch.

'Aren't you going to invite me in for a while, Marion? A cup of coffee would be welcome, and,' he patted his pocket, 'I haven't yet broached the flask of whisky my father gave me for an emergency.'

'What emergency?' she asked, but she allowed him to follow her into the small, sparsely furnished room, with a bed under the window, two hard Windsor chairs, a small card table, an armchair with twanging springs and a Primus stove. 'You can make the coffee, Bruce; cups are on the draining board, and luckily I have two of everything. Do you mind turning your back while I change out of this dress, and then I can relax in my dressing gown and slippers.'

Bruce was wondering what this might lead to, but he obediently looked away. 'Kettle's steaming, hurry up,' he observed.

They sipped the hot coffee, and emboldened by the fact that the beer she had drunk earlier didn't seem to have affected her, she accepted the tot of whisky he offered. Suddenly he observed, 'You are a beautiful girl, Marion. I don't know how your husband could be so foolish as to part with you.'

'I couldn't give him what he wanted, I suppose.'

'I must say that Kathleen was not what I expected; she's no femme fatale. She's obviously happily married, and a good mother. Well, I suppose I must make a move . . .' When she giggled, he added, 'And go to my room.'

Was it the whisky that made her say, 'Don't go – please stay, Bruce.'

'You really want me to?'

'Yes. I'm not sure if I'm ready, but . . .'

'I am certainly not going to force myself on you,' he said, but he took off his jacket, pulled off his tie and unbuttoned his collar. 'I did have a childhood sweetheart, but she didn't wait for me while I was at university, and . . . well, I am aware of the proper procedure. As a medical student, that was drummed into us, but you must tell me if you change your mind.'

'I won't, Bruce. It seems incredible, but I think I have been waiting for someone like you ever since I grew up.'

'Well, I knew you were the girl for me the moment I met you.'

'Just a few weeks ago,' she said softly. 'Turn the lamp low, will you, please?' She couldn't help wondering, though, what Danny would think. His love for Kathleen was unrequited.

Bruce left quietly at dawn. Later, Marion discovered a note under her pillow: *I will always remember last night. We must be discreet from now on, especially when we are working together in France.*

TWENTY-SEVEN

'Marion will have arrived in Boulogne by now.' Mrs Amos sighed heavily at the breakfast table.

'With Dr Gillespie,' Kitty said cheerfully. 'So she's not alone.'

'That's what I'm worried about . . .'

'He seems very nice, doesn't he, Heather? He'll look after Marion, won't he?'

'Stop talking and eat your breakfast, or you'll be late for school,' Kathleen said hastily. 'I must get back to work – be a good boy, Jimmy, and I'll see you all later.'

Thank goodness the young ones didn't realise that Marion wasn't on holiday, thought Jessie, but instead was about to be involved in the war, like Danny and Sam.

Marion soon discovered the reality and dangers of her situation. There were qualified nurses and doctors, including Bruce, in the field hospital some distance from the trenches, but the volunteer nurses were part of a mobile medical unit: a horse-drawn ambulance emblazoned with a red cross, driven by a member of the Royal Army Medical Corps, who was in charge. There were two stretcher-bearers who could perform first aid on injured soldiers; the nurses also provided temporary care for casualties on the spot. The first time the VADs were called upon was after an episode of fierce hand-to-hand fighting; they spent the journey in silence, contemplating what they might find among the fallen infantry.

The nurses were dressed in white, with caps completely covering their hair. After her first experience of treating the wounded, Marion's skirts were streaked with blood, matching the red cross on her bodice, but she carried on. She saw injured or dying horses too, but had to avert her eyes, because there was nothing she could do for the animals. An Alsatian guarded a mortally wounded man and whined to alert the rescuers. Dogs were used to find casualties and stayed by the fallen to comfort them. The injured were sorted into three categories: the slightly injured, who could go back to the front line after treatment; priority cases to be transferred to hospital; and those beyond help.

Shifts usually exceeded fourteen hours a day, and sleep was often broken at night. When Marion was off duty, she rested up in the deserted farmhouse nearby with her fellow volunteer nurses. The only habitable rooms were the big kitchen downstairs, where copper pans still hung on the walls, and the main bedroom upstairs, which was used as a dormitory for up to six nursing auxiliaries at a time.

Outside there was a well and a tarred black barn, still full of decaying hay, where rats had taken over. There was no livestock apart from the scavengers.

She met up with Bruce only once during those first weeks, when she was accompanying casualties to the field hospital. She was settling her patient carefully into his bed when suddenly she turned and he was there. They exchanged a long look, and then Bruce said, 'Thank you, nurse.' As she turned to go, he murmured softly, 'I remember our last meeting . . .'

'So do I, Dr Gillespie,' she replied. That was all, because the sister in charge bustled over and Marion was summarily dismissed.

Back at Home Farm, they avidly perused the newspapers that Daisy brought home from the village every day. Mrs Amos passed the *Times* on to Kathleen; it was grim reading, and Kathleen anxiously checked the casualty lists. Jessie preferred the village news, though that was all about war now too. Women were told it was their duty to keep the home fires burning and to take over the jobs their husbands had left. By this time, half of the British army horses were in France. The rest were in the Middle East, Egypt and Italy.

Kathleen asked Doc how their own beloved horses were likely to be employed. He replied, 'The strongest will move general supplies and ammunition; some fast horses like Grasshopper will be ridden by dispatch riders, and when there is a charge by the cavalry, they will be on the front line.' He added, 'Shire horses, in tandem, pull the heaviest loads, like the big artillery guns.'

'Will some of them be injured?' she asked fearfully.

Doc said slowly, 'It is inevitable, Kathleen. But the Army Veterinary Corps will carry out medical treatment.'

That evening, after Kathleen had taken a much-needed bath, she asked Jessie, 'Would you cut my hair? Not too short, but to my shoulders, so I can just brush it through and not bother with putting it up or plaiting it. Easier to wash, too, I think.'

Jessie didn't demur. She fetched her sharp scissors and swathed Kathleen's shoulders with an old towel. She bit her lip as she released Kathleen's long black locks from their restraint. What would Sam say? She banished her misgivings as she concentrated on the job in hand.

When Jessie had finished, Kathleen shook her head so that her hair bounced on her shoulders. 'Freedom! I love it, Jessie, thank you!'

Jessie was collecting up a bundle of hair from the floor, but she looked up to see Kathleen dancing around. 'It suits you, Kathleen,' she said softly.

Heather and Kitty crowded round. 'Oh Mummy you look lovely! Like a Dutch doll! Will you cut our hair like that, Grandma?'

'Not this evening,' Jessie said. 'Time you got washed and went to bed, isn't it?'

Later, Jessie, Doc and Kathleen were joined in the living room by Mrs Amos, who said pointedly, 'I haven't had a spare minute to read my paper yet. I hope I dug enough potatoes for you, Jessie . . . we'll need them, as there is a shortage of them already. I reckon I earned my keep today. Whatever have you done to your hair, Kathleen? You've lost your crowning glory . . .'

Kathleen refused to be ruffled. She was concentrating on knitting socks for Sam. She paused for a moment and then said, 'I'm a liberated woman now, Ann. You might want to follow my example. Well, any good news today?'

Mrs Amos gave an exclamation. 'That great ship I saw in Sydney harbour . . .'

'Has it been sunk?' Jessie asked.

'No – there was a battle off the Cocos Islands, where a German cruiser, the *Emden,* was causing havoc. The article says that the crew captured and sank several ships, French and Russian. Apparently the Germans landed a raiding force on the islands but were attacked and overpowered by HMS *Sydney*, the vessel I was telling you about, Most of the German crew were killed or taken prisoner. A victory for the Australians, eh?'

'No good news then,' Doc observed. 'Well, I'm off to bed.'

'I'll let Bobby outside for five minutes,' Jessie said. 'There's still some cocoa in the jug, Ann, if you'd like it. Kathleen, are you coming up?'

'I want to write to Sam first. The girls have given me their notes to enclose.'

'Tell him you've been shorn like a sheep,' Mrs Amos said, but Kathleen ignored the jibe. The old girl's bark was worse than her bite, she told herself, and at least she was pulling her weight; she'd got dirt under her fingernails to prove it.

After the first big battle of the war, the Battle of the Marne, Allied troops had stopped the advance of the Germans through Belgium and France, and both sides were optimistic that the war would soon be over. However, hostilities continued and more trenches were dug. Sam was now working in muddy conditions and miserable damp weather.

There were three lines of trenches constructed in a zigzag pattern, the front line being located fifty yards from its enemy counterpart, with machine guns in action on both sides. Steps were built up to the machines; when facing the enemy, the brave gunners were exposed, and grenades were thrown as the other side advanced. There were communication trenches and shallower positions that extended into no-man's-land, with observation posts protected by cruel barbed-wire fences. When men went over the top, they were all too often caught in the tangle of spikes and became a sitting target.

The second trenches were several hundred yards behind the first, their occupants waiting to support the front-line combatants. The final trenches held the reserve forces. There were dugouts beneath the trenches fitted out with rudimentary furnishings for the officers. Their safety was paramount, as they were in charge of planning, plotting and decision-making.

Sam was involved with digging more trenches further along the line. Some of his fellow workers were Welsh miners, muscular men skilled at tunnelling, who sang lustily as they toiled underground to keep up their spirits. Sam worked alongside a carpenter who had a pencil behind one ear and the nickname of Woody, while Sam himself was known as Digger. It was far removed from digging clay pits at the brickyard. Despite the cold and the rain, he thought ruefully that he was in a muck sweat. He wondered where Danny was, and if they would ever meet up again. He thought about Kathleen and the children, and Jessie and Doc at Home Farm, but was thankful they could not see him in this situation. They would know about it one day, though, because he had a little notebook in his pocket in which he wrote random thoughts. This was a parting gift from his daughters: *To Dad, come home soon, love from Heather and Kitty*.

The latest scribbled entry read: *This is a bloody hellhole. I feel as if I am digging my own grave. Perhaps I am. What is this war all about? It makes no sense. No sense at all* . . . He had broken the point of his pencil underlining that.

*

Danny, meanwhile, was stationed just a few miles away from where Sam was labouring in the mud. He had not been reunited with Grasshopper; his favourite horse was with the cavalry. King Cole, the big black horse he rode to deliver messages to the front line, had distinctive white socks and was a feisty animal but also very speedy. They tolerated each other, but if Danny became too familiar, the horse would bare its teeth and shy away. King Cole was a superb jumper who seemed to fly over any obstacle.

Danny was in touch with Marion and was aware that when their divorce went through, that part of his life would be over, apart from the link with their son. He wished she had not told him there was another man in her life. *We will remain friends, I hope; may you also find someone else*, she had written. Kathleen is the only woman I want, Danny thought, but that's an impossible dream.

On their rare days off, he and some of the other men visited villages beyond the war zone that amazingly had not been ruined by the fighting. Life seemed almost normal there, but of course it wasn't. Brothels had sprung up, where some of the men went seeking comfort. Danny told himself he couldn't pass judgement on that. He must continue to be resolute and fight for his country.

TWENTY-EIGHT

By Christmas 1914, food rationing had not yet been introduced in Britain, though after the initial rush by customers to stockpile goods, shopkeepers clamped down on bulk buying and tried to be fair to rich and poor alike. They were all aware of the loss of food supplies from overseas, as many supply ships were torpedoed by enemy submarines.

At Home Farm, they had always been more or less self-sufficient, with land set aside for essential crops – strawberries as well as vegetables of all kinds – and meat provided by pigs and spring lambs. They had increased the number of chickens and ducks, and Mrs Amos became their chief adviser after her years on the poultry farm. The strawberries were manageable without outside help, and the girls and Kathleen enjoyed being involved in what they considered the highlight of the year. Jessie was aware, though, that strawberries would not reach peak sales nowadays.

Daisy was now the designated housekeeper, as her nursemaid days were almost behind her, and she already cooked wholesome meals for the family. Bobby the dog did his bit, but mainly dug holes where they were not needed in the expanding kitchen garden. Jessie organised the girls, foraging in hedgerows and fields for blackberries, wild plums, rosehips, chestnuts, mushrooms, edible plants and elderberries and elderflowers for the Christmas wine, and took them gleaning in the fields at harvest time.

'We can grow most things here, but we can't grow sugar cane, and although we have decided – some of us anyway – to give up sugar in our tea, what about the Christmas baking? It will be a very small cake this year, not much dried fruit either,' Jessie sighed. 'We'll have to improvise, Daisy.'

The humble carrot was no longer limited to stews, but was grated into puddings and cakes as a sweetener. Potatoes were in short supply in towns, but in the country they maintained their vegetable clamps, and the humble spud remained a vital part of their diet. Mashed potato was added to the flour when making pastry, as imported wheat from the Commonwealth had drastically reduced. Tea was another commodity that must be used sparingly. Daisy decided to put one less spoonful in the teapot and save used tea leaves. But how many times could she reuse them? she wondered.

On Christmas morning, Kathleen woke early in the bed she now shared with her daughters. After Sam had gone to war, she had found sleep difficult. Now, as Jessie remarked fondly, 'You are like three giggling girls together!'

'Well, we are looking after Mum, as we promised Dad,' Heather said solemnly. She was growing up fast, Jessie thought, and promised to be a beautiful young woman. Kitty was very much like her own daughter Mary had been; full of fun.

There was wrapping paper all over the bed and excitement over presents. Kathleen had been busy knitting, while Jessie's sewing machine had been whirring. Heather and Kitty had red woolly caps with saucy white bobbles and matching mittens, as did Jimmy, who had joined them for the delving into parcels.

Daisy took Wilf to his grandparents' room to open his pillowcase of presents, while she volunteered to make the morning tea. The adults were thinking of Sam and Danny but were determined to make this Christmas as normal as possible. There was a tentative knocking on Jessie's bedroom door and Mrs Amos came in bearing gifts. 'You don't mind me joining you?' she asked.

'Of course not,' Jessie assured her. 'Wilf is your grandson too. We are all one family here. Move the rocking chair over . . .'

On Christmas Eve, Marion collapsed with exhaustion and the duty doctor at the hospital was asked by the sister in charge to call in at the farmhouse.

Sister ushered Dr Gillespie in and pointed up the stairs. 'Nurse Amos is in the first bed. I took her temperature just now and it is still up. I expect you know each other?'

He nodded. 'Yes. We do. She trained at my hospital back home.'

Marion was dozing, her face turned into the pillow. He bent over the bed. 'Marion, I was asked to check you over . . . Can you sit up?'

'I . . . I don't know,' she murmured. 'Pain in legs . . . all over . . .'

He lifted her gently and propped her up with a second pillow from another bed. He checked her heart with his stethoscope, and then turned her on her side so he could move the cold metal over her back. Her skin was hot and dry. She shivered and he tucked the blankets back round her.

'You have a chest infection, Marion; I will give you something to bring your temperature down.' He was puzzling over a swelling on her right arm, which was red and puffy. It came to him that he had seen something similar on a young soldier with minor injuries but a raging fever. The lad was now battling for his life. Could this be the start of an epidemic?

He rummaged in his black bag. Sister arrived with a cup of coffee for him and a glass of water for Marion. 'I'll leave you to it, Doctor . . . Any instructions?'

'She should be given quinine four-hourly, please. I don't think she is infectious, but she must rest up for a few days. I wonder, was she bitten by something?'

'Bitten? She didn't say, but most of the patients have lice when they arrive at the hospital. Marion has to remove their clothing, of course.'

'She must have bed rest,' he emphasised once more. 'I'll give her the first dose now and then I must get back to the hospital.'

They were alone for a precious few moments. He bent and stroked her flushed cheek.

'You'll be all right, Marion. No hugs or kisses tonight, I'm afraid, but I will come again when I can, I promise.'

'I love you, Bruce,' she whispered.

He wanted to say that he felt the same, but he was, after all, still on duty, with more patients to see. 'Goodnight, dear Marion,' he said, and then he was gone.

Sam was not part of the amazing Christmas truce, when soldiers from both sides joined together for an impromptu football match in no-man's-land, but he and Woody were due to join some of the other diggers and Welsh miners for Christmas dinner. Prior to that, he had a surprise visitor; Danny rode over on a borrowed motorcycle with Christmas greetings and some post from home. Sam left an official letter until last, after the loving messages from his family.

'Aren't you going to open that one?' Danny asked. He lit a cigarette. He was a regular smoker now, whereas Sam had not succumbed to the habit. When Sam felt stressed, he would feel the rosary beads in his top pocket and think of his beloved Kathleen.

The letter was from a firm of solicitors; the name seemed familiar. Sam realised that it was Kathleen's uncle's firm. He read it twice without saying anything, and then cleared his throat. 'Kathleen's uncle has died and left her some money. This is a copy of a letter she received, but she didn't mention it to me.'

'This would help your present situation regarding the brickworks?' Danny guessed.

'Kathleen has asked that the money be put in trust for the children and used for their further education . . .' Sam sounded bemused. 'I have to sign this and send it back to the solicitors to say I agree.' He added, 'Money is of no importance when you're stuck here in all this stinking mud far from home, eh?'

'I had a letter too,' Danny said. He seemed to have something in his eye, which he was rubbing. 'I heard from Marion's . . . friend, Dr Gillespie, that she is very ill. He asks if I would be able to go and see her, given the circumstances.'

'Will you go?' Sam asked.

'If I can. I still love her, you know.'

Is it possible to love two women at the same time? Sam wondered. There was no answer to that.

Woody appeared. 'Dinner's arrived! We're having it in the officers' mess. Bring your brother.' The mess was a glorified dug-out, but brick-built.

Danny gave a wry smile. 'It doesn't *smell* like Christmas, Sam, not like Mother's kitchen back home.'

'The cooks do their best,' Sam said, 'but it is all thrown in the same pot . . . rather like us,' he added reflectively.

When it was time for Danny to leave, they exchanged small gifts. Sam gave his brother a crumpled packet of cigarettes and Danny presented Sam with a small French dictionary.

'I may not be here much longer,' Sam said slowly. 'These bloody dugouts I helped to establish mean the front line now extends from the North Sea to Switzerland. I have asked to transfer to a fighting regiment; I need to be involved with the real action.'

'But what about Kathleen? You are much more likely to be injured or . . .' Danny took a deep breath; he had to say it, 'killed.'

'She gave me this.' Sam brought out the rosary from his pocket. 'I say the prayers we learned as boys . . . Danny, if the worst happens and you survive me, will you look after Kathleen and the children? I was the fortunate one, I married her, but I know you loved her too.'

'I promise you I will,' Danny said solemnly, 'but I hope it will never come to that.'

Danny had to wait until New Year's Eve before he was able to visit Marion. He borrowed his friend's motorbike again and arrived in the afternoon. A nurse answered his knock; one glance at her face, and he knew what had happened before she managed to tell him: 'Marion . . . passed away this morning. You must wear a mask and gloves before you are allowed in the sickroom. Sister's orders. We are not to touch the body. I'm so sorry; please follow me . . .'

Marion had been isolated in a small room upstairs. Bruce was waiting for him, masked and gowned too. 'May I call you Danny?' he asked.

Danny nodded. He looked towards the bed. Bruce gently pulled the sheet down.

'She looks peaceful,' Danny said after a long moment. 'She was my wife for ten years, the mother of our son.'

'I know.'

'It wasn't an unhappy marriage, but Marion knew I was in love with my brother's wife. I never betrayed her, though, because you see, I loved her too.'

'I know.'

'What caused this to happen?' Danny wanted to know.

'I'll tell you all I know, which isn't much. But first I'll leave you to say goodbye to your wife. Come downstairs when you are ready.' Bruce went quietly from the room.

Danny knelt by the bed. 'I can't kiss you, Marion, I can't touch you, but I'm sorry I failed you. You are at peace now, and you will always be with me in spirit, I know that.'

Later, he learned that this mystery illness was spreading. 'Some call it trench fever,' Bruce told him.

Marion was buried a few hours later, at dusk. There was a brief service conducted by the chaplain, and Danny stood tall among Marion's fellow nurses as the Last Post sounded. He did not cry then, but he felt despair. This would affect the family back home badly, he thought. How would Wilf deal with it? He would ask Sam's friend, the carpenter, to make a simple wooden cross.

The family at Home Farm received the sad news shortly after New Year. Mrs Amos did her grieving in the privacy of her room, and Wilf, bewildered by all the tears shed by the women, clung to Daisy, who vowed silently never to leave him.

Heather and Kitty were worried about their young cousin. They observed Daisy washing out his damp bed-linen most days; poor Wilf, he couldn't tell anyone, not even Daisy, how much he missed his mother, who he knew would never come back.

The girls took him to one side and Heather told him, 'You have us, Wilf, and we think of you like another brother – Jimmy does too. You will always be part of our family.'

'Will Kathleen be a sort of mum to me?' Wilf wanted to know.

'Of course she will. And when your dad comes home, he'll be proud of you, I know.'

Kathleen overheard this conversation. She was missing Marion too, and she was proud of her girls for comforting

Wilf. Heather was growing up fast, such a beautiful girl, and Kitty, who was very like Jessie in looks and manner, had an impish sense of humour. We'll be all right so long as we all stay together until Sam and Danny come home, she thought.

TWENTY-NINE

In February 1915, the relentless rain and damp turned to bitterly cold weather. Conditions worsened and trench fever became all too familiar.

Back home, the headlines in the newspapers reported that German battleships had shelled the coastal towns of Whitby, Hartlepool and Scarborough; there were many civilian casualties from these attacks. Gallipoli, which the girls looked up on their world map, was much in the news too; the war was reaching places they had never heard of before. Mrs Amos, who was proud to be an honorary Australian, related how the Anzacs were involved.

The first night-bombing raids were not on London as expected but on the east coast of England at Great Yarmouth and King's Lynn. The original target was Humberside, where many wartime factories were based. The blackout imposed all over the country from 10 p.m. had proved its worth, but now the Zeppelins carried incendiaries that could be thrown overboard to light their way.

Another official visitor called at Home Farm – something Doc had warned Jessie might happen. Daisy answered the knock on the door. A short man stood there; he removed his bowler hat and said in a high-pitched voice, 'Good morning, are you the lady of the house?' He tapped his bulging briefcase. 'I have a document for you to sign, may I come in?'

Daisy, flustered after being mistaken for her employer, despite her apron and headscarf, opened her mouth to reply, but Jessie appeared behind her. She too wore an apron, and she had a trowel in her capacious front pocket as she had come in from the garden.

'May I ask why you are calling?' she said. 'I can see to this gentleman,' she added to Daisy, who escaped thankfully. The visitor wore a pince-nez, which was unusual in these parts, and he had a sharp look about him, Daisy would tell Kathleen later.

'You are Mrs Kathleen Mason?' The visitor stepped inside the hall.

Jessie put him right. 'No, I am her mother-in-law, Mrs Wiseman. This is my house. Kathleen is at the stables where she works with my husband. May I ask why you are here?'

'I am one of the billeting officers for the area. My name is Cyril Gosling. Is there somewhere we could sit and talk?'

Jessie opened the parlour door. She suddenly thought, if Kitty had heard the name she would no doubt have nudged Heather and whispered: "Quack, Quack!" She quickly composed herself. 'Take a seat, Mr Gosling, pull up that small table . . .'

Mr Gosling clicked the lock on his briefcase. 'I understand that your son, Sergeant Samuel Mason, is with the army in France. He owns two properties: a new house and a converted barn at a brickworks. These properties are empty at the current time. Is that correct?'

'Yes, but—'

'I have to tell you that these empty dwellings will be requisitioned in the near future, unless you can tell me that they are likely to be reoccupied soon. Everyone must be prepared to help the war effort.'

'I understand, but it could be that we might take in our own evacuees if London is bombed – we have friends there who work among the families in the docks area.' This was true; something Olga had mentioned in her last letter.

'Well, that is very laudable, but I still need confirmation from you that you will co-operate with us if necessary. Have you a pen in your desk?'

'Yes,' Jessie said. Mr Gosling gave her the paper he wished her to sign, and she dipped her pen in the inkwell.

'I will need another signature from your daughter-in-law; may I call on her at the stables?' Jessie nodded. I must write to Olga right away, she thought, and also to Min and Josh, and explain the situation to them.

Doc told her later that he thought Mr Gosling came from the government property office in the big Nissen hut that had replaced Mrs Amos's farmhouse at the beginning of the war, rather than from the council offices as she had supposed. It was all very mysterious, they agreed, but you didn't ask too many questions nowadays or you could be suspected of having an interest in matters you shouldn't have.

In April, poison gas was used for the first time by the Germans, to devastating effect. Chlorine gas was followed by the even more deadly mustard gas. The men in the trenches donned gas masks, but often it was too late. There were many casualties, and those who survived would be left with irreparable damage to their lungs. It was not long before the Allied troops retaliated with the same weapon. This was a very different war from those that had gone before. Incendiary bombs were dropped on the troops from aeroplanes, targeting the trenches and the armoury. Fires blazed and were tackled by the firefighters, a chain of weary men with buckets of water.

Overhead, it became commonplace to spot reconnaissance aeroplanes, with cameramen on board who took photographs of the trenches. Shortly after the initial gas attacks, there was frequent aerial combat between the warring factions.

Danny was transferred to the cavalry along with his horse, King Cole, and joined a new battalion of the Buffs – the Royal East Kent Regiment – who were in France to back up the British Expeditionary Force. Sam, meanwhile, was no longer stuck down his hellhole. He drove a truck ferrying troops around, and delivered ammunition and supplies to the front line. Danny had taught him to drive; it was ironic, Sam thought, that his brother had himself chosen to stick to horsepower.

In the spring of 1915, the long-anticipated onslaught on London from the skies began. Bombs began to rain down on the capital, and on strategic targets in other cities all over the country.

Doc kept his promise to his dockland friends and arranged to drive to London to collect a large extended family who had been made homeless and bring them to live with Olga in the Brickyard House. This would necessitate two journeys, for there were four young children with their mother, an aunt and a disabled grandmother; three older girls had already been sent to a munitions factory in the Midlands. The aunt's husband would stay in London to be involved with the firefighting, but the children's father had recently been killed in France.

Kathleen and Jessie went over to the house to open it up and air the rooms. They collected blankets knitted by the group Daisy belonged to in town, and there were donations of household linen from the community. At last the stacks of platters, bowls and mugs in the barn would be put to good use, as well as ornaments made by the girls to make the place look more homely.

The stove and fires were lit to warm the house up, and Daisy came over to clean the windows and banish the dust and cobwebs. 'The house has come alive again,' she told Jessie. 'There was a huge spider in the bath, but I captured it and put it outside – it's unlucky to kill spiders, isn't it?'

Tins of food appeared on the Home Farm doorstep, along with boxes of vegetables. 'People are so kind,' Jessie said.

The girls were doing their part by cutting an old felt hat into strips to make wicks for the oil lamps. 'Waste not, want not,' Jessie quoted. 'These last much longer than the wicks you can buy.' She also showed them how to polish the brass fittings on the lamps. 'Clean with ordinary polish, then rub the brass with furniture cream using a soft cloth; they will gleam for much longer!'

'How will the children get to school? It's a long way to walk,' Kitty said. She looked at the cloth she was using. 'Oh, I rubbed the brass so hard this big hole appeared – sorry, Grandma.'

'It was an old piece, don't worry,' Jessie said. 'School? We have an idea about that – Grandpa has suggested the old Barn House could be a schoolroom and they can be taught there . . . Your mother is finding out about that.' She didn't enlighten them further.

The next day, Saturday, a letter arrived for Kathleen and she read it over breakfast, after she had returned from the stables. She looked the part of a stable girl now, in her new fawn jodhpurs, in which she could bend over without fear of them splitting like the old pair that had been returned to the ragbag. However, she retained Danny's cap, which he had presented to her before he left for the Front. 'This is the one Sam gave me on my birthday all those years ago,' he'd said. Kathleen wore it at a saucy angle on her bobbed black hair.

Heather had the same style now, and Kitty was trying to cajole Jessie into cutting her hair too, but Jessie said, 'A shame to lose those curls, Kitty – next year perhaps.'

'I always have to wait for things, it's not fair,' Kitty moaned. 'I'm nearly ten years old, remember!' She still had to share Heather's bike.

Kathleen was smiling. 'Good news!' she said, waving the letter at them. 'Min and Josh have said they'll come back here to live in the Barn House, and Josh will teach the children while Min helps Olga run the house!' She was excited at the thought of being reunited with Min and her husband.

'Will they bring the harmonium with them?' Kitty asked. 'I'd like to learn to play it.'

'That will come by carrier,' Jessie told her. She looked around for Jimmy, who sat up at the table now and was always eager to go out to play when he'd finished his breakfast. 'Where's Jimmy disappeared to?'

A head emerged from under the table, and the crockery rattled at the disturbance, then the rest of the little boy appeared. 'I was only giving Bobby my bacon rinds,' he said airily.

'He's so like his father,' Jessie said fondly. 'Determined to do what he wants.'

Heather surprised them all by standing up and shouting at her grandmother: 'You never say that about me! Don't you think I take after Dad too?' Then she stomped out of the room.

Silence for a moment, before Kathleen made to follow her daughter. Jessie put out a restraining hand. 'No, Kathleen, this is not the time to say anything – she's getting to a certain age, thinks she's grown up, but she isn't. She'll get over it, just be patient.'

'Let me go after her,' Kitty offered. 'I'll get round her.'

Kathleen nodded. 'Yes, you go.'

Jessie gave Kathleen a concerned look. 'It's all right,' she mouthed.

Mrs Amos had refrained from saying anything until then, but now she muttered to herself, 'That girl needs putting in her place.'

Kathleen overheard this and was furious. 'Some people need to mind their own business!' she cried. 'I'm going back to the stables now; Doc will be wondering where I am. It may be Saturday, but *I* have to work every day of the week!' With that, she went out of the front door, slamming it behind her.

Doc didn't ask her why she was pale and her face tear-stained. 'Will you hold the mare, please, while I have a look at her feet? She seems rather lame, and it's probably time we called the blacksmith to fit her with new shoes.'

Later, when their morning's work was done, he said, 'Would you like to tell me why you are upset? It will go no further, I assure you.'

They sat on a hay bale, side by side. 'Oh Doc, I know I ought to tell Heather that Sam isn't her father. I've been waiting for the right time, but now she's growing up. What do *you* think I should do?' she appealed.

'My dear, she has to know sometime, but it is bound to upset her whenever you tell her. What does Sam think?'

'We discussed it a while ago, but he didn't think she was old enough to know the truth at that time.'

'It's something you should do together, I think, so he can reassure her, but of course, that's not possible with him so far away. I think you will know when it is the right time, Kathleen, but not just now, eh?'

'Thank you, Doc.' Kathleen rose and dusted herself down. 'I'll take your advice.'

When she arrived back, the girls were out in the garden with Jimmy, throwing Bobby's ball for him to fetch. 'The children from London are coming to our house soon!' Heather called to Doc. 'And guess what? Min and Josh are going to stay in the Barn House!'

'I'd better fill the motor with petrol then,' he called back.

THIRTY

Early one Saturday morning, Doc travelled to the East End to collect the first of the evacuees, who had been taken to the refuge set up by Min and Josh. The O'Brien family had few possessions because their dockside home had been gutted by a bomb, but today they would have a home again, although the future was still uncertain.

Kathleen and Heather cycled over to the brickyard to make sure everything was ready, while Kitty helped Jessie at Home Farm and kept an eye on her young brother. Jessie fried bacon for breakfast; Daisy and Wilf would be home soon with the milk. She yawned; she had been up since dawn making sandwiches for Doc to take to London, and for Kathleen and Heather, who would get the stoves going and light the fires in both houses. The kettle would soon be singing and mugs were lined up for tea. Where was Mrs Amos? she wondered. Still in bed? She hadn't done much to help since they heard the sad news about Marion, though that was understandable.

She turned the sizzling rashers over, and thus preoccupied, didn't hear the tentative knocking on the door. Kitty, holding Jimmy firmly by his left hand as he clutched a soggy rusk in his right, called out, 'Who is it?'

'It's Dennis. Is Kathleen there?'

'Oh,' Kitty said casually. 'Come in. I thought you were in Devon. Mum's gone over to the brickyard this morning. We are expecting visitors, but we didn't expect *you*!'

Dennis had shot up in height and looked gangly and awkward. He was fifteen years old and his voice was breaking. 'I called at the Barn House last night, just in case, but there was nobody there. I had to sleep in the big barn where the pottery was made; someone had left the door unlocked.'

'Oh, all the pottery is now in the big house. But why are you back?'

'I was homesick, I suppose.'

'How on earth did you get here?'

'On my bike; it's taken me nearly two weeks. I had to find places to sleep after blackout. All the signposts have gone, but I had my compass that I got in the Boys' Brigade – us lads in the workhouse all belonged; I played the drums, I wasn't no good with a bugle.'

'Well,' Kitty said, 'come in the kitchen. Grandma's here – she's cooking breakfast – so you can explain it all to her!' She looked him up and down. 'I expect she'll say you need a bath!' She wrinkled her nose.

'Well I did sleep in a pigpen one night,' he said ruefully.

Jessie was kind enough to give him a hug, then directed him to the bathroom. 'I expect you'd like to wash and freshen up. Have you any clean clothes?'

'In my rucksack.'

'There's a fresh towel on the hook and a flannel in the drawer under the sink. Your breakfast will be cooked shortly, but I should get in there quick – here come the troops! They'll be surprised to see you, but I reckon they'll be glad of your help.'

Fortunately, Dennis had gone to make his ablutions before Mrs Amos appeared. She had become very thin and gaunt in the face since losing her daughter, but she didn't talk about Marion any more. She kept those feelings to herself.

Heather was excited when she heard about Dennis's return. 'He can stay with Min and Josh, I expect, can't he?'

'We'll see. You'll have to wash your hands in the sink . . .'

'The bathroom will stink,' Kitty put in. Jessie looked at her reprovingly.

'Everything shipshape, Kathleen?' she asked.

'Nearly! I'm starving,' Kathleen said.

'I made all those sandwiches,' Jessie said mildly.

'I ate most of them,' Heather admitted, 'and Bobby was hungry after running after us all that way.' Daisy emerged from the pantry, having deposited the milk and eggs. 'How long will that boy be in the bathroom? Wilf needs to go . . .'

Mrs Amos surprised them all with her comment: 'The privy is still outside where it always was. Wilf, stop making a fuss. You're not the only one with a weak bladder.'

Jessie mopped her brow. It all seemed too much today, she thought.

Mrs Amos gave Dennis a stern look as he wolfed down a large plateful of bacon and eggs. 'Anyone would think you hadn't had a square meal for some time!'

'I haven't,' he said truthfully. 'All I got was a bite or two of cow cake.'

Jessie said hastily, 'Would you like some bread fried in the bacon fat, Dennis?'

'Oh yes please!'

Later, Kathleen took Daisy, Jessie and the girls back in the buggy to greet the newcomers at the brickyard. Dennis accompanied them on his bicycle. Shy Wilf elected to stay at home with Jimmy and the dog, under the watchful eye of his Grandma Amos.

Just as Kathleen was conjecturing whether the O'Briens came from Ireland originally, like herself, Kitty and Heather, who were on the lookout for Doc's car, called out: 'They're here!'

Olga was the first to step inside, followed by Mrs O'Brien, carrying her youngest child, a little boy. Clinging to her skirts were three older children, a girl of about ten, and twin girls a few years younger, which caused a flurry of excitement. How would they be able to tell them apart?

Mrs O'Brien, a slight woman of perhaps forty, had retained a slight Irish accent, with overtones of Cockney; as she told them later, 'I came over here to marry my Tom. I was only seventeen then and he was nineteen. Tom was called up because he was in the Army Reserve, and then . . .' Her eyes suddenly brimmed with tears.

Jessie held out her arms for the baby. 'I know, my dear; we have had a bereavement too, we understand how you feel . . . What a lovely lad – is he Tom as well?'

'Yes, how did you guess?' Mrs O'Brien said, smiling now.

'He's your only son, isn't he? After six girls! I have a grandson, Wilf, named for my first husband, Wilfred. And two wonderful sons in the army, fighting for their country. This is Kathleen, my Sam's wife; she's an Irish girl too, from County Clare. Kathleen and the children are with me while Sam is away.'

Jessie introduced the rest of the family one by one, including young Dennis, whom Olga said she remembered. 'Kathleen will take you over the house so you can choose your rooms. There are three good bedrooms upstairs and one downstairs, which we thought would be ideal for your relatives as they are elderly.'

'I can share with Bridget,' Olga suggested. 'Mrs O'Brien will be with the baby, of course, and the twins will want to be together.'

'I'm Bridget too,' said Mrs O'Brien, 'but please call me Bridie.'

'If there's anything you need, just ask Olga and we will try to oblige,' Jessie said. 'My husband is about to return to London to collect Josh and Min and your aunt and grandmother. He'll arrange a carrier for anything he can't manage in the car. He needs to be back here before dark.'

Bridie suddenly shivered and looked afraid. 'I wonder if there will be bombs in London tonight . . .'

Kathleen hugged her old friends warmly once they arrived. 'It's so good to see you again; I've missed you!'

'It's good to be here,' Min said. 'Josh is all ready to renew his teaching career; the carrier will deliver his desk and chair, blackboard and easel, several boxes of books and some old school desks next week. Oh, and my harmonium. And the local priest has offered to say Mass here for the O'Briens once a week.'

'I'm afraid you will have to go over to the big house when you want a bath, and there's only an outside privy,' Kathleen apologised.

'My dear, remember we are Primitive Methodists, and the manse was certainly that!' Min replied.

'How are the boys?' Kathleen asked tentatively.

'You have heard, of course, about James and John . . . David was sent home to hospital here. The other boys are in the conflict in the Middle East. Our youngest is still over here, training for the ministry. We need to keep busy ourselves, with all that going on. And praying helps.'

'That's how I feel too, about Sam – and Danny,' Kathleen said. 'Well, I'll leave you to settle in and will see you all tomorrow. I have to go to the stables first thing, though.'

'We are well provided for here,' Min said gratefully. 'Thank you, for everything.'

Olga was giving the three O'Brien girls an art lesson when Jessie called in after a couple of days to see how they were getting on.

'It fascinates me to see the twins painting one picture between them,' she observed to Jessie while the children were engrossed. 'One is left-handed and one right-, so they don't cross paths – or rather hands – do they?'

'Which is which, so I can tell them apart?' Jessie asked.

'Louisa is right, and Lucy is left,' Olga said, and both girls looked up and giggled.

'Heather is hoping you will be able to finish her portrait – of course she's grown up a bit since you started it, but it's a lovely memory of a little girl, I think.'

'Tell her to come over this weekend, and after I've completed her picture, I'll find out if Kitty would like me to paint her too.'

'I'm sure she'll say yes. But I don't think Jimmy can sit still long enough yet to be painted!' Jessie smiled. 'Abraham managed to get a photograph of the three children for Kathleen to send to Sam, though.'

'They are a lovely family. And how is Danny? His little son must miss him, especially since he lost his mother.'

'Danny and Marion had . . . parted some time ago. Wilf has spent more of his life with us at Home Farm; he has a devoted companion in my housekeeper, Daisy. It is sad, but she is more of a parent to him than Danny and Marion ever were.'

'It wasn't a happy marriage?'

'Marion's mother . . . well, she interfered too much. I hope *I* didn't . . .'

'Kathleen obviously thinks of you as her mother.'

'She means the world to me, Olga,' said Jessie, adding briskly, 'Well, I'll leave you to your lesson and see how they are getting on at the big house.'

'Josh is chopping wood, I believe, and Min is cooking the meal today; we will join them later on.'

Jessie met Auntie Lou and Grandma for the first time. She knocked on their door and introduced herself, and was surprised to find that Auntie Lou was younger than she had expected. 'Are you Bridie's sister?' she enquired.

'I suppose you could call me her mother-in-law, because she married my adopted son, Tom. My husband and I couldn't have children of our own, and Tom was eight years old when he came to us. We fostered him to begin with, and he called me Auntie. This is my mother, Lily . . .'

The old lady reclining in the bath chair suddenly spoke. 'They call me Grumpy Grandma; they think I don't know, but my hearing is sharp enough.'

'Well,' Jessie improvised, 'grandmas are entitled to be grumpy sometimes, eh? And aches and pains come with age, as we all know, but you're smiling now, so . . .'

'It's a shock to leave somewhere you've lived for seventy years because of Kaiser Bill and his bombs, but we're lucky to be here, due to your kindness. Prop me up, Lou, I want to shake hands with the lady!'

Jessie suddenly had a flash of inspiration. 'I know someone who needs a friend; she's a bit grumpy too, since she lost her only daughter over in France, so she needs cheering up. I'll bring her next time I come.' She mentally crossed her fingers – surely two grumpy grandmas would get on? But would Mrs Amos agree?

Dennis was wondering how he could be usefully employed; the pottery was in abeyance until the war was over, and whether the brickyard would ever be a thriving concern again was doubtful. He was fortunate in that he was now back in his old bedroom in the Barn House. Min had said to Jessie, 'Of course he must come to us; it is the only real home he knows. You are chock-a-block at Home Farm. I can guess your thoughts, Jessie, but I imagine that Josh, tolerant though he is, would it find it difficult if Mrs Amos joined us . . .'

It was Doc who came up with a solution; he suggested that Dennis could be the woodsman over at the brickyard. 'After all, he worked with Herbie and learned a lot. Then Josh wouldn't be responsible for the firewood needed in the colder weather – Min mentioned to me that he has heart problems. Dennis is a big strong boy, and he thinks of this part of the world as his home ground.'

Not only did Dennis prove his worth and earn his keep as well as a small wage, as the weather worsened there were requests from old customers for logs, so he was busy from dawn to dusk and was paid a percentage of every order. He delivered the logs in the brickyard cart, and the old horse appeared to be glad to be back in harness.

Heather and Kitty went over to the Barn House most weekends, as Olga was putting the finishing touches to Heather's portrait. Kitty had made friends with the twins, and Heather now had a best friend too – Bridget, a year her junior.

'I wonder if Dad will get leave at Christmas,' Kitty said to Heather hopefully.

'Dad is in the desert, Mum says, in Egypt, driving the troops around. It must be boiling hot there,' Heather said.

One Sunday afternoon, when the priest was coming over, Bridget shyly asked Heather if she would like to attend the service in the Barn House. 'I expect your mother is Catholic, coming from Ireland, isn't she?'

'I'm not sure,' Heather said. 'She never talks about religion, or about Ireland, and Mum and Dad were married in the minister's chapel not far from here. We go to the local church with Grandma sometimes, but I'd like to come. Does Min play the harmonium?'

'Auntie Lou plays it for our services,' Bridget said.

The schoolroom was transformed, with Josh's desk covered in a snowy cloth. The chalice and the prayer books were on display, along with religious pictures and a small figurine depicting the Virgin Mary. The big Bible rested on a wooden stand, marked at relevant pages. There was a dish of small wafers, not pieces of bread as Heather remembered from the chapel. 'Stay in your seat when we are called up to the table to receive the sacrament,' Bridget advised her.

The young priest arrived and removed a dark cloak and hat, revealing his colourful robes. Heather was impressed. The prayers and singing began. Auntie Lou had a sure touch on the harmonium and Heather was impressed by the priest's rich baritone voice when he sang the responses. In fact, she was entranced by the whole ceremony. She plucked up courage to speak to the priest as he was preparing to leave. 'I would like to join in again,' she said.

He looked at her for a long moment and then smiled. 'I would welcome you, Heather.' He paused before asking, 'Have you been confirmed in the Anglican Church?'

'No, you see I haven't even been baptised . . .'

'You feel drawn to the Catholic faith?'

'I . . . I don't know.'

'Talk to your mother about it; she is the one to advise you.'

Heather didn't confide in her sister regarding her experience. She waited until she was alone with Kathleen. 'Mum,' she said earnestly, 'I would like to become a Catholic.' When Kathleen didn't respond immediately, she added, 'I know you were one in Ireland, because you gave Dad a rosary to take with him to war.'

Kathleen said faintly, 'Have you spoken to Josh about this – he is the best person to counsel you, Heather.'

'I just know that it is something I must do,' Heather said. 'Like you said when you came here in the snow.'

'I was seeking redemption.'

'Does that mean forgiveness? What for?'

'I found it Heather, that's all I need to say . . .'

THIRTY-ONE

While the O'Briens were busy settling in at the brickyard house, Sam was conveying troops across the desert in a rattling truck. In the searing heat, men dropped like flies, not from gunfire, but from mosquito attacks; malaria was a nightmare. Sam even wished sometimes that he was still wallowing in mud in the trenches.

He'd always had an interest in Egyptology, but had never thought he would see the ancient wonders pictured in his books, and now here he was, though as a soldier rather than a tourist. In letters home, he described the pyramids and the camel trains. Kitty, in reply, asked naïvely, *Have you seen a mummy, Dad, in an ancient tomb?*

They reached their destination, Mesopotamia, at last. Long before the war, the region had been part of the Turkish Ottoman Empire, but now Turkey was allied with Germany. In Great Britain, there was much rhetoric from Lloyd George and Winston Churchill advising Parliament that a victory over the Turks was essential after stalemate on the Western Front. Most of the men thought it an impossible mission.

The task force had to leave the trucks to be ferried across the water in a big carrier boat because there were no proper roads; passenger boats conveyed the troops and equipment along the river. Baghdad was still over five hundred miles away, upstream from the Gulf.

The only water supply was from the river, and dysentery was rife. Some men, already weakened by illness, succumbed and did not survive the journey. Kathleen would have been shocked to see how thin her beloved Sam had become, how much older he looked. The heat had been exhausting, but the troops had been told they now faced a bitter winter. Sam organised a team to dig latrines in the desert, but their services were also called upon to dig graves.

At last the British forces closed in on Kut, where the garrison was under siege. Those inside were near starvation. Supplies of food and ammunition dropped by the Royal Flying Corps mostly ended up in the River Tigris or in the hands of the enemy. A bloody battle ensued, which in April 1916 ended in an Ottoman victory. British forces surrendered.

In June, the family at Home Farm heard that Sam was a prisoner of war. Heather found it difficult to communicate with her mother; Kathleen was often in tears over Sam's misfortune.

'Oh be quiet about what *you* want,' she cried in exasperation when Heather mentioned the word Catholicism.

'I haven't said no, but you need to speak to your father about it.'

'How can I?' Heather shouted, before rushing upstairs and banging her bedroom door shut. Kitty wisely disappeared outside with Jimmy and Wilf. She was upset because her sister no longer seemed to want her company. Only Jessie seemed to understand.

'She's just finding her feet, Kit. She's growing up and you've got left behind, but it'll happen to you too one day, and you'll become close again.'

Heather calmed down, and alone in the bedroom, she felt like poking around. She knew Kathleen's bundle was kept in the washstand drawer, and that she shouldn't touch her mother's private things, but she untied it anyway. The contents were mostly uninteresting, though she had a look at the documents: her mother's birth certificate among them, as well as her parents' wedding certificate – Heather's eyes widened as she realised she must have been a year old when they married. There was a prayer book, mostly in Latin, for Roman Catholics; her mother's name was inscribed at the front in childish handwriting, *Kitty Clancy*, and Heather said aloud, 'That's not fair, she called Kitty after herself!'

The third document that she picked up was an adoption certificate. She had to read it twice before she understood what it said: that her beloved father, Sam, was not her natural father. With trembling hands, she replaced everything in the bundle and put it back in the drawer. Then she lay on her bed and sobbed her heart out.

Much later, Kathleen ventured upstairs and found that her daughter had succumbed to an exhausted sleep. She touched her shoulder hesitantly. Heather stirred and opened her red-rimmed eyes.

'Mum, why didn't you tell me that Dad isn't my real father? I know it was wrong looking in your bundle, but I . . .' Tears suddenly coursed down her cheeks, and Kathleen sat down on the bed and took her in her arms, rocking her like a baby.

'I'm so sorry, Heather, but what could I say? Sam always thought of you as his flesh and blood; you *are* his daughter as far as we are all concerned.'

'I want to know who it was,' Heather said. 'Didn't he want me?'

'Heather, I was only seventeen at the time. He . . . was much older.'

'Was he a bad man?'

'No, but he was a weak person, afraid of causing trouble. I was sent to England after my mother died in Ireland, to a cruel employer who terrified me. The man . . . he lived there too; he was an Italian artist. I thought he was trying to protect me, but he . . . took advantage of me.' She paused, swallowed convulsively. 'I ran away, that's all I can tell you, and Danny found me in the snow, then Jessie took me in and I met Sam and they all cared for me. After you were born, I never wanted to leave my new family. Please don't blame me for something that was not my fault.'

'But you love Sam – Dad – don't you?' Heather demanded.

'You know I do. But we wanted to tell you the truth together. Sam always says, "Heather is my daughter, and I am her father," and he means it. Oh Heather, I miss him terribly.'

'So do I,' Heather whispered. 'Will you forgive me, Mum, for looking at your personal things?' She added, 'We won't tell Kitty yet, because she's not old enough to understand.'

'Oh Heather, I love you so much.'

'I love you too, Mum. Now I know I'm half Italian . . . well, that's a Catholic country, isn't it?'

'If you want to become a Catholic, I won't stand in your way,' Kathleen said.

That evening she told Jessie what had happened. Doc had gone to see Josh after a phone call from Min to say her husband was not well.

It was Kathleen's turn for a hug. 'My dear girl,' Jessie said softly, 'you became my daughter when you arrived here in such distress. I always felt my Mary would have loved to have you as a sister. It was the same for Sam; he accepted Heather as his child and that was that.'

'Oh Jessie, I can't bear to think what might be happening to him now. I wish there was more news . . . When is this war going to end?'

'All we can do is pray for peace. I had a telegram this morning while you were at the stables; I knew you would be upset when you heard the news, so I was waiting for the right moment . . . Danny has been injured and is in hospital in France. He may be sent home. No details yet. I told Daisy, because of Wilf, and Abraham. I haven't said anything to Mrs Amos yet, but she had some news of her own: she is going to stay with Lily at the Brickyard House while Aunt Lou visits her husband in London. The bombing seems to have abated for a bit.' She heard a noise from outside. 'Oh, is that Abraham back?'

Doc walked in. 'Any chance of a hot toddy? It's chilly out tonight.'

'How is Josh?' Jessie bustled about.

'He said Min was making a fuss about nothing, but I'm not so sure. He might have had a slight stroke. He is doing too much, I think.'

'Like you, old dear,' his wife said fondly as she passed him a glass of whisky with hot water, a spoonful of honey and a squeeze of lemon.

There were more sad events to come nearer home. Auntie Lou had been reunited with her husband in Stepney, but the very next night a bomb destroyed the house where he had temporary accommodation. 'They died together, as they would have wanted,' Mrs O'Brien repeated over and over.

It was Mrs Amos who broke the news to Lily – her fellow grumpy grandmother, as she now referred to her. She took Lily's hand in hers and told her, 'Don't worry, I promise I won't leave you, my dear.'

'But your job . . . your family . . .'

'I'll get the vegetable patch here going again; I've still got my health and strength. We'll have a goat and a few hens, and young Bridget and that lad Dennis will help us to be independent.'

'You are a good woman,' the old lady said tremulously.

No one has ever called me that before, Mrs Amos thought. Marion would have been happy to hear it . . .

It was almost Christmas, and Danny was back in England after two years away – not at home, but in a nearby military hospital. His horse had collapsed from under him when the cavalry was involved in a charge against the enemy, and as he fell to the ground there was a barrage of shots and he received wounds to his head and chest. He remembered no more until he recovered consciousness in a field hospital and heard a disembodied voice. His sight was still blurred and words would not issue from his mouth.

'Danny, I was told you were here. Can you hear me? Just press my hand if you can . . .'

He grasped the doctor's hand. The voice continued. 'It's Bruce Gillespie – do you remember me?'

Danny squeezed the doctor's hand again.

'You're going to be all right, Danny, but it may take a long time for you to recover.'

'Marion . . .' Danny managed.

'The wonderful girl we both loved . . . I had hoped I would meet you again, though not like this. Fate has brought us together.'

There was still no news of Sam. Kathleen now slept on her own in the room Mrs Amos had vacated. She could cry in there, she thought sadly, and not disturb the girls; it was a comfort and relief to her that she now had no secrets from her elder daughter. Life had to go on. She worked hard, and that helped, but at night she had vivid dreams of the time before Sam went away to war.

Sometimes she dreamed of being in his arms, and then she would wake and stretch out to the space in the bed where she had imagined him to be, and find it empty, the sheets cold to the touch. She knew she wouldn't be able to go on without the support of her adopted family and the children, two of whom were the result of such a loving relationship.

One night, the wind was howling outside and she slept uneasily. She awoke screaming, and Jessie came, followed by Doc. She could hear them asking what was wrong, and she held on tight to Jessie as she whispered, 'He's gone, Sam is gone. He won't come home ever again . . .'

They received the official news in the new year, 1917, after a subdued Christmas: *We regret to inform you that Sergeant*

Samuel Mason died of cholera on 15 December 1916. His effects will be sent home to you in due course.

They learnt that Sam had been among the prisoners of war who had been forced to march to Aleppo. Some had fallen on the way. Sam had arrived at the prison camp, but like many of his comrades, he did not survive prolonged imprisonment due to the cholera epidemic.

'I knew,' Kathleen cried out. 'I just knew . . .'

THIRTY-TWO

It was July 1917, and back at Home Farm they were picking the luscious strawberries. It was almost like old times, before the war. The three O'Brien girls were eager to help and worked alongside Kitty. Wilf, who had grown up quite a lot, kept an eye on Jimmy, who was always up to mischief, while Jimmy's inseparable companion, Bobby the dog, waited patiently in the shade of the hedgerow with his ball between his front paws.

Dennis, the only young man they could call on now, carried full trays of strawberries to the house and stacked them in the cool pantry, ready to be taken to market the following morning. If the war dragged on, the family were aware that Dennis would be eligible to be called up the following year.

Heather was now at the posh all-girls school, having passed her entrance examination, the fees funded by the legacy from Mr Bartholomew. Although schools closed earlier now for the summer holidays, she was mostly with her mother at the stables, for Doc was now semi-retired at his wife's insistence.

'I don't want to lose you too,' Jessie told him. Besides, he was the only one who could drive the motor, and they needed to visit Danny regularly in hospital. Mrs Amos kept her word, and she and Olga were in harness, as she put it, over at the brickyard. Josh and Min were always there if advice or help was needed.

Dennis helped himself to a glass of milk and sat down in the kitchen, having earned a break after depositing the heavy trays. The door opened and Heather came in. 'Oh, I was hoping for a cup of tea; I thought Grandma would be making one by now,' she said.

'I can take a hint,' Dennis said, but he didn't move.

'Why are you staring at my bosom?' Heather asked indignantly. 'Or do I smell bad after seeing to the pigs?'

'I'm sorry,' he blurted out. He drained his glass of milk. 'Kettle's boiling. I'd better make a couple of pots; they'll be glad of one out in the field . . .'

Dennis thought Heather was very beautiful, but rather stuck-up, and he knew she would never be interested in him. He was trying to grow a moustache, but he really needed a beard to disguise all his spots. Heather didn't have any of those, though she did blush quite a lot, which he found attractive. She was growing up fast; she was approaching fourteen now, and was obviously a young woman, and he couldn't help noticing the change. She no longer had a straight-up-and-down figure.

He said awkwardly, 'You and Kathleen look more like sisters now than mother and daughter.'

Jessie appeared and noted the awkward silence between the two young people. 'Oh thank you, Dennis, we all need to take a few minutes off for a cup of tea. It's so hot out there, but what a wonderful crop this year, eh? I hope we'll have finished picking before the rain comes . . .'

'Doesn't look like it'll rain,' Dennis said. 'I'll take the teapot out, and milk and sugar; they've got mugs, haven't they?'

'It's wet over most of the country, the papers say, but we've been lucky here so far. Heather, Daisy will be here, of course, but could you keep an eye on Wilf and Jimmy for me this afternoon? We won't be picking then, so the O'Briens will be off home and I reckon Kitty will go with them, don't you?'

'Are you going to see Uncle Danny?'

'Yes, we'll take a tray of the strawberries over to the hospital; a treat for the patients, the ones who are able to eat them . . .' Jessie paused, then added, 'I've persuaded Kathleen to come with us. Danny would like to see her.'

'Are you sure Mum is up to it?'

'To be honest, I don't know; she will probably be upset, but Danny will understand.'

'I wondered,' Heather said, all in a rush, 'if Mum and Uncle Danny would, you know, get together when he is well again.'

'I wouldn't mention that to her,' Jessie said, but she was wondering the same.

Doc drove them to the hospital in Sussex. It was a large manor house that had been requisitioned early in the war, and straight away they spotted Danny in a bed chair on the veranda. It was soon after lunch, so he had not yet been joined by his fellow patients.

'I'll park round the side,' Doc said. 'You'll want a few moments on your own.'

'I'll go with you, as I want to leave the fruit in the kitchen for the staff to share out,' Jessie told him. 'He's seen us and is waving – you go and say hello, Kathleen.'

Kathleen walked slowly towards the veranda and climbed the steps to where Danny sat. She felt too choked up to say anything, but he held out his arms and said simply, 'Oh Kathleen, is it really you? You look so pale and tired.'

She could have said, 'So do you, Danny,' because close up, apart from his bright copper hair, he looked so much older. Instead she simply bent over to kiss his cheek.

He said softly, 'You can do better than that,' and she allowed him to briefly kiss her lips.

'Hello, Danny, how are you?' she managed.

'My right lung is fine, but I wheeze on the other side!'

She winced. 'Nothing to joke about.'

'No, but it makes things bearable if you do. You'll be glad to hear I have given up smoking.'

Kathleen straightened up and moved a chair nearer so that she could still hold his hand. 'Danny, you lost dear Marion, and now I have lost my wonderful Sam.'

'I loved him too; he was my brother after all. He was a brave man, Kathleen – and he was a lucky one, because you chose *him*, not me.'

She was silent for a long moment; then, as Jessie and Doc approached, she said quietly, 'I made the right decision then, Danny, but I am grateful for your love now.'

'Sam asked me to look after you if anything . . . Well, I'm not capable of doing so at the moment, but when—' He broke off as his mother and stepfather greeted him.

Jessie was relieved to see that Kathleen was not crying as she had expected. 'How are things?' she asked Danny.

'They tell me I should be able to come home in a week or two, although it will mean extra work for you, Mother, I know.'

'We will look after you between us,' Jessie said, and she was the one shedding tears now, of relief. 'Won't we, Kathleen?'

Kathleen nodded. She suddenly realised that she was still holding Danny's hand. 'Jessie, come and sit here and I'll draw up a chair next to Doc,' she said.

'Then you can hold my other hand,' Danny said with a flash of his old spirit.

Jessie and Doc retired to bed earlier than usual after an eventful day. They talked about the visit to Danny. 'It's a shame,' Jessie said. 'He's got a bald spot on his head where they had to insert that plate – I don't suppose he can see it in a mirror, though.'

'Does it matter if he *has* noticed it? He's lucky to be alive.' Changing the subject, he continued, 'Did you notice that young Dennis seems smitten with Heather?'

'But she's only fourteen!' exclaimed Jessie.

'Maybe, but I think she is old enough to make her own decisions, whether we agree with them or not,' Doc said gently.

In the next room, Kathleen lay awake thinking about what Danny had said to her: how Sam had asked him to look after her if anything happened to him . . .

Josh and Min called a meeting at the Barn House to discuss the future plans of the evacuees now that the bombing of London was no longer such a threat. The maroons still alerted the population when necessary, but the war continued on the Western Front and in the Middle East rather than on home ground.

'Sam and Kathleen were very generous and agreed to minimal rent, as you know,' Josh said to Olga, who was representing the O'Brien family. 'Sam, sadly, will not be returning home, and Danny will be unable to return to the army and will need time to convalesce; he may not be fit to work for some considerable time. The family have seen their business cease to be profitable, but all are working long hours. Kathleen has a little money put by for the children's future, but that is all. Her only real asset is the house her husband built; it may have to be sold. It is unlikely that the brickyard will be viable again. I would be grateful for any suggestions for a solution . . .'

Olga was the first to speak. 'We could get the pottery going again, perhaps, and give the profits to Kathleen? Or I have been thinking of using the barn as an art studio and taking in students of all ages . . . Heather could come along, with Kathleen's permission, of course. Again, profitable for the family. We could pay more rent, I'm sure.'

Josh put in, 'The O'Briens have no home to return to in London; I know they hope to stay here as long as possible. I have advised Bridie that her girls should be enrolled in the local school; they need to be involved in village life, as we are very isolated here, and my wife insists I should resume my retirement. Young Dennis is a hard worker and is building up the sales of wood, besides keeping the home fires burning. Was Kathleen hoping to return here at some point?'

Min shook her head. 'No, she needs to be with her family, and Home Farm lives up to its name; it *is* Kathleen's home.'

'I'll pass this all on to Jessie, Doc and Kathleen, then,' Josh said. 'What about Mrs Amos? She obviously wants to stay on here too.'

Olga said, 'She still has money invested in the bank; I'll tell her this is a good cause!'

Everyone smiled at that. Ann Amos had surprised them all recently.

It was September, nine months since they had received the terrible news about Sam. Kathleen had slept alone in the big room since her bereavement, but now she was moving back into the girls' room, because Danny was returning home. She and Jessie prepared the room for him. The washstand and commode would be back in use as the bathroom was downstairs. Nurse Buss would be a regular visitor, and Doc would watch out for any problems.

The children were all at school now, Jimmy included. Kitty was not academic like her sister; she preferred the village school, where she had lots of friends. So the house was quiet when Doc helped Danny out of the car and handed him his crutches. Jessie was waiting on the door-step, but Kathleen was finishing her work at the stables. Daisy was in the kitchen, waiting for the call to brew a big pot of tea.

Danny swung himself along the path; his legs were still weak from all his inactivity. He saw his mother coming towards him, wiping her eyes. 'Oh, I shouldn't be crying,' she said, 'but I am so thankful you are home at last, Danny.'

'Don't try to help me, Mother, I have to do things for myself if I can,' he said. 'It's so good to see you, and to be home, but is there no one else to greet me?' he joked as he manoeuvred himself over the threshold.

'Wilf wanted to stay at home but decided Jimmy needed him at school, as he only started there this week. Kathleen will be back shortly; she had more to do this morning as Doc was collecting you.'

'I need to sit down,' he said ruefully.

'Come into the living room. I lit the fire; there's an autumn nip in the air,' Jessie said, taking his crutches as he lowered himself into the chair. At once, Bobby came over, wagging his tail, and licked his hand.

'You remember me, do you?' Danny said, stroking the dog.

'Welcome home, Mr Danny,' Daisy beamed, bringing in the steaming cups of tea. 'I'm just going to meet the children from school; Wilf will be so excited to see you.'

When Daisy had gone, Danny said quietly to Jessie, 'I haven't seen my son for nearly three years, but it seems *he* is eager to see *me*.'

'He's a credit to Daisy, who is the one who has really brought him up. She made sure he would remember you by talking about you and Marion, and he is very proud of you both. He's a bright boy; he loves learning, like his

Uncle Sam, but I see a lot of you in him too. I don't think he'll be tall like you, but you never know, boys shoot up later than girls. You probably won't recognise Heather and Kitty now, but young Jimmy is the spitting image of his dad.'

'Where's Doc?'

'He's gone to the stables to help Kathleen finish up there and will bring her back.'

'She looked very tired when I saw her – I hope she's not doing too much.'

'It takes her mind off her loss,' Jessie said.

When Kathleen arrived home, she just looked round the door and said, 'Good to have you home, Danny,' then added to Jessie, 'I must have a bath, if that's all right? I forked up a lot of manure today!'

By the time the children came rushing in to see him, Danny was feeling weary. Doc beckoned Jessie. 'We need to get him upstairs; he can have a nap before supper, eh?'

When Kathleen returned, having changed and washed her hair, she was disappointed that she hadn't had a chance to talk to Danny.

'A parcel came today from the Red Cross,' Jessie told her. 'Keep it to yourself until you feel like showing us what's in it.'

'I'll take it upstairs and look through it before the girls come to bed,' Kathleen said. 'I'm sure there is something in there for you too, Jessie.'

There was indeed a letter addressed to 'Mother'. Kathleen put it to one side, unopened, with two other notes, one for 'My girls' and the other for 'My son'. Then she took a deep breath, blinked away the tears, and opened the letter with her own name on. It was written in pencil and was very creased, as if he had reread it many times, and added to it too.

My dearest Kathleen, the love of my heart,

I endure the life here, if I can call it a life, because of you and our children. I dream of you often, and you are in my arms and I think how fortunate I was to marry you and of the passion we shared. Not everyone can say that. If I am unable to come home again, and that seems increasingly likely, I promise I will always be with you in spirit. If Danny should be more fortunate, I hope that you two will come together; after all, he loves you too.

Darling, don't be sad, remember all the happy times together.

All my love,

Sam

After she had dried her eyes, she examined the items wrapped in a cloth streaked with mud. The rosary she put to one side; she would give that to Heather, she decided. There was a Bible with turned-down pages, obviously much read, and the notebook in which he had written about the mud of Flanders. There was also the photograph of Kathleen and the children, which she thought she would frame, and his silver pocket watch, which was dented in places but would be given to Jimmy when he was older. Finally, at the bottom of the bundle, she discovered the lucky heather that Min had given her all those years ago.

THIRTY-THREE

By October, Danny was showing signs of making a good recovery. However, as it was proving a wet and windy autumn, with hoar frost in the mornings, he was not encouraged to venture outside as he had hoped, or to visit the horses and other livestock at the stables. Instead, he sat in the kitchen talking to Jessie and Daisy, or put his feet up on the old sofa in the living room with Bobby, now his constant companion, and read the newspapers, which were full of the Russian Revolution. Russia was no longer involved in the war.

He wrote letters, mostly to his old comrades still at the Front, and enjoyed the warmth from the crackling fire, which he replenished with bundles of twigs brought in by Dennis. He saw Kathleen only now and then, for she was always busy, but he welcomed the company of the children after school each afternoon. He realised ruefully that he had never been close to Wilf in the past, but this was slowly changing, and he was glad. He thought of Marion, and recalled the happy days of their youth. No one could take those memories away. The lively girls made him smile, and Jimmy looked on him as a father figure.

'My family,' Danny would say to Jessie.

'You don't know how much it means to me to hear you say that,' she replied.

Night-times were his biggest problem. He still called for help when he needed the commode. Nightmares were a regular occurrence and Jessie was always on the alert, which meant that she and Doc slept intermittently.

One night he awoke, sweating and anxious, in the dark. The night light had gone out; Jessie had mentioned that it needed a new wick. He was afraid of stumbling and falling over if he got out of bed.

Jessie, for once, was fast asleep, but Doc heard Danny's cry. He nudged his wife gently. 'Danny . . .' he murmured. It took a few minutes for Jessie to come to, and she had just opened the bedroom door when she saw that someone else was hurrying along the corridor. She hesitated a moment, before returning to her warm bed.

Doc yawned. 'He's stopped calling?'

Jessie said, 'Yes. Kathleen's with him.'

Kathleen put her candle on the washstand and bent over the bed. 'Danny, are you all right?' She felt his damp brow and helped him sit up. 'There. You had a bad dream; would you like me to stay with you for a while?'

'Please,' he said.

She stretched out beside him, on top of the covers. He put out a hand and said with concern, 'You're shivering, Kathleen.'

'I didn't have time to put on my wrapper.' She folded her arms across her chest.

Danny relaxed and lay down beside her. He made no attempt to touch her. Then he became aware that she was crying silently, and he tentatively put an arm round her. 'Oh Kathleen,' he murmured. 'Am I dreaming?'

'No, Danny. You needed me . . . and I need you too.' She was still trembling, but she was warming up, inside and out.

Kathleen was up early as usual; she joined Jessie at the table for a bacon sandwich. The girls came through en route to the bathroom. Heather paused to ask, 'Where were you last night, Mum? Daisy woke us up and told us to get washed and dressed for school.'

Jessie answered for Kathleen. 'Your mum is going to look after Uncle Danny at nights; he needs someone with him, and she's younger than me, as you may have noticed. All right? Now hurry up before the boys come downstairs, eh?'

In the bathroom, Kitty said innocently to Heather, 'Where's Mum going to sleep? There's only one bed.'

Heather, well aware of the facts of life, said loftily, 'It's none of our business. She's Uncle Danny's night nurse, I suppose . . . That's my toothbrush, not yours, Kit!'

'We can have more larks without Mum telling us off,' Kitty said smugly.

'Midnight feasts or pillow fights?' Heather giggled. She was an avid reader of schoolgirl stories nowadays, like her friend Bridget O'Brien.

Danny too had had an early awakening. He discovered that Kathleen was already up and about, so it was Daisy who brought him hot water to wash with and helped him out of bed. 'Can you manage, Mr Danny?'

'Yes, I think so; thank you, Daisy. I know you're busy getting the children off to school.' He hesitated. 'Kathleen . . .?'

'I expect she's on her way to the stables by now. Doc goes down later. She'll be back with the milk in a couple of hours as usual.'

Danny lathered his face, steadied himself and applied his razor. Kathleen didn't like beards, he recalled; that was why Sam got rid of his. Last night nothing happened, he mused, but don't they say that love conquers all?

The family at Home Farm were hosting Christmas lunch for their friends over at the brickyard. Only Min and Josh had declined the invitation, for they were travelling to see their youngest son, now a minister himself: he had a heart murmur so had been turned down for active service. Three of their other sons would be reunited with them too, as they were being sent back to Blighty after being wounded, no longer fit for active service. Two of their brothers had been killed in action early in the war and were buried in Flanders.

Jessie confided in Doc, 'I have a feeling our dear friends will not come back.'

Dennis was now on his own in the Barn House, but joined the family at the Brickyard House for meals and the use of the bathroom. He too had been turned down for conscription, because he had flat feet. He said dolefully, 'I knew I had big feet, but they say I can't wear army boots and march.'

'We can't do without you, Dennis, so that's a relief,' Jessie told him.

'You're one of the family now,' Doc added.

'I hope to be,' Dennis said boldly, looking over at Heather. She made a face at him, but it was a cover for her unexpected feelings: was this what they called puppy love?

On Christmas Eve, Kathleen didn't go to bed until almost midnight; she had to wait until the children were asleep to dole out the stockings. She spent the evening with Jessie and Daisy, preparing the vegetables for Christmas dinner.

When she tiptoed into the room she shared with Danny, he appeared to be asleep, so she undressed quickly and stood for a moment looking down at him. His eyes opened and he grinned. Kathleen snatched at her nightgown.

'You seem to find it funny, catching me . . . well, with no clothes on!'

'I thought you were doing it on purpose,' he said mildly.

'I haven't got a lovely figure like . . .' She paused.

'You can say her name, you know: Marion . . . But you are desirable too, Kathleen. Aren't you coming to bed?'

'Why, what do you have in mind?' she asked.

'What do you think?' he returned.

'I think . . . perhaps we shouldn't . . .'

'And I believe we should. It's what Sam wanted for us both. I'd marry you tomorrow if I could, but I know it's not possible – are you aware that a man cannot marry his brother's widow?'

'It's a ridiculous rule that will be changed soon, Jessie told me.'

'Why did she tell you that?'

'Because she knows you love me, and that I love you – yes, I do, Danny. It's different from the way I felt about Sam – that was a passionate relationship between two young people, and it was wonderful – but I can't help longing to be close to you.'

'Come here,' he said quietly. 'It's been so long, and I don't know if I can live up to his memory, but I can try.'

She threw the nightdress to one side and said simply, 'I'll try too.'

He reached out and held her close. Nothing happened for some time, and she waited patiently. Their lovemaking was tentative at first, but quite suddenly they were both aroused.

Much later, he asked hesitantly, 'Were you disappointed, Kathleen?'

She gave him a long, lingering kiss. 'It's just the beginning; we'll get better at it, I am sure! Practice makes perfect, as they say.'

'Did you feel . . .?'

'I'm not disclosing all my secrets! We must get some sleep now before we hear the chorus of "Happy Christmas!"' she said, and kissed him again.

It was an austere Christmas this year, despite the optimism regarding the outcome of the conflict that had blighted so many lives. With fears that food supplies were at a dangerously low level, there was more panic-buying and strong rumours that rationing would be introduced in the new year.

However, Jessie and Daisy had been hoarding sugar and tea for months, and they had been careful not to waste food. There was no turkey or goose this Christmas, but a brace of pheasants appeared, though Jessie wasn't revealing where these came from. Carrots were plentiful and swelled the Christmas puddings and cake, but flour was a precious commodity nowadays.

There were fewer bottles of elderflower wine and cordial due to the sugar shortage, but there had been a bumper crop of apples, plums and blackberries, which they had preserved by bottling the fruit and making jam and pickles, while Mrs Amos had tried her hand at sloe gin for the first time.

When all the presents had been opened, mostly home-made this year, and the cards put up on every available shelf, Dennis moved two large tables into place. One was for the eight children: Heather, Kitty, Jimmy, Wilf, Bridget and the twins, plus the youngest O'Brien, Tom, now three years old; the other for the grown-ups: Jessie, Doc, Danny, Kathleen, Daisy, Mrs Amos and her companion Lily, Bridie, Olga and Dennis. Kitty counted them all up – eighteen in all! She and Bridget had fashioned paper hats from a pile of *Daily Mirror*s, and Heather and Wilf had made a large Christmas cracker as a table decoration.

Kathleen sat next to Danny; he smiled at her and she blushed, thinking of the intimacy of the night before. Jessie, observing them, gave a little sigh.

Danny was recalling the day when he had seen Kathleen lying in the snow, and how he had felt when Heather was born. He bit his lip; that first Christmas Day he had upset Marion, and despite the episode in the hayloft afterwards, when he was, he realised now, tricked into marrying her, he loved her too. Marion never believed me when I told her that, he thought sadly. Sam was the lucky one, and Kathleen was right to marry him – can we be as happy in time as they were then?

'Danny, you're supposed to be passing the plates along the table,' Kathleen reminded him.

'Sorry, I was remembering past Christmases,' he said.

It was midnight again before anyone got to bed.

'I wonder what the new year will bring,' Kathleen said, yawning.

'Peace, I hope,' Danny said. The candle was snuffed; he waited for a few moments, while she snuggled up to him. 'Kathleen?'

'Mmm?'

'Will you marry me when it's possible?'

Kathleen cried out, careless of being overheard. 'I have prayed every night that you would ask me that!' She flung her arms round him and hugged him tight. 'Of course I will! I love you, Danny. I will never forget you lifting me out of the snow that day; when I looked up at you as you carried me in your strong arms, I wondered if you were an angel – and I now realise that was the moment I fell I love with you. It wasn't the right time, I know, and later . . . well, Sam and I came together, and that was a real love story. It's sad that it wasn't like that for you and Marion.'

Danny's mind filled with thoughts of his brother and his wife; of loved ones lost.

'Danny, please don't feel guilty about not . . . well, waiting, you know. Sam wanted us to be together if he didn't come home. You told me that he asked you to look after me if anything happened to him, didn't you? We will be one big family with our children. We won't forget Sam or Marion ever.'

Danny nodded, too choked with emotion to speak.

'And when we have our honeymoon,' Kathleen continued, 'will you take me home?'

'To Ireland? I promise I will. Like the old song, eh, "I'll Take You Home Again, Kathleen". I know it's what Sam wanted to do too.' And with that, she kissed him again.

Later, still encircled in his arms, Kathleen realised that he had fallen asleep. He's happy now, she thought, and so am I. Life is good again.

Epilogue

In 1926, marriages between couples in Danny and Kathleen's situation became possible. They wed the following spring.

Doc had passed away in his sleep a year earlier; he had touched so many lives, and many people joined Jessie and her family at the service of thanksgiving. He was much missed.

In 1921, Heather had married Dennis. They had been childhood sweethearts since she was fourteen; 'Just like Danny and Marion,' Jessie said fondly. Heather was eighteen, and the marriage took place in the Catholic church, where Dennis was also a member. They were now proud parents of two boys – Sam aged four, and Danny aged two. The little family lived in the Barn House, where Dennis made a good living from the wood. Heather sold a painting or two; she was aware she had inherited her artistic talent from her natural father, and told Kathleen, 'It's actually nice to be different.' She was proud to be known as 'The Winter Baby', and to hear the now familiar story of how her mother had struggled along in the snow before her birth.

Wilf was at university, studying ancient history; Jimmy was about to leave school and wanted to work with the horses; bubbly Kitty had a job in a London hotel as a receptionist, and had a queue of suitors. They all missed her at home. Danny was slowly building up the stables again with Kathleen, and Jessie and Daisy were still busy cooking in the kitchen.

The Brickyard House was unoccupied, and would remain so. The O'Briens had returned to London after the Armistice in 1918 and were reunited with their elder daughters. Lily had passed away by then, so Mrs Amos went back to her friends at Home Farm. She was very proud of Wilf, nowadays referring to him as 'my clever grandson at university'. She considered herself retired, though she still made the elderflower wine for Christmas. Olga was now teaching at a London art college, and as Jessie had anticipated, Min and Josh did not return to Kent.

There were still piles of bricks in the courtyard, but the clay pits were no longer dug. It was the end of an era.

A day after their quiet wedding, Kathleen and Danny were at sea. He was taking her back to Ireland, but she assured Jessie she would return to Home Farm.

'It is my real home; you are my family, and always will be,' she told her.

They saw the farm where Kathleen had lived until she was seven, and to her delight, there were horses there again. She shared with Danny her memories of living in County

Clare before she moved to Dublin with her mother and stepfather. She vowed that the one place she would never visit again was where she had been a victim of malicious ill-treatment.

'I still don't want to remember that time,' she told Danny, and he understood.

Although Kathleen and Danny were now both over forty, with grown-up children and young grandchildren, there would be another winter baby nine months after their honeymoon in Ireland – a tiny daughter, dark-haired with blue eyes, named Clare, after the place where Kathleen had been born.

Acknowledgements

Ian Mitchell of Tatsfield history project, for information on the early twentieth century in the area.

Jean Pearce Edwards, author of *Little Jean's War* and other good books.

Virginia Whitnell, artist/teacher, my daughter, for valuable information on potting!

Welcome to the world of *Sheila Newberry*!

Keep reading for more from Sheila Newberry, to discover a recipe that features in this novel and to find out more about what Sheila is doing next . . .

We'd also like to introduce you to Memory Lane, our special community for the very best of saga writing from authors you know and love and new ones we simply can't wait for you to meet. Read on and join our club!

www.MemoryLane.club

Meet Sheila Newberry

I've been writing since I was three years old, and even told myself stories in my cot. So it came as a shock when I was whacked round the head by my volatile kindergarten teacher for daydreaming about stories when I was supposed to be chanting the phonetic alphabet. My mother received a letter from my teacher saying, 'Sheila will not speak. Why?' Mum told her that it was because I was scared stiff in class. I was immediately moved up two classes. Here I was given the task of encouraging the slow readers. This was something I was good at but still felt that I didn't fit in. Later, I learned that another teacher had saved all my compositions saying they inspired many children in later years.

I had scarlet fever in the spring of 1939, and when I returned to our home near Croydon, I saw changes which puzzled me – sandbags, shelters in back gardens, camouflaged by moss and daisies, and windows re-enforced with criss-crossed tape. Children had iron rations in Oxo tins – we ate the contents during rehearsals for air-raids – and gas masks were given out. I especially recall the stifling rubber. We spent the summer holiday, as usual, in Suffolk and I remember being puzzled when my father left us there, as the Admiralty staff was moving to Bath. 'War' was not mentioned but we were now officially evacuees, living with relatives in a small cottage in a sleepy village.

On and off, we returned to London at the wrong times. We were bombed out in 1940 and dodging doodlebugs in 1943. I thought of Suffolk as my home. I was still writing – on flyleaves of books cut out by friends – and every Friday I told stories about Black-eyed Bill the Pirate to the whole school in the village hut. I wrote my first pantomime at nine years old, and was awarded the part of Puss in Boots. I wore a costume made from blackout curtains. We were back in our patched-up London home to celebrate VE night and dancing in the street. Lights blazed – it was very exciting.

I had a moment of glory when I won an essay competition that 3000 schoolchildren had entered. The subject was waste paper, which we all collected avidly! At my new school, I was encouraged by my teachers to concentrate on English Literature and Language, History and Art, and I did well in my final exams. I wanted to be a writer, but was told there was a shortage of paper! True. I wrote stories all the time and read many books. I was useless at games like netball as I was so short-sighted – I didn't see the ball until it hit me. I still loved acting, and my favourite Shakespearian parts were Shylock and Lady Macbeth.

When I left school, I worked in London at an academic publisher. I had wanted to be a reporter, but I couldn't ride a bike! Two years after school, I met my husband

John. We had nine children and lived on a smallholding in Kent with many pets (and pests). I wrote the whole time. The children did, too, but they were also artistic like John. We were all very happy. I acquired a typewriter and wrote short stories for children, articles on family life and romance for magazine. I received wonderful feedback. I soon graduated to writing novels and joined the Romantic Novelists' Association. I have had many books published over the years and am over the moon to see my books out in the world once again.

MEMORY LANE

A Day I'll Never Forget . . .

I was inspired to write *The Winter Baby* years after visiting the deserted house and brickworks near Westerham in Kent. Here is an earlier memory of an historical walk I took to Westerham just after the war ended . . .

We girls at Lady Edridge School were excited that our education now included outings to museums and art galleries, a trip down the Thames and to the *Britain Can Make It* exhibition in London. Until the terrible twins boarded a tube train going in the wrong direction and the teacher in charge "flapped." But this time we would be more or less on our own!

Our popular history teacher – the charismatic FF as she was known – suggested the walk, as we had been studying the Siege of Quebec, where General Wolfe, who was actually born in Westerham, commanded an army sent out to capture the capital of the French Colony in North America. Both he and the French Commander, Montcalm, were mortally wounded, but it was a victory for the British.

One Saturday, my best friend Maggie and I caught a bus to Croydon and met up with our group. We began the long trek to Westerham to culminate at General Wolfe's statue. We walked along in pairs in a straggling crocodile, referring to the map and wondering when we could open our gas mask cases, which were now used to carry our packed lunches. This was not permissible until we reached Westerham. FF and another teacher were travelling by car and, unbeknown to us, were checking our progress.

We finally reached our destination and sat on a patch of grass opposite the lofty statue of the General – who naturally ignored us – to eat our spam sandwiches. A girl called Marion casually produced a banana, brought home by her recently demobbed father. She sliced the banana into six portions and generously shared this treat with us. None of us had tasted a banana since before the war. Just a mouthful each, but we felt we were the luckiest girls on the walk. The banana was the most memorable part of the exercise.

You will see that I have named a character Marion in my book after that long ago friend . . .

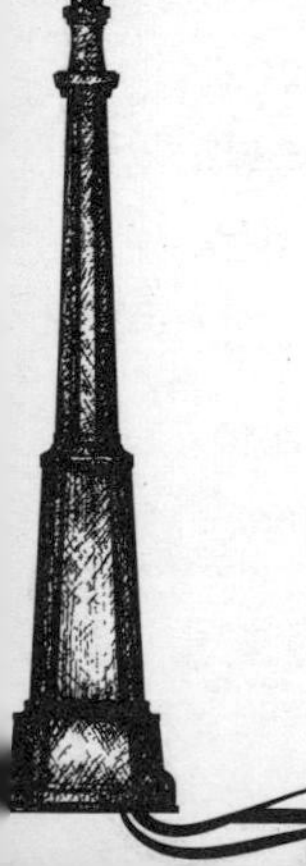

Elderflower Cordial and Wine

During the glorious summer of 1914, Mrs Amos – who disapproved of most children – recruited half a dozen village boys and girls to help with harvesting the elderflower blossoms. She was famous for her elderflower cordial and wine, and reserved bottles for Christmas lunch with her nearest neighbours – the Mason family at Home Farm.

Method

Rinse the elderflower heads with cold water and dry with a tea towel before use.

Cordial

- Pour 2 ½ pints of boiling water onto 24 elderflower heads in a large pan, which must be scalded before use.
- Add 3 ½ pounds of sugar and 1 sliced lemon.
- Stir until the sugar dissolves, skim off any scum, then cover.
- Stir twice a day for five days. Strain through muslin, then bottle.

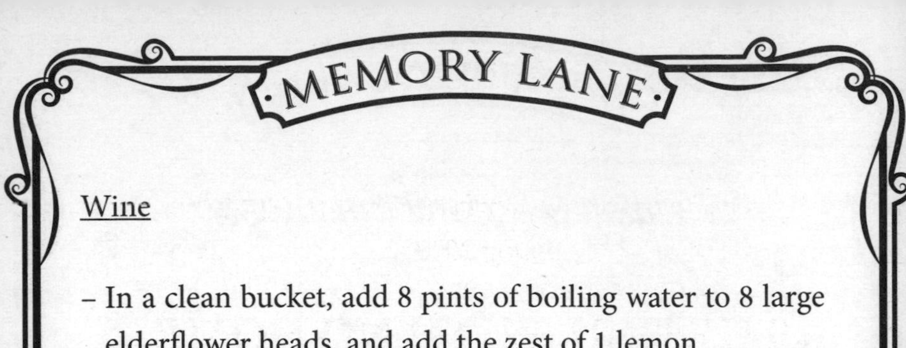

Wine

- In a clean bucket, add 8 pints of boiling water to 8 large elderflower heads, and add the zest of 1 lemon.
- Cover and leave to stand for four days, stirring occasionally. Strain through muslin.
- Stir in 3lb of sugar, the juice of 1 lemon and ½ oz of yeast.
- Allow to ferment at room temperature.
- When the contents have ceased to bubble, stir the wine and leave it to settle for three days.
- Pour into a demijohn to mature for three months before bottling.

Raise your glass to Mrs Amos!

MEMORY LANE